# Fiona

## A HISTORIC NOVEL OF THE CIVIL WAR IN CHAMBERSBERG

# Eileen Dougherty Troxell

ISBN: 1536995525

ISBN 13: 9781536995527

Library of Congress Control Number: 2016914237

CreateSpace Independent Publishing Platform

North Charleston, South Carolina

# Dedication

*To my dear husband Gene and my family for their love and support.*

Editors
Warren Hope
Colleen Troxell

Cover Artwork
Jake Troxell

# Part One

# Chapter One

As sixteen year old Fiona McKenna walked along the road, she lifted her skirts to keep them out of the spring mud. She was wearing her good corded skirt, and it would not do to arrive at her first day of work in muddy skirts. As she struggled to hold on to her small satchel, she lifted her face to the warm sunshine. It felt so good after the long winter. Her heart felt as light as the breeze that swirled around her. She was headed into town to work at Mrs. Mary Ritner's boarding house.

Fiona had seen Mrs. Ritner around town. She was what Da called a real lady in reduced circumstances. Her husband was from a prominent family. His father, Joseph Ritner, had been the governor of Pennsylvania back in 1839. Mrs. Ritner's husband, Abraham, had died leaving her with little money. She had several grown stepchildren and three young daughters to rear and needed an income. Taking in boarders was the only respectable thing that a lady could do. Judge Flood, Fiona's father's boss, had recommended Fiona for the job.

"The Ritners are known to be abolitionists," the Judge explained, "but they are good people."

Fiona smiled when she remembered hearing Judge Flood talk to someone about her father, "He's Irish, but you can trust him."

*The Judge had a way of qualifying his prejudices*, she thought. The fact that the Ritners were abolitionists did not bother Fiona. Her father did not believe in slavery. He often talked of how the British treated the Irish like slaves. She had grown up hearing his tales of the old country.

Da had seen her off at the cottage. He put his finger in the small holy water font that hung by the door and blessed her on the forehead. "God bless you on your way my darlin' only child. I hope you find what you're lookin' for in this new endeavor. Always remember that no person is better than you." He took her face in his hands, "You are a true black Irish beauty like your dear mother Kathleen."

"Oh Da, I'm not black."

"That means black hair and blue eyes, a lovely combination. Beware the wags in town. I'm sorry I can't drive you in, but Judge Flood needs me in the north field early today."

Fiona smiled up at him; "It's all right Da, it is a lovely spring morning and you know I like to walk."

She knew in her heart that her father didn't want her to take this job, but he would never show it. He recognized her restless spirit and always wanted what was best for his daughter. As long as Fiona could remember, it had been just the two of them looking after each other. She never knew what it was like to have a mother, so her Da had been everything to her. He sent her everyday to the nuns at the local convent where she received a good education. Now she wanted to earn some money and do something for Da and for herself. She wanted to go out and see the world even if it was only Chambersburg.

Da put his hands on her shoulder and said, "I hope you like livin' in town. Chambersburg has been good to me. After your mother died in Philadelphia, they were startin' with the riots against the Irish Catholics. You were just a babe and I wanted to find a safe place for you. Me friend Barney was livin' here, so I came, and when I saw this place it felt like home. The rolling green hills and lovely streams reminded me of Ireland. I got the job with Judge Flood and made a life for us."

"That you did and it's been a great life, Da"

*Not such a great life for you Da,* thought Fiona. It's been a life with plenty of hard work and a lonely one with no wife. Fiona hugged her Father and started down the road. She waved to him in the door way.

"Make sure to stop at Kate Gormley's," he called.

"I will," she called back and turned for one last look. He was a tall man with a fine brow and a wide face. He was only fifty, but his hair was snow white. It was a fine head of hair as the Irish said. Fiona thought him a handsome man.

As she walked, Fiona thought about what it would be like living in town. She wanted to meet people her own age and talk to others with different ways of looking at life. She often felt isolated in their small country cottage. Riding into town with Da in the wagon was always exciting. Chambersburg was a bustling place with lots of people and shops. There was the great courthouse square called The Diamond surrounded by many fine buildings. Besides the courthouse there were several hotels, a bank and Franklin Hall where many prominent speakers appeared. Chambersburg had neighborhoods of fine houses and neighborhoods of middle and working class people.

The Cumberland Valley Railroad had its headquarters there and the town had become an important transportation center. The railroad depot was just off the square. Fiona liked to see the people getting off the train from Philadelphia and she wondered what their life was like in that great city. Da had settled there when he first came from Ireland and she was born there, but she had no memory of it.

Fiona would live at the boarding house and work as a hired girl with another country girl. She would get to go home every other weekend. That suited Fiona. Judge Flood often sent Da into town for supplies and she would get a chance to see him then. It would be the first time she had ever been separated from her Da. They had been a team for as long as she could remember.

Thomas McKenna was born in County Kilkenny, Ireland in 1809. As a boy he roamed the green hills looking after his father's sheep. The family rented the land from Lord Bromley. Thomas's father often told him that all of the surrounding land had belonged to their family many generations back, but the English had seized it and made it their own. Thomas loved his family, but as long as he could remember, he wanted to get away. He wanted to be his own man and not have to bow and scrape to the English land lords. He would stand on the highest hill and look out over the sea.

He dreamed of crossing the sea to America. What a great adventure that would be. He could get rich and come back and buy up all the land. A rich American could do anything. He hired himself out to the neighbors and worked their fields. Finally, in 1836, he had saved enough money for the passage. All the neighbors gathered at the house the day he was leaving and held an American wake. When a loved one left for America, there was a good chance they would never be seen again. They all blessed him and said their goodbyes. As in most wakes there was music and laughter and reminiscences of old times. His friend Jack reminded him of the time they had climbed the fence and picked the apples from Lord Bromley's trees when they were boys.

"We ran like the divil himself was after us and got away. We went back many times after that and did what mischief we could."

Tom laughed and said, "The only time we got caught was the time we decided to take a swim in his mill pond. We got chased by the man and ran off naked into the woods and we couna go back for our clothes."

"Aye," Tom's sister Annie shouted, "You came to the kitchen window, and begged me to get you both some clothes. I did, but I made you pay dearly for months by doing my chores."

"And you boyos thought I didn't know what was going on," Tom's mother chimed in.

All too soon it was time to leave and their laughter turned to tears. His mother kissed him and begged him to be careful. "Thomas darlin' promise me you won't get a job on the railroad. I hear that it is dangerous work."

Tom assured her that he would not do anything dangerous. His father drove him in the cart to the great ship in New Ross harbor. His mother could not bear to see him off. Before he boarded the ship, his father took him into his arms and said, "God bless you my dear son. Work hard and be a good man. Always remember your family and your faith. Be true to your self and always remember where you came from and that you are a McKenna. You come from a great family and no person is better than you."

Thomas kissed his father good bye. He promised him that he would come back with money to give them a good life. The last thing he saw was his father's wave as he sailed out on the evening tide.

Fiona thought of the sadness that her father carried in his heart. He never got rich and never saw his home or his family again. The great famine came soon after he left and his father was driven off the land. His parents both died and his brother, Michael, got in trouble with the English and was sent to Australia. His sister Annie married and died in childbirth. He lost track of his other relatives in the many troubles that swept over Ireland. Thomas McKenna may have carried sadness in his heart, but he always carried himself with dignity. He was a man who believed in himself and thought no other man his better.

Lost in her reverie, Fiona looked up and noticed the road was descending through the hills. Great pine trees grew along the hill side and the warm spring air carried their fragrance. Fiona inhaled it all and her excitement grew as she climbed a small rise and saw the town nestled in the valley below. The mountains rising up behind created a beautiful backdrop. When the sun hit the trees on the hills just right, they were enveloped in a beautiful blue haze. The locals called them the Blue Mountains.

The town of Chambersburg nestled in the Cumberland Valley, surrounded by the foothills of the great Appalachian Mountains. It was a pretty town and had always been a crossroads of history. It was on the frontier at the time of the French and Indian War. A stone fort was built for protection from the Indians. During the Whiskey Rebellion in 1794, the citizens of Chambersburg raised a liberty pole in support of the rebels who opposed the tax on whiskey. Whiskey making had always been an enterprise on the frontier. This was George Washington's first test as president and he sent troops to put down the rebellion. Washington himself passed through Chambersburg on his way to Bedford where he sent the troops toward Pittsburgh under General Harry Lee. He returned to Chambersburg where he stayed overnight. The townspeople welcomed him with great respect. He politely ignored the liberty pole. Now, in 1859, it was a prosperous town and the county seat of Franklin County.

As Fiona entered the town, the sights and sounds of Chambersburg surrounded her. On this Saturday morning, horses and carriage wheels clattered over the cobblestone streets. Lawyers in stove pipe hats came and went from the courthouse. Women moved from shop to shop with their market baskets and young men stood on the corners eyeing the crowds.

"Hey pretty miss, can I be of service to you?" a young man said as he tipped his hat.

"No, thank you," she primly replied and walked on.

*The wags Da had warned me about*, Fiona laughed to herself. Mrs. Gormley's house was on East Queen Street just off The Diamond. Kate Gormley was a family friend and kind of the leader of the small Irish community in Chambersburg. Fiona had known her as long as she could remember. She stepped up to the large wrap around porch and knocked at the door.

"Is that you, Fiona?  Come on in, I've been expecting you."

Fiona stepped into the small hall and Kate Gormley gave her an affectionate hug. She was a nice-looking plump woman about her father's age. Her faded blonde hair was pulled back into a bun. She wore small gold ear bobs and a gold brooch was pinned on her blue dress.

"Your Da said you would be coming in today. You must be tired from your walk. Take off your bonnet and shawl. Go out back and use the privy and then take off your shoes and I'll wipe the mud off. There's a cloth at the pump where you can wash your face and hands."

Fiona smiled at Mrs. Gormley's motherly instructions as she finished her absolutions and returned to the house. They went out on the front porch where Hattie, Mrs. Gormley's maid, served them lemonade. Hattie was a freed slave. She was a beautiful woman.  She had large black soulful eyes and her complexion was light. She and her husband, Enoch Williams, had worked for the Gormleys for years.

"Hey Mis Fiona, good to see ya," Hattie said as she handed her the glass.

"Thank you Hattie, that's just what I need. How's Enoch?"

"He's doin fine thank ye Mis," Hattie said and returned to the house.

Fiona gratefully sipped the cooling drink and rocked back enjoying the shade of the porch.

Mrs. Gormley smiled at her and said, "Your Da will miss you. I'm surprised he let you go, but I think he understands that you're like him. As a boy he was wantin' go off and find new adventures. That's why he left Ireland. He's glad that you're like your mother in looks, but he never talks about her much. I think it hurts too much. He's one of those one-woman men." she said with a sigh and started on one of her stories. Fiona sat back contentedly. "You know an Irishman was one of the first to come to Chambersburg way back in 1730. His name was Benjamin Chambers and he was Scotch-Irish. They called themselves that so it would be known that they were not Catholic," Mrs. Gormley emphasized. "Anyway, this place was known as Falling Springs back then. Chambers started a grist mill down there at Falling Spring Falls where it meets the Conocacheague Creek. All of the land belonged to the Penn family. They got it from the king of England because he owed them money." She sat back in her chair and paused. "The Penns wanted people to settle the land. It was all wild back then; how beautiful it must have been. Old Benjamin did very well for himself and was around for a long time," she turned to Fiona and said, "Some of his descendents are still around here."

Mrs. Gormley continued. "Them old Lenape Indians were here long before. The Penns were always signing treaties with them. The Indians had no idea what them papers meant. They did not understand land ownership. The land did not belong to anybody. It was just something that their Great Spirit had created for them to use and care for. To them the land was sacred. But ownership was important to the white folks. The Penn family owned Pennsylvania and the Calvert family owned Maryland. In 1750, there was a dispute over the boundaries. They complained to the courts in England and they sent over two surveyors named Mason and Dixon. They drew the boundary line between Pennsylvania and Maryland." Mrs. Gormley leaned forward in her chair and pointed down the street, "That line is just thirteen miles south of here."

"Chambersburg became a transport center when the Great Wagon Road from Philadelphia passed through. Now we have the railroad and we're doing all right."

Fiona loved to visit Mrs. Gormley and hear her stories. She knew the widow was lonely living alone in the big house. Her husband had been dead for many years and she had no children. Her husband had been an Irish immigrant like Fiona's father. Her family had lived in Chambersburg for generations, but originally came from Germany. They objected to her marriage to the Irishman, but Patrick Gormley soon won them over. Her father even loaned him the money to buy a store. Her Da told her that Kate became "more Irish than the Irish after she married Pat." She sold the store after his death and invested the money. It left her in comfortable circumstances.

Fiona finished her lemonade and stood up. Mrs. Gormley was just getting started on politics and the troubles with the South. Fiona knew she had to make a getaway.

"I'm sorry, but I really must be going. Thank you so much for every thing."

"Of course, dear, you must be on your way. Bless you and good luck to you. Let me know if you need anything and stop by whenever you can."

She pointed the way to the Ritner House and Fiona found her way to a narrow tree lined street. She passed the county jailhouse on her way and remembered that her father's friend Barney had spent some time there after one of his drunken binges.

Fiona soon found herself at 225 East King Street. She looked up at the two story house. The white overlapping clapboard and green shutters looked freshly painted. There was a clump of red tulips growing by the doorstep. Fiona thought it a fine looking home. She wondered about Mrs. Ritner and hoped that she would be nice. It must have been difficult for her to give up her privacy and rent out her home to strangers. Fiona thought *dear Lord, what am I doing standing here? I must go around back. I'm a hired girl now.* She walked through the narrow passage between the Ritner house and the one next door. There was a small fenced yard and an alley way. Beyond that the land sloped down to a small creek. She was startled when she heard a bark. There was a mean-looking, large brown dog tied in the yard next door. He growled at her menacingly.

A young man came out of the house and looked at her also menacingly. She quickly opened the gate to the Ritner yard. She walked up the garden path and saw green shoots just coming up. They looked like beans. The back door was open. She took a deep breath and called, "Hello, it's Fiona McKenna. I've come to start work."

"Come in, Fiona," a voice called from within.

Fiona stepped inside and it took a while for her eyes to adjust to the dark kitchen after the bright sunlight. She saw a young girl, about her own age, kneading bread at a table in the center of the room. She was a tall big-boned girl. Her bright blonde hair fell in ringlets under her mop cap. She had a round face and large blue eyes. She was not pretty, but there was a sweetness and wholesomeness in her face. She had such an open and welcoming expression that Fiona was immediately drawn to her.

"Hello, I'm Helga Myers the other hired girl. Welcome to the Ritner house. I've been working here for a year. We will be sharing a room in the attic. Mrs. Ritner said you were coming. She'll want to see you. You can hang your things on the peg by the door."

All this was said at a fast past while Helga pounded the bread into submission. Fiona suppressed a laugh as Helga wiped her hands and went to fetch Mrs. Ritner. Helga soon returned and announced, "She'll be along soon. Don't worry; she is kind but overworked, poor thing. Those daughters of hers could do more to help, but she wants them to be ladies."

Helga stopped speaking quickly when the kitchen door opened and Mrs. Ritner walked in. She was a thin woman with an air of grace about her. Her face was pretty, but care worn. Her hair was pulled back in a crocheted net and two large black curls dangled behind each ear. She wore a cotton print dress with a high collar and her only jewelry was a mourning broach.

She spoke very softly. "Welcome Fiona, we are glad to have you here. You will be working with Helga in helping to prepare meals. You will do the washing and clean the house. Helga will show you what to do. We only have two guests here right now but, with the warm weather coming, we will be expecting more. Helga will show you to your room. You may rest for a while until it is time to serve luncheon. Please feel free to come to me if you have any questions. Thank you."

Mrs. Ritner quietly left the kitchen and Helga smiled at Fiona. She showed her the cooker where a pot of soup was simmering. Fiona had never seen an iron cooker before. She and Da still had an old fashion stove for cooking. It was free standing iron stove with two burners on top and an oven underneath with a door decorated with beautiful scrolls.

"That's the soup for dinner, they call it luncheon. We have the bread from yesterday to serve with that." She covered the bread she had been kneading and left it to rise, "Come on. I'll show you up stairs."

They went up the back staircase for two flights and entered a small room under the eaves. There was a large feather bed with a bright cover-let, a stand with a chamber pot, and a small clothes press. One window faced the back garden.

"This is it," chimed Helga. "We share the bed and the clothes press. You're so tiny! You won't take up much room in the bed. There's no fire-place up here, so it will be nice to have a warm body next to me. Unpack your satchel, there's room in the press."

Fiona had only brought two lawn dresses, some undergarments, stockings and her night gown. She would get the rest on the next trip home. She put away her things and the two girls started downstairs. When they reached the second floor, Helga remembered that Mrs. Ritner had asked her to fetch her bonnet as she had to go out later. She went into her mistress's room for the bonnet and Fiona waited in the hall. A woman came out of a room down the hall. She was an elegant looking middle-age woman. She was dressed all in black in the latest fashion with a large hoop skirt and ruffled bodice. She walked with her head held high and with an air of imperious superiority. Fiona smiled as she passed, but the woman took no notice of her.

"Dear Lord, who was that lady?" she asked Helga as they continued back down to the kitchen. "She walked right by as if she didn't see me.

"Oh that's Mrs. Knight. A dark night she is. She looks at servants as if they were bed bugs. She used to be rich and lived in a big house in

Maryland. They had slaves. Her husband got involved in some kind of swindle. They say he would have gone to jail, but he died first. She's poor now and living here, but you would think she was queen of the land the way she acts. I don't know how Mrs. Ritner puts up with her."

"The other boarder is Mr. Adamson," Helga continued. "He's just the opposite, a real gentleman. He treats everybody the same. I think he's an old friend of the family. He has a carpenter business in town. He helped Mrs. Ritner put on this addition to the house," she said, pointing around her to the kitchen and the rooms upstairs.

Helga and Fiona donned aprons in the kitchen and were busy cutting the bread and dishing the soup into elegant bowls. Helga told her that Mrs. Knight was the only border who got a meal at noon. The others only got breakfast and supper. They made several trips to the dining room where Mrs. Ritner and Mrs. Knight were seated. The Ritner daughters were in school. They served the soup and bread and tea and cakes for desert. On one of the trips Fiona heard Mrs. Knight say something about servants loitering in the hall.

Mrs. Ritner answered, "She's new."

The rest of the day was filled with cleaning up the kitchen and preparing supper. The Ritner girls, Laura, Emma Jane, and Ella, returned home from the nearby King Street School and came into the kitchen looking for snacks. Helga gave them cookies and introduced Fiona. They were nice girls and had their mother's good manners.

Helga explained that Mrs. Ritner was the second wife. "Mr. Ritner had three children when they married. The oldest, Mary, is married and lives in Connecticut. The boys John and James are away at college. The three girls are fourteen, twelve, and little Ella is eight. She was born after Mr. Ritner died."

Mr. Adamson later stopped in and introduced himself. He was a tall dignified man with long graying side whiskers. He welcomed Fiona with a warm smile and bowed slightly. He made her feel like a lady, not a hired girl.

Helga put on a pot of stewed chicken for dinner. She showed Fiona how to make dumplings to drop in the pot. Helga had learned to cook from her German mother. She lived on a farm out near Gettysburg with her parents and six brothers and sisters. She and Fiona were both sixteen.

Fiona told her about her life with her father. She had cooked for him as soon as she was old enough to tend the fire. Da taught her but his knowledge of cooking was limited. Fiona learned more from Annie Kelly, their neighbor down the road. She showed her how to make preserves and put up peaches and applesauce.

After serving in the dining room, Helga and Fiona ate their supper in the kitchen. When they were through, Helga took her into the parlor and showed her how to light the gas lights. They were another first for Fiona. She looked around in their soft glow. There was a small piano in the corner and several chairs with needlepoint covered seats around the room. Some of the chairs had arms and some had no arms. Helga explained that the armless chairs were for the ladies so that they could spread out their skirts. A large round table stood in the center of the room and an opened bible lay on top. A turkey rug covered the floor. Fiona thought it was a beautiful room but she was more impressed with the many books on a shelf that covered one wall. She wondered if she would be allowed to read them.

The family, Mrs. Knight and Mr. Adamson retired to the parlor while Fiona and Helga cleaned up the dinning room and washed the dishes. Fiona could hear Mrs. Ritner reading to the group. It sounded like something from Mr. Dickens. She felt a slight pang, thinking of Da. He used to read to her every night. Thomas McKenna had no schooling, but he could read. There were no schools for the Irish, but he had learned from Father McGrath who had a secret school where he taught the local children. Da often spoke of how Father McGrath had inspired him to learn. Da always had books. They never had much money, but he always managed to buy or borrow books. They had read Mrs. Stowe's *Uncle Tom's Cabin* and discussed the slavery issue. Newspapers were another source of knowledge. They always read the papers and discussed what was going on in the world. They read about the debates between Mr. Lincoln and Mr. Douglas out in Illinois. Fiona knew she would miss her evenings with Da.

This evening, her first in the Ritner house, was coming to an end. She and Helga used the privy out back and washed at the pump. They took a candle, climbed the stairs and got into their night gowns. Fiona knelt down and said her prayers. She could hear Helga saying her prayers in German on the other side of the bed. The girls climbed into the big bed.

"You know the Ritners used to hide slaves up here," Helga whispered. "They say this was a stop on the railroad."

"How could this be a stop on the railroad?" Fiona giggled.

"It was the underground railroad, silly. Runaway slaves stayed here 'til they could go farther north. It stopped when Mr. Ritner died or it could have been before that. They couldn't keep it up when the slave catcher moved in next door."

"Next door," Fiona exclaimed, "where that mean looking dog is?"

"Yep, that's old Mr. Gross. He uses that dog to run down slaves and then returns them for a lot of money. He says that the dog can smell them."

"There was a mean-looking boy too."

"Oh that's his son Ralph. He's harmless, a little stupid and has an eye for the girls. Wait 'til he gets a good look at you."

Helga was still talking when Fiona fell asleep. She dreamed of gaslights, books, mean dogs and mean ladies in hoop skirts.

# Chapter Two

The days passed quickly for Fiona. The work was hard but Mrs. Ritner worked right along with the hired girls. She was in the kitchen when they came down in the mornings and started the fire going in the stove. The girls went out to the pump to fetch water and put on the coffee. Mrs. Ritner had the porridge bubbling in a large pot. Mrs. Knight was served breakfast in the dining room whenever she arose. Mr. Adamson ate breakfast in the kitchen with the Ritner girls before he left for his office. The girls would go off to school and Helga and Fiona would go about their daily tasks.

On wash days Mr. Adamson always helped the hired girls get the fire going in the yard. He would lift the great copper boiler over the fire grate and fill it with water before he left for work. When the water was hot, Helga and Fiona began the washing. They would scrub, rinse and ring. They would giggle over Mrs. Knight's fancy linen undergarments that had to be carefully washed.

"We're not good enough for her majesty to speak to, but we can wash her drawers," Helga shouted with a laugher as they hung the washing on the lines to dry.

Ralph usually hung over the fence next-door. He was a plump boy with slicked black hair and pimpled face. He looked them over and shouted, "Need any help girls?"

"Not from the likes of you," Helga returned.

At least they didn't have to wash the sheets. Mrs. Ritner sent the sheets out to be washed by a Negro laundress called Old Molly. Molly would return them neatly folded. She would wheel the baskets of linens up the back alleys in her pushcart singing:

*When Israel was in Egypt' Land,*
*Let my people go,*

*oppressed so hard they could not stand,*
*Let my people go.*
*Go down Moses,*
*Way down in Egypt's Land.*
*Tell ol' Pharoah,*
*Let my people go.*

Fiona couldn't keep herself from clapping to the tune when she heard Old Molly coming down the alley. She would go out and help her carry in the sheets. Molly always wore a red bandana around her head and two large round gold ear bobs. Her handsome finely chiseled face was the color of bronze and people said she was part Indian. They also said she could tell fortunes and Fiona and Helga was always begging her to tell theirs, but she would say,

"Not yet childs. You too young"

The next days, as Fiona was putting the linens away in the upstairs closet, Mrs. Knight called her into her room.

"Girl, come in here, I need assistance."

Fiona entered the room and found her standing by the side on the bed, struggling with her corset.

"Lace up my corset," she ordered.

Fiona laced her up with much difficulty. Mrs. Knight was not a small woman and the corset was very tight. As she worked, Fiona looked around the room. On the dresser there was a picture of a grey bearded gentleman in a fancy frock coat. There was a silver comb and brush and cut glass perfume bottles on a mirrored tray. *Things from her past life,* Fiona thought.

"All done Mum," Fiona said as Mrs. Knight turned around.

"My fingers are getting a bit stiff and I find it difficult to lace myself. I would like you to assist me in the future."

"I'll have to ask Mrs. Ritner, it may interfere with my other duties," Fiona replied as she left the room.

When Helga saw Fiona coming out of the dreaded Mrs. Knight's room, she put her hands to her mouth in shock. "What were you doing in there?"

"Lacing up her corset," she replied with a smile. "She said her fingers are getting stiff and she needs help."

"Ha, her middle is getting bigger, more likely. Be careful, she'll have you waiting on her hand and foot." Helga said as they finished putting the linens away.

Later that day, Fiona encountered Mrs. Ritner in the parlor and asked to speak with her. She told her about Mrs. Knight's request and the landlady smiled and asked her to sit down.

"I think it would be all right to help her each morning. She is getting older and having difficulties. She is a distant cousin, that's why she came here after her husband died. I know how she puts on airs but don't let her treat you as her personal servant. I will make her understand that. I don't think she can afford to pay you anything."

"That's all right; just lacing her up mornings takes little time. I'm just surprised she asked me. She never spoke to me before."

"Well, it's funny, the other day she spoke of you. She said that she thought you had a look of dignity about you and could be trusted."

Fiona thanked Mrs. Ritner and returned to the kitchen. She told Helga what Mrs. Ritner said and they collapsed in giggles.

"Well, Miss Dignity," Helga said. "Have fun lacing the old girl up. I'm glad she didn't think I was dignified."

It soon was the weekend for Helga to go home and Fiona knew she would miss her. Mr. Meyers and Helga's brother Hans called for her. Mr. Meyers was a large man with a grey beard. He was dressed in overalls and a plaid shirt. He greeted Fiona warmly and introduced Hans. A young man with straight blond hair stepped forward. He just stood there staring at Fiona with a silly grin on his face.

"Hans," Helga shouted, "Mind your manners."

"Oh, sorry," said Hans. "Pleased ta meet ya miss."

"Hans is shy with girls," Helga whispered as she hugged Fiona good bye.

Fiona laughed and hugged her back.

One of Fiona's favorite tasks at the house was walking up town to purchase supplies. She would carry a shopping basket and a list from Mrs. Ritner. Most of the shops were on Main Street that ran through The Diamond. Mr. Hughes sold groceries and Mr. Denig ran the drug store. Mr. Armstrong had a dry goods store on South Main. Fiona enjoyed chatting with the shopkeepers and customers. Mr. Hughes told her about Mr. Heneberger who lived just up the street. He had been a soldier in the Revolutionary War. Fiona was thrilled to hear that. *He is living history*, she thought. She loved to walk by his house. Sometimes he would be sitting outside and she tried not to stare. He looked very old and she thought of the stories he would have to tell, but she was too shy to ask.

The best shopping days were the times Mrs. Ritner sent Fiona and Helga together. They would make the purchases, and then browse in the other stores. Bishop's photography displayed photographs and Fiona planned to have her portrait taken for Da someday. They looked in Mr. Aughenbaugh's jewelry store and admired the ear bobs and watches. Glosser's Tobacco Shop was next to the shoe shop. Fiona planned to buy Da some nice tobacco when she got paid. They would always stop at Granny Reisher's shop for penny candy.

Some days they would have time for visits. Helga would take Fiona to visit friends of her family. Some of them, like the Wenzes, could speak only German and Fiona would enjoy listening to them. Fiona would take Helga to visit Mrs. Gormley. Helga was impressed with her parlor. There were lace curtains on the windows and potted plants everywhere. The chairs were all red velvet and every surface was covered with lace doilies. Helga and Kate got on very well and had a great time gossiping. They would then stop to see Enoch and Hattie. Helga had never been in the home of a black person before and she liked them very much.

One day they ran into Mr. Adamson as they were headed home. He took their baskets and carried them. He asked, "Is Mrs. Ritner well? I did not see her this morning."

"She's fine," Helga replied, "she was busy in the larder."

"She is such a fine woman and she works too hard. It is not a good life for a gentle woman."

Fiona could not believe that she had been at the Ritner house for two weeks and it was time for her weekend off. Da was coming on Saturday morning to pick her up in the wagon. Fiona was up early and ready to go when she heard his knock at the back door. She almost cried when she saw him; she had not realized how much she had missed him. She gave him a great hug and pulled him into the kitchen to meet Helga.

"Helga, this is my father, Thomas McKenna."

"Please to meet ya, sir. Your girl and I have become great friends."

"I'm happy to hear she has a friend here," he replied as he removed his cap.

Fiona beamed with pride at her father. He was dressed in his best clothes and looked just fine. As they were leaving, Mrs. Ritner entered the kitchen and Fiona introduced her father.

"Very nice to meet you sir," she said in her nice way. "I'm very pleased with your daughter's work. She is a fine girl."

Mr. McKenna bowed and thanked her and they were on their way. He had parked the wagon at Mrs. Gormley's house. They walked over and she insisted that they stay for a noon dinner. Hattie served them fried chicken in the dinning room and Fiona enjoyed being waited on for a change.

Da and Mrs. Gormley wanted to know all about her life at the Ritner house. Fiona told them about her work and described all the people who lived there. She told them that the work was hard, but that Mrs. Ritner was kind and worked right along with them. She laughed when speaking of Helga and the fun they had together. She spoke of the young Ritner daughters and described the two boarders.

Thomas put down his fork and said, "Oh yes, Charles Adamson is a fine gentleman. He is very well thought of around town."

"Not so that Agnes Knight," chimed in Kate. "She gives all the shop-keepers a hard time with her highfalutin ways. She used to be rich, but now she has to live on a small inheritance from her father. She can't get over her come down."

Fiona told them about her morning services to Mrs. Knight and Kate laughed.

Both she and Da reminded her that she was not her servant and Fiona assured them that she would not let her take advantage. Hattie entered with dishes of early strawberries and cream and Thomas asked her about Enoch. He knew they were living in Wolftown, the colored section of Chambersburg, but there were some blacks in the vicinity of Third Street. Enoch had been looking at property there.

"He's doing very well, Mr. Thomas. He was able to rent that small shop on Third Street to set up his barber shop."

"Aye, that's wonderful Hattie. I'll stop in to see him soon."

Thomas and Fiona thanked Kate for the meal and said there good byes. They headed down the Baltimore Pike to their cottage.

"Aye, I've missed you, macushla," Tom said as the old horse Roisin trotted along the road. "I'm a happy man today," he said and broke into one of his songs:

*Wid my bundle on my shoulder,*
*Faith! There's no man could be bolder,*
*I'm lavin' dear ould Ireland widout*
*warnin,*
*For I lately took a notion*
*For to cross the briny ocean,*
*And I'm off to Philadelphia in the*
*Mornin.*

Fiona laughed and said, "Well that was you, Da." And they sang together:

*In Dublin's fair city,*
*Where the girls are so pretty,*
*I first set my eyes on sweet Molly*
*Malone.*
*She wheeled her wheelbarrow*

*Through streets broad and narrow*
*Crying cockles and mussels, alive,*
*alive, oh.*

Fiona laughed and sang. She did not realize how much she had missed these times with Da. When they arrived at the cottage, she looked around at the dear room with the table and chairs that Da had made. Fond memories of the times they had spent there flooded back.

"I'll start the fire and we can have some tea," Tom said as he busied himself.

"I'll do it. You sit in your rocker," Fiona said as she smiled up at him.

They sat with their tea and some soda bread that Annie Kelly had sent over, and relaxed. Fiona realized that she had not felt so relaxed in many weeks. It was good to be home.

The weekend passed too quickly. Many neighbors stopped by and wanted to hear all about the happenings in town. Fiona regaled them with all the news and the wonders of town life. Even Judge Flood stopped by for a short time. Fiona was surprised to see him in the doorway. He filled the door with his presence. He was tall and rotund with a neatly trimmed grey beard. He had the look of a man of importance. He inquired on how Fiona was doing at the Ritners.

"Just fine, sir," she assured him.

"Well, well, I was sure you would," he replied in his gruff manner. "Tom, I need you first thing Monday morning to oversee the planting in the west field."

*Of course he didn't come here just to ask about me*, Fiona thought. Tom answered that he had already planned to do that and the Judge left reassured.

Howard Flood was a man of many enterprises. He was a retired judge and to most people, he was still the Judge. He owned a house in town plus a large farm on the north side of the pike. The house there was one of the largest in Franklin Country, sitting on a rise overlooking Falling Springs. It was the largest farm in the area with many crops plus peach and apple orchards. He also owned several businesses in town and was a trustee of the bank. He was a widower in his sixties and had a daughter that he rarely saw. He did not approve of the man she married. Through the years, Thomas McKenna had become his right hand man. He was responsible for a great deal of the operation of the farm. Fiona always felt that her Da was underappreciated by the great man.

Fiona was glad when everyone had left and she and her father sat by the fire. He had a copy of a Philadelphia newspaper and began to read the headlines to her. The new mayor Robert Conrad had been backed by the Know-Nothing or American Party. He was recruiting a police force of 900 men and specified that they must all be of American birth.

"Their still trying to keep down the Irish," Thomas grunted.

Other stories related to the coming election, the new Republican Party and the growing fear of a schism with the south.

"I like what this fellow Lincoln has to say," Thomas reflected. "When I got my citizenship, I became a Democrat because they helped the immigrants, but I don't like their stand on slavery. This country needs to end this god awful thing."

On Sunday morning they left early to make the 11:00 o'clock mass at Corpus Christi. Fiona wore her best blue dress and bonnet. After mass, Father Mahoney greeted them warmly and congratulated Fiona on her new position.

"Are they treating you well there, dear?" he inquired.

She replied that they were and that she liked work.

"Take care out there among the Protestants," he said with a wink.

Tom and Fiona walked around town and greeted friends as they passed. Tom wanted to stop off at Third Street to see Enoch's new barber shop. Enoch and Hattie welcomed them and proudly showed them around. The shop faced the street with a large window in front. They had a small apartment in the back and their faces beamed with pride as they showed the new place to their friends. They sat and talked for a while. Fiona noticed as they sat side by side that Enoch was as black as Hattie was white. They made a handsome couple. As a neighbor's child wandered in, Hattie picked him up and put him on her lap. Fiona noticed the look of sorrow that came over her face.

When she was still in slavery, Hattie had two children. They were sold to another planter and she never saw them again. Enoch had been born free up north. He met Hattie when her mistress brought her north on a shopping trip. He always said that he fell in love with her at first sight and was determined to work hard and save enough money to buy her freedom. He did manage to do that but they never found her children and were not able to have children of their own.

Hattie once told Kate Gormley, "The mistress sold them because she knew her husband was the father and she could not stand to look at them."

Fiona always noticed that even when Hattie was smiling, there was a look of longing in her eyes. They chatted for a while and then Tom and Fiona stood up to leave.

"God bless your new home and may your business prosper," Tom said and shook hands with Enoch.

"Thank you Mr. Tom. Stop in any time."

As they left, Fiona noticed that Old Molly's laundry was right next door. They strolled back along Third Street and Fiona saw a familiar figure ahead and rolled her eyes, "Oh no, there's Barney."

Tom's reaction was quite different. He laughed and called out, "Hello old friend, good to see you."

"And the same to you, darlin'man," Barney replied, as he gave Tom a great hug. He made a sweeping bow to Fiona and said, "She walks in beauty like the night."

Fiona laughed in spite of herself. Barney soon broke into song and Tom joined him.

*Come back to Erin, Mavorneen,*
*Mavoreen,*
*Come back Aroon to the land of thy*
*Birth.*

*Come with the shamrocks and spring-*
*time, Mavorneen,*
*And Killarney shall ring with our*
*mirth.*

Barney Carney was a short man of some forty years. His hair was red and stuck up at odd angles. His ruddy face held a permanent smile and his eyes were usually red rimmed. He rented a room over the shoe shop and did odd jobs when he was sober.

"Too bad it's Sunday, all the pubs are closed," Barney said laughing at their singing. "Won't you come up to my room and have a drink with me? I'll get some lemonade for the lass."

"Sorry, Barney, I must be getting Fiona back to the Ritner house soon," Tom replied.

"I heard she had taken up employment there. Well, another time," Barney said as he tipped his hat and went on his way.

"He should be taking up employment," Fiona said with a frown. "I don't know why you bother with him."

"Aye, he's from Kilkenny," Tom replied. "And now, I have a surprise for you daughter. I'm takin' you to dinner at the hotel."

"Oh Da, that's too expensive."

"Not atall, atall, Flood gave me a bonus for getting the crops planted on time. I know you think he doesn't treat me well enough, but he does show a bit of appreciation now and then."

They entered the Montgomery House on the Diamond. Just as they were being shown to a table, they encountered Mr. Gross and his son Ralph. Fiona always thought Mr. Gross looked like a grizzly bear. He had a large brown beard that surrounded his face and small beady eyes. He spoke in a gruff manner.

"Well McKenna, I see that daughter of yours is at the Ritner house," he announced loudly. "Better warn her not to get involved in any of their activities. I keep a close watch on them."

"Thank you, Gross, she can take care of herself," Tom replied.

"You look lovely, Fiona." Ralph said with a wink as they headed out the door.

Tom and Fiona sat down and Tom said, "I hope I did the right thing by letting you go there dear. There could be trouble."

"Don't worry, Da. The family has not been involved in anything since Mr. Ritner died, especially with that one next door."

"What about that obnoxious boyo? Has he given you any trouble?"

"Hey, you just said I can take care of myself."

Fiona repeated Helga's observation that he was harmless and a bit stupid. They enjoyed their steak dinner and did not give the Grosses another thought.

Tom escorted Fiona back to the house. "Good bye Macushla, take care and God bless. Send word if you need anything. I'll be coming into town more often now. There's always supplies needed with the growing season."

"I'll be fine, Da. Don't worry. You take care and don't work too hard."

He kissed her good bye and walked back to the stable to pick up the horse and wagon.

When Fiona entered the house it was very quiet. Mrs. Ritner and the girls were out on their Sunday calls. She guessed that Helga was out for a walk and the boarders were off some where or in their rooms. Fiona sat at the kitchen table, looked around and reflected on the time she had spent there. She was happy here, even though she missed Da. She thought that what she was doing had some worth. She was helping Da and doing a good job. Mrs. Ritner was pleased with her work and she and Helga had become good friends. Suddenly she thought of Mr. Gross and was filled with a kind of foreboding. It wasn't just about him. It was something else. She wasn't sure what. *Oh good Lord, I'm becoming fey*, Fiona thought. *That's the word that Da uses about people who can see into the future.* She shook her head and she went up stairs to change her clothes.

# Chapter Three

The days passed quickly and the lovely days of spring were turning into the warm days of summer. Fish were splashing in the creek and the green beans in the back garden were getting tall. One day Mr. Adamson came home with poles to stake them up. He liked to help with the garden, because Mrs. Ritner was so fond of it. Fiona continued to help Mrs. Knight with her corsets each morning. A kind of grudging respect had grown between them and Fiona was beginning to understand the relationship between the two widows.

"Mrs. Ritner and I like to chat about our dear departed husbands," Mrs. Knight said one morning. "When you lose a loved one, others get tired of hearing about your grief, but one who has also suffered a loss understands. We comfort each other."

Mrs. Knight did not object when Mrs. Ritner invited Fiona and Helga into the parlor on some evenings. Helga usually found them boring but Fiona enjoyed them. They would listen to Mrs. Ritner or Mr. Adamson read from the bible or the latest book. Sometime Mrs. Ritner or Laura would play the piano and they would sing hymns. Fiona liked the Protestant hymns and would sing along. She especially enjoyed singing "Shall We Gather by the River."

> *Shall we gather by the river,*
> *The beautiful, beautiful river;*
> *Gather with the saints by the river*
> *That flows by the throne of God.*

Fiona smiled when she thought of Father Maloney's warning about the Protestants. Best of all Mrs. Ritner gave Fiona permission to borrow any book she wanted. She found the works of Mr. Dickens and many of Shakespeare's, she read Jane Austin's and dreamed about Mr. Darcy. Fiona was careful to take only one book a week and put it back properly.

One day as Fiona was returning a book to the shelf in the parlor, she heard a knock at the front door. She went to open it and saw a strange man on the door step. He had a long white beard and deep-set, penetrating eyes. Behind him in the street a wagon with a white canvas covering was parked. He wore a wide brimmed slouch hat and a long white coat.

He removed the hat and said, "Good afternoon, Miss. May I see your mistress? I would like to rent some rooms."

"Yes sir," she replied and went to fetch Mrs. Ritner.

*What a strange looking man*, she thought. *He spoke kindly, but there is something about him that is frightening.* She wasn't sure what it was and she had a feeling of foreboding again. Mrs. Ritner asked the man to step into the parlor and closed the door.

Fiona went back to the kitchen and told Helga about the man. Helga answered in her down-to-earth way.

"Hey, as long as he's a paying customer, who cares if he's strange. We need more boarders."

A little later, Mrs. Ritner came into the kitchen looking pleased. "Mr. Isaac Smith is going to rent several rooms for the summer. He and his business partners will be coming and going, but they want us to keep the rooms ready at all times. They are developing iron mines in Maryland and Virginia and will be receiving shipments of tools here in Chambersburg." She instructed the girls to get the rooms ready.

"They will use the big room in the back on the second floor and also the small adjoining bedroom. There is one man who will be here all the time overseeing the shipments. His name is Mr. Henry. We will put him in here," she said as she pointed to the small room off the kitchen.

Helga and Fiona set to work airing and cleaning the rooms and making up the beds. At the end of the day they sat in the kitchen exhausted.

Helga said, "This is going to be a lot more work, but it's good for the Misses. She needs the money."

"I don't know if I will like having a gentleman in this room right next to the kitchen. It won't be very private for him or for us," wondered Fiona. She had that same sense of foreboding.

When Mr. Adamson arrived home that evening, he came into the kitchen and the girls told him about the new boarders. He looked concerned. Later, Fiona heard him speaking to Mrs. Ritner in the dining room.

"Mary, what do you know about these men?"

"They are business men, Charles, and will be receiving shipments here"

"That's all? Should you not make more inquiries?"

"Mr. Smith and I had a long conversation. He is a very religious man and studied to be a minister. He is a gentleman."

"Well, I hope his men aren't ruffians," Mrs. Knight said in her disdainful way.

A few days later, Mr. Henry arrived. Fiona's mood changed as soon as she saw him. He was a young man of medium height with brown hair and nice grey eyes. His smile was kindly and he had the look of a man with a gentle nature. Fiona showed him in to the room off the kitchen. A narrow bed, a dresser, and a small desk were the only furnishings. She apologized that it was so small and barren.

"This will be fine, Miss, my needs are simple. I will be comfortable here. Thank you."

He smiled at her sweetly and Fiona left the room with a lighter heart. "I guess it won't be so bad having him here," she told Helga.

Several of Mr. Smith's other associates came and went in the next few days. Three of them were Mr. Smith's sons Wilson, Oliver and Owen. The others names were Tidd, Merriam, Hazlet, and Coppoc. They stayed upstairs and rarely took meals. However, Mr. Henry was a constant presence. He spent a great deal of time working at the desk in his room. He would usually leave the door open and talk to the girls while they worked. Mrs. Ritner and her girls also enjoyed his company. When she learned that he had been a teacher, she asked him to instruct her daughters in French and penmanship and he readily accepted.

Fiona and Helga loved to hear him instructing the girls in his room while they worked. Mr. Henry taught them all French songs and they sang:

> Frere Jacques, frère Jacques,
> Dormez vous, dormez vous?
> Sonnent les mantines, sonnent les mantines:
> Ding dang dong, ding dang dong

Sometimes, Mr. Henry asked Fiona about the books she was reading.

"They are all fine, but I'll lend you some books of poetry by Ralph Waldo Emerson. You should read some American literature"

Fiona read the book, but found some of the poems hard to understand. She liked "The Rhodora."

> In May, when sea-winds pierced our solitudes,
> I found the fresh Rhodora in the woods,
> Spreading its leafless blooms in a damp nook,
> To please the desert and the sluggish brook
> The purple petals fallen in the pool,
> Made the black water with their beauty gay;
> Here might the red bird come his plumes to cool,
> and court the flowers that cheapens his array.
> Rhodora! If the sages ask the why
> This charm is wasted on the earth and sky,
> Tell them, dear that if eyes were made for seeing,
> Then beauty is its own excuse for being:
> Why thou wert there, O rival of the rose!
> I never thought to ask, I never knew:
> But, in my simple ignorance, suppose
> The self-same Power that brought me there brought you.

Mr. Henry tried to explain the poem to Fiona. "It answers the question of what is so special about this ordinary flower. It shows the mystical unity of God throughout all of nature. God guides the flower in the world just as he does all of us. We are all connected and responsible for one another. Man and nature are one."

"What a beautiful thought," Fiona replied with wonder.

"Mr. Emerson is a Transcendentalist. They are creating a new form of American literature showing the mystical unity of God's love through all of nature. Many of them are abolitionists. They look not only at Christian beliefs, but also Hindu and Buddhist beliefs of the oneness of all creatures."

"It is a bit difficult to understand, but it is a very beautiful concept," Fiona said enthralled.

"There is a new poet named Walt Whitman that I would like you to read. I'll show you his book when I get it and also the essays of Thoreau. They are very good."

Fiona could not wait to discuss all of this with Da. She knew he would find it interesting.

Mr. Smith was not at the house very often. When he was there he would sit in the parlor after supper and read from the bible. His voice was usually quiet, but when he read from the bible, it was like thunder. He always read from the Old Testament, fire and brimstone chapters, Fiona's father called them. Mr. Henry would look over at Fiona and wink and she would stifle a giggle.

Mrs. Ritner had great respect for Mr. Smith's preaching. When the minister for her church, Falling Springs Presbyterian, was away she invited him to preach there one Sunday. People said his preaching was very well received.

One afternoon, Mr. Smith was having a cup of tea with Mrs. Ritner. Fiona was bringing in some biscuits. Mrs. Knight never joined them for tea when Mr. Smith was present. Suddenly little Ella burst through the door carrying a small black boy who was crying profusely.

"Oh Mama, I found him alone in the street. He is lost. Isn't he beautiful? Can we keep him?"

Before she could answer, Mr. Smith grabbed the boy and set him on his lap. He hugged him fiercely and said. "He is one of God's chosen."

Mrs. Ritner looked slightly alarmed and told Ella to take the boy out-side and find his mother.

The summer days were growing longer. Da came into town often and always stopped to see Fiona. He met Mr. Henry and thought him a fine gentleman. When their chores were done in the evening, he would take Fiona and Helga for a ride in the wagon out in the country. Sometimes Mr. Henry would go with them and Fiona loved to sit next to him and chat. She loved to hear about his life. He told her he was twenty-four and was born in Ohio. He had taught school in Virginia and saw slavery there first hand. His voice changed when he spoke of that experience and it would frighten Fiona a little. But soon, his gentle voice would return and they would talk of pleasant things. He told her about trips out west, the beauty of the land out there and the wild Indians he had seen. Fiona told him of her longing to travel and have new experiences.

After one ride, he put his hands around her waist and lifted her down from the wagon. Fiona felt a warm glow pass through her body. She fell asleep that night dreaming of Mr. Darcy, but in the dream, he became Mr. Henry.

That summer the Ritner girls were constantly underfoot when not tak-ing lessons with Mr. Henry. Fourteen year old Laura was usually helping her mother, but the younger ones ran free. Sometimes Mr. Henry took them back to the creek and they would wade. Fiona and Helga, working in the kitchen, could hear their delighted screams. One day he took them fishing and brought home fish for supper. Mr. Henry helped Fiona and Helga clean them on the back porch.

July faded into August and Mr. Henry told them he would be very busy the next few weeks. He spent a great deal of time in his room writ-ing. Mr. Smith's other associates were in and out. He would give them notes to deliver to Lemnos Edge Tool Factory. One day he asked Fiona to take a note there for him.

"It's an order for tools for our mining operation," Mr. Henry told her. "Please take this note and give it to George Stork."

The tool factory was over the Loudon Street Bridge down by the Conochocheague Creek. Fiona had passed by there, but had never been inside. When she opened the door, she was almost thrown back by the heat and noise. There were rows of roaring fires and the ringing sound of hammers beating on anvils. At first she thought it a horrific scene, but soon found it interesting. Men wearing large leather aprons were pounding iron into axes and other tools. Some of them stopped when they saw a girl at the door.

A man ran up to her and gruffly asked what she wanted.

"I have a note for Mr. George Stork," she replied haughtily.

He pointed to an office in the corner and she found a man seated at a desk.

"Mr. Stork? I have a note for you from Mr. Henry."

He looked up at her and frowned, took the note and read it.

"That group is certainly ordering a lot of tools, but they're paying in gold. Must be a big operation. How come he's sending a little girl on his errands?"

"I work at the Ritner house where he is staying. He was busy and none of the other men were around," she replied with great dignity.

"All right girlie, tell him we'll let him know when the tools are finished. We'll send them over to Oakes and Caufman's Warehouse for storage."

Fiona walked back through the factory and smiled at the stir she was causing. She looked back and the entire ceiling reflected the glow of the fires. She thought it looked like a weird and beautiful Purgatory.

"Why did you send me there?" She asked Mr. Henry when she returned.

He laughed and said, "You always say you're looking for new experiences. I thought it would be an interesting experience for you. You remember I told you about the Transcendentalists. They not only believe in abolition, they also believe in the equality of women. Someday the slaves will be free and women will be free to do whatever they want."

"Well, I didn't feel like I belonged in Lemnos. I felt like an alien in that place but it was interesting. You are a strange man, Mr. Henry."

There was some talk around town about Mr. Isaac Smith and his associates. People wondered what kind of business they were in. Young Emma Jane wandered into the kitchen one day talking about them.

"Mama says they are in the mining business, but I heard people saying they were making bad money."

Helga laughed and asked, "Do you mean counterfeit money?"

"Yes that's what they say and I'm gonna find out."

"Don't you be goin' in their rooms. Your Mama won't like that."

"I won't go in," she replied as she went out the door. "I'm going to my friend Anna's house."

Helga looked at Fiona and said, "Those two are trouble."

A few days later Mr. Smith was at the house along with several of his associates. They were all up in the back bedroom. Mr. Henry had gone down to the depot to check on a shipment. Emma Jane and her friend Anna were playing dolls in the front hall. Fiona and Helga were peeling potatoes in the kitchen. A few minutes later the girls burst into the kitchen with gales of laughter.

"What are you girls up to?" Fiona asked.

They both collapsed into giggles, composed themselves and Emma Jane announced, "We crept up stairs to spy on Mr. Smith. We looked in the key hole and all we saw were the men sitting around looking at a map. That's all. It was disappointing."

"Well, you deserve to be disappointed, spying on people indeed," Fiona said.

"You better not do it again or we'll tell your mother," Helga scolded.

"We won't" Emma replied. "I guess he's just a nice old man like Mama said."

In August, Mr. Smith started moving their mining supplies to a farm down in Maryland. He told Mrs. Ritner he was renting the Kennedy farm to store his supplies until they could begin their mining venture. Mr. Smith and the Ritner girls were old friends by now. He was especially fond of little Ella. He took the girls for rides in his wagon when heading for Maryland. He let them off at the edge of town and they walked back.

"We had so much fun and Mr. Smith told us stories," they told Fiona and Helga when they returned.

Fiona was still tending to Mrs. Knight each morning. She was not happy with the new boarders.

"They all look like ruffians to me." she complained to Fiona.

"Well, Mr. Henry is a real gentleman." Fiona said.

"Then why is he associating with them?" Mrs. Knight asked.

"They're in business together," Fiona replied. "And Mrs. Ritner thinks highly of Isaac Smith. He preached at her church."

"Well, that's the Presbyterians for you. My Episcopal Church would never let just anyone preach. They must be ordained."

"They're just like the Catholics in that regard," Fiona replied.

"Hardly," Mrs. Knight replied icily.

One day Mrs. Knight surprised Fiona when she asked her about Judge Flood

"I understand your father works for him."

"Yes, he's worked for him for many years."

"I have heard that he's a man of substance."

"Substance, you mean wealth?"

"Well, yes and property."

"He has plenty of both," Fiona replied

Mrs. Knight thanked her and dismissed her.

Later, when Fiona told Helga about the conversation, she wondered what it was about. Helga laughed and said:

"I bet she's setting her cap for him."

"Why would she be setting her cap for that old man?"

"The oldest reason in the world: he has money."

On her next visit home, Fiona spoke with Da about the books Mr. Henry gave her to read and the Transcendentalists.

"Oh yes, I've read about them. There're New Englanders, very active in the anti-slavery movement. They also believe in women's right to vote."

"Women voting, that will never happen," Fiona exclaimed.

"Oh, it will come someday. Probably not in my lifetime, but maybe in yours. But first the slaves must be free."

"Da, are you an abolitionist?"

"Yes, I think I am. Not an active one, but I am against slavery."

"Mr. Henry and the men at the house are all abolitionists, I hear them talking."

"Tis an issue that will be coming to a head soon and there will be a terrible price to pay," Thomas Mckenna said almost to himself.

The weekend passed quietly for Fiona and her father. As usual they headed into town on Sunday for mass. After mass, they stopped to see Hattie and Enoch. They found several neighborhood people gathered in front of their house.

"Mr. Tom," Enoch said, "we heard that Fredrick Douglass is here in Chambersburg."

"Frederick Douglass, the former slave? He has become quite a famous speaker."

"Yes sir. Ol' Molly here saw him herself."

Molly was sitting on a bench in front of her house. She looked at Tom and Fiona and said, "Ay was making my deliveries and saw him talking with Shields Green out by the quarry."

Enoch said, "Green's a colored man who came to town with that Mr. Isaac Smith. He's stayin' with some folks in Wolftown."

"They was a white fisherman with a long white beard there too," Molly added.

They all wondered what a famous person like Douglass was doing in town and why he would be down by the quarry. Tom and Fiona stayed and chatted for a while, then as they were leaving, Old Molly grabbed Fiona by the arm and whispered:

"Ya all be careful young un. Ay have a feelin' there's gonna be big trouble."

"What did she say to you?" Tom asked.

"Oh nothing, just some of her silly predictions," Fiona replied. "I better get back to the Ritner's."

When they arrived, they could hear voices in the parlor. Fiona said goodbye to Da and went in to see if they needed anything. Mrs. Ritner,

Mr. Henry and Mr. Adamson were standing and talking excitedly. Mr. Smith sat on one side of the room and Mrs. Knight sat on the other.

"Hello Fiona," said Mr. Henry, "Wonderful news, Frederick Douglass is in town and will be speaking at Franklin Hall tomorrow evening at seven o'clock. I think you would enjoy him. Is it all right if she goes?" He said, turning to Mrs. Ritner.

Before she could answer, Mrs. Knight stood up and announced, "Well, I certainly won't be attending," and swept out of the room.

Mr. Smith remained strangely quiet.

"Of course you may go, Fiona, as long as you get your work done," Mrs. Ritner finally replied.

Fiona thanked her and returned to the kitchen. Helga was just coming down stairs and Fiona told her the news.

"Frederick who?" Helga said with a frown.

Fiona explained who he was and told her about the lecture.

"Lectures are not for me. They make me fall asleep like sermons in church. You go and I'll stay and clean up after supper."

Fiona thanked her and just then Mr. Henry and Mr. Smith went into Mr. Henry's room and closed the door. A little later, Fiona was getting water from the pump in the yard and heard them talking through the open window.

Mr. Henry said, "He's not going to join us?"

"No," Smith replied, "he said that it would not help the cause and it would be sheer folly."

Fiona quickly went inside, not wanting to be caught eaves dropping.

On the night of the lecture, Franklin Hall was packed. A negro had never spoken in Chambersburg before and there was great excitement in the air. Fiona entered with Mrs. Ritner and her daughters, escorted by Mr. Adamson. Mr. Henry and Mr. Smith were already seated. She could see Hattie, Enoch, Molly and several blacks standing in the back. She waved to Mrs. Gormley on the other side of the hall. Gas lights lined the edge of the stage and a podium stood at the center.

All grew quiet when Frederick Douglass came out on the stage. Fiona thought she had never seen a more impressive looking man. He had an air of great dignity in his movements. He was well dressed and looked like a gentleman. With his thick main of grey hair and a broad face with high cheek bones, he reminded Fiona of a proud lion.

He started to speak in ringing tones. "Thank you for having me here. I know that this is not exactly an abolitionist town, but I have been welcome by many folks."

He went on speaking about his life as a slave and about the evils of the system. Fiona looked around at the expressions on the faces of the audience. Some were enraptured and nodded their heads as they listened. Some sat with their arms folded, not agreeing with what he said. Fiona looked around at the black folks in the back and their faces beamed with pride. She tried to remember everything that Mr. Douglass said, so she could tell Da. She knew she would never forget what he said about slavery at the end of his speech:

"Be warned, a horrible reptile is coiled up in the tender breast of your nation's bosom."

The audience exited quietly, each in their own thoughts. Outside they gathered in small groups and spoke excitedly. Mrs. Gormley came over and said to Fiona, "Wasn't he magnificent?"

Fiona just nodded. Their group started walking home in the cool night air. Mr. Henry and Mr. Smith walked ahead, speaking softly. Mr. Adamson walked with the ladies and spoke of an incident in his boyhood.

"When I was a boy in Baltimore, I had a playmate who lived next door. We played together every day, but one day he was not there. I asked everyone where he had gone, but no one knew. Finally I asked my mother and she told me that he was a slave and his master had sold him. That was my introduction to slavery."

Mr. Henry came back and walked beside Fiona. He asked what she thought of the speech.

"I think I am an abolitionist," she replied.

# Chapter Four

The warm days of summer were winding down. The green beans were ready. They picked them and Mr. Adamson took down the polls and leaned them against the back of the house. It was a bumper crop. Mrs. Ritner gave baskets of them to the neighbors. They cooked the rest and had them for dinner every night. The cucumbers were in and Mrs. Ritner made summer pickles. They had lost some of the vegetables due to Mr. Gross's dog, who was constantly digging under the fence and getting in the garden. Mrs. Ritner was always complaining about that dreaded slave catching dog.

"I think he lets that dog in my garden just to taunt me. He knows my views on slavery."

One evening as they sat in the parlor, Mr. Henry heard her, and said, "I'll take care of him."

Later, as Fiona and Helga were cleaning up in the kitchen, Mr. Henry went into his room. They suddenly heard a shot and he came out with a pistol in his hand. He laid the pistol down and went out the back door. They ran to the door and saw the Gross dog lying on the ground dead. Mr. Henry had shot him through his window. He calmly picked the dog up and threw him into the Gross's yard. He washed his hands at the pump and came in.

"That dog won't bother anyone again," he said and went into his room and closed the door.

Helga and Fiona stood there with their mouths agape. The others in the house came running into the kitchen and Helga told them what had happened. They soon heard shouts from the Gross's yard. Fiona ran out and looked over the fence.

"What happened, Mr. Gross? We heard a shot."

"Somebody killed my dog. Did you hear where the shot came from?"

"Yes, from over there," Fiona said pointing toward the creek.

Mr. Gross and Ralph ran in that direction.

"Well aren't you the cool-headed one," Helga said when she came back in.

Fiona didn't feel that cool. Inside she was shaking

"I think we had all better go to bed," Mrs. Ritner said.

"Let's go upstairs," Fiona gasped.

The girls sat on their bed and Helga took Fiona's hand.

"You're sure actin' foolish over Mr. Henry. You know nothin' about him."

"Oh Helga, I think I love him."

"Love, that's foolish. My mama told me to be practical about who ya marry with. I'll probably marry Fritz Yeager."

"Fritz, who lives on the farm next to you? You're always making fun of him."

"I know," she laughed, "He's not real bright, but he's a good man and a hard worker. Its good to marry your own kind, and my Papa would be happy. The Yeager farm and ours would be joined. Another thing, Fritz is pliable."

"What do you mean by that?" Fiona said.

"He's easy goin', he won't rule the roost. He'll let me have my say. Mama says that's important."

"Well, I didn't say I was going to marry Mr. Henry. I just like him very much. I never knew anyone like him."

"You should marry my brother, he's mad for you."

"I'm not going to marry Hans!"

"Well, just go easy, my little friend. You don't know much of the world."

"Neither do you my friend. I'm tired, let's just go to bed."

They climbed into bed and it took a long time for Fiona to get to sleep. Her mind was whirling with the thought of Mr. Henry with the gun in his hand. How could someone who believed in the unity of all living things have no problem shooting a dog?

The next morning, the household was abuzz with talk of Mr. Henry's great shot. Mrs. Ritner thanked him, but asked that he not fire guns in or near the house again.

Mr. Henry replied, "I'm sorry, ma'am, I just wanted to rid you of that cursed animal."

He left to check on a shipment at the depot before Fiona could to speak to him. Mr. Adamson left for work with a look of concern on his face. Mrs. Knight came down for breakfast looking unconcerned. She must have not have heard the shot, Fiona thought. She went out to the pump to fetch a bucket of water and Ralph was hanging over the fence with his usual sneer.

"We never caught the bastards who shot Pa's ol' dog. Pa already left for Virginia to get another. He's gonna get a blood hound this time. Major was just a mutt, but he was a great catcher. Can I help you with the water, Mis Fiona?"

"No thank you," she replied and went inside with visions of that dog catching slaves. *I'm glad he's dead* she thought.

Mr. Henry returned later that afternoon and asked Fiona to take a walk down by the creek.

"I know you're upset with me," he said, as they walked along the stream.

"It was just a shock to see you shoot that animal after all you told me about the oneness of all in nature. I think I understand though that it was your hatred of slavery that made you do it."

"Yes, and I just wanted to help Mrs. Ritner. She's a great lady. I am a flawed man, Fiona, I do try to believe in those things I've read, but I also believe in some causes fervently and will do anything to help that cause and eliminate villainies. Slavery is the sum of all villainies."

He said this with a look of great determination on his face. They continued walking and he spoke of more pleasant things, but Fiona did not feel comforted. She had never been in love, but this feeling she had for him felt like love. Sometimes it was a comforting warm feeling. Other times it was an uneasy worrisome feeling. Mr. Henry was not an easy man to understand.

September was upon them and the Ritner girls were back in school. Things were quieter around the house. The trees were turning early and the valley was aflame with red and gold. Mr. Henry spent a lot of time down by the creek reading. Mr. Smith and the others were around more often. Fiona was feeling a sense of normality again. That is, until, one day she answered the front door and found Judge Flood on the doorstep. He was dressed in his finest suit and top hat. His best horse and carriage stood in the street.

He removed his hat and said, "Good afternoon Fiona, I'm here to see Mrs. Knight."

Fiona tried to suppress a look of surprise and asked him to come in. Mrs. Knight was already coming down the front stairs. She was dressed not in black, but a lovely shade of lavender. She had put on her best lace collar and cuffs and was carrying a parasol.

"Mr. Flood and I are going for a carriage ride," she said as they swept out the door.

Fiona stood there for a moment dumfounded, before running to the kitchen to tell Helga.

"I told you she was setting her cap for him," Helga chortled.

After that, Fiona's morning sessions with Mrs. Knight were more interesting. It was all about what Mr. Flood said and did.

"We met at the Episcopal Church. He is one of the most prominent men in town. He took me out to see his home in the country. It is quite large."

"Yes, I know," Fiona replied.

Mrs. Knight loved the fact that the Judge knew everyone of prominence in town and talked about all of their goings on.

"Mr. McClure told him that Mr. Henry brought Mr. Merriam into his law office the other day. He wanted to make out a will."

"Who did?" Fiona almost shouted.

"Who did what?"

"Make out a will."

"Oh, that was Mr. Merriam. He said he was going on a journey south and that accidents will happen. He has some property in Boston and wanted to leave it to the Abolition Society. Can you imagine?"

"Should a lawyer be giving that information out? Isn't that privileged?"

"Oh no, the Judge said that wills are a matter of public record."

Fiona was left with that uneasy feeling again. Why were they making out wills?

The next weekend was Helga's turn to go home. Mr. Henry and all of the men were down at the Kennedy Farm making preparations for their mining venture. On Saturday, Mr. Adamson was taking Mrs. Ritner and the girls to visit mutual friends in Mount Alto. Mrs. Knight was having dinner with Judge Flood. Mrs. Ritner suggested that Fiona take the day off.

"Well I could spend the day with Mrs. Gormley...."

"Oh no," Helga shouted. "You must come out to the farm and spend the day with us. Papa's going to pick me up and Hans will bring you back tonight. Mama will love to meet you and we'll have a good time."

"Well, I guess...."

"No guesses about it. Come on, let's get ready."

Before she knew what was happening, they were ready to go and Helga's father was at the door. They climbed into the wagon and were off along the Gettysburg Pike. The trees were in their full magnificent fall colors and when they rounded a bend in the road, the valley below and the distant hill presented a blaze of red and gold. Fiona sighed and felt herself relaxing. That uneasy feeling was fading away.

"There's our farm," Helga shouted as the Meyers's place came into view.

"Oh, it is so beautiful," sighed Fiona as she gazed on the green fields.

There was a large red Pennsylvania bank barn with a painting of a six pointed star surrounded by colorful birds.

"Oh what a beautiful hex sign," Fiona exclaimed.

"Americans call them hex signs, but we call them sechs," Mr. Meyers said. "To them sechs sounds like hex. They are not to keep evil spirits away, but to bring good luck and happiness."

"Sechs means stars and the birds are called destilfinks," Helga said with a grin.

"Well, whatever you call them, they are beautiful," Fiona replied.

They pulled up to the two story farm house and the girls jumped out. Helga ran in and shouted,

"Mama, Mama, I brought Fiona home with us!"

Fiona entered the front room and was greeted by a large woman who looked very much like Helga. She wore a mop cap and apron and a huge smile.

She gave Fiona a great hug. "Velcom, Velcom, little one. Look how skinny you are. Ve must feed you."

Helga's brothers and sisters and several dogs stormed in the back door. Amid the children's shrieks and the barking dogs, Fiona was introduced to Maria, Madeline, Peter, Johann, and little Gertie. Hans stood in the back and just nodded and tipped his cap.

"Back to your chores children," Mrs. Meyers scolded. "Helga you may show Fiona around the farm. Maria you stay here and help me wid' supper."

The children scurried off and Helga and Fiona strolled out to the barn followed by little Gertie. She skipped along beside them with her pigtails flying. Fiona inhaled the smell of fresh hay and petted the horses in their stalls. The Meyers also kept pigs and goats and she delighted in the sight of them. They walked past rows of corn stalks now being cut down after the harvest. Hans, swinging a sickle, grinned when he saw the girls walk by. The young girls were feeding the chickens and Johann and his father were off in the fields.

"Gertie, Mama's calling you. Go home," Helga scolded.

Gertie stuck her tongue out. "You're mean Helga, you're always chassin' me off."

Fiona watched her run, her little bare feet a white blur, as she crossed the field. "You didn't have to get rid of her," she said

"Oh, yes I did. She can be a pain and this is our day."

They reached the stream that ran through the property and sat down under the trees.

"Oh Helga, it must be wonderful to live in such a lovely place!"

Helga spread out her skirts and sighed, "It's not always so wonderful. Farming is very hard work. My poor father works the land day after day but doesn't always make a profit. Everything depends on the weather. If there is no rain there is drought. If there is too much rain, the crops rot in the field. Then there's the bugs. One year the locust came and destroyed everything."

Fiona was familiar with the woes of farming. Her father handled all of them daily on the Judge's farm, but it was a huge operation. It was so big that if some crops failed, there were many more to fill the gap.

Fiona looked at Helga and said, "You all work so hard. You all have so many chores to do."

"Yep, the only reason I got out of chores today was because you were here. That's why working at Mrs. Ritner's is like a picnic to me. That work is not nearly as hard. I was glad to go when Papa needed the money. The crop had failed that year and he owed money to the bank."

"You must miss it so."

"Sure I miss the family like you miss your Da. I like living in town, but I know I'll be back here someday."

Fiona poked her and said, "When you marry Fritz?"

Helga laughed, "Who knows? Where do you think you'll end up?"

"Who knows," she sighed. "Let's wade in the stream!"

They took off their shoes and stockings and splashed in the cool water. For the rest of the afternoon, they were little girls again, climbing trees and picking wild flowers.

The dinner bell called them back to the farmhouse. Suddenly aware of their appearance, the girls ran to the pump and washed. They entered the house smoothing back their hair.

Mrs. Meyers looked at them and smiled. "Did you have a gud time yung uns?" She asked.

"We sure did. Thank you Mama," Helga said

They all sat at the large table in the kitchen. Mr. Meyers said the blessing and great steaming bowls were passed around. There was sauerkraut with great chunks of pork, boiled potatoes, corn, and applesauce. Fiona had two large helpings, but it wasn't enough for Mrs. Meyers.

"Eat, eat, little one. You must have more."

Fiona protested that she could not eat another bite. The girls jumped up to clear the table and ginger cake was passed around. It smelled so delicious that Fiona was able to eat a piece and she saw Mrs. Meyer smile approvingly.

All too soon it was time to go. Hans pulled the wagon around and they all stood at the door saying goodbye.

Mrs. Meyers handed Fiona a wrapped ginger cake and said, "Take this for the Ritners."

Fiona hugged her and said, "Thank you for everything. It was a wonderful day."

She climbed up on the wagon next to Hans and they were off. Hans was very quiet for a while and Fiona wondered if he would be silent for the entire ride. Fiona was startled when he finally spoke.

"It's starting to get a bit chilly, isn't it?"

"Yes," Fiona replied, "The evenings are getting cooler. It's almost October."

"Are you cold?" He asked.

"No, I'm fine, I have my shawl. I really enjoyed today. The farm is so beautiful."

"It will be mine someday. I'm the oldest," he said with pride.

"Well, you are very lucky."

They went on in silence for the rest of the journey and Fiona smiled to herself and thought, *I guess he's said everything he wanted to say.*

When they arrived in Chambersburg, Hans drove the wagon into the alley behind the house. He stopped the wagon and came around to help Fiona down. He took her hand and smiled. The light was fading fast, but she could see his face was red.

"Thank you, Hans, for seeing me home."

"You're welcome Miss. It was a nice ride."

"Yes it was," she said as he climbed back on the wagon and she waved goodbye.

As she entered the house, Ralph called from next door, "Is that your beau?"

"No, he's not. Don't you ever mind your own business?"

"Pa says it's my job to watch the house. Hey, I could be your beau."

Fiona ignored that and slammed the door. She set the ginger cake on the table and walked to the front hall. She lit the gas light on the table by the door. Just in time, she thought, as Judge Flood's carriage pulled up. Mrs. Knight would not have liked coming into a dark house.

Fiona opened the door and greeted them as they came up the steps.

"Good evening, Fiona." The judge said. "Thank you for a lovely afternoon, Agnes," he said as he guided her through the door.

"Goodnight, Howard. I had a very nice time."

Fiona returned to the kitchen and soon heard the front door close and Mrs. Knight's footsteps going upstairs. *Well, I guess they are courting,* Fiona laughed to herself.

Soon there was a great commotion at the front door as the Ritners returned. The girls and Mrs. Ritner came into the kitchen.

"Mr. Adamson is returning the hired horse and carriage to the stable. Don't lock up until he gets back," she instructed Fiona. "How was your day at the farm?"

Fiona regaled them with tales of life on the farm and the little girls loved it. Fiona sliced up the ginger cake for them and they wanted to hear more.

"It is a beautiful place and there are lots of children and animals there to play with."

Little Ella chimed in, "Oh, Mama, can we go there some day. It would be much more fun than visiting the Wiestlings in Mount Alto."

"Hush," her big sister Laura scolded. "Let me tell about Mr. Smith."

Fiona leaned forward at the table and said, "Was he there?"

"No," Laura answered, but he stayed there last spring. He was working on the South Mountain Railroad and he stayed there for a while."

Mrs. Ritner added, "The Wiestlings thought very highly of Mr. Smith. He set up a Sunday School for negro children at the Emmanuel Chapel."

"Were any of his other men there with him?" Fiona asked.

Mrs. Ritner looked at her sharply and replied, "No."

Fiona started to clean up the kitchen and the Ritners went up to bed. Mr. Adamson returned from the stable and she offered him some ginger cake.

"Thank you, Fiona, I think I will."

He sat down and had his cake with a mug of milk and they discussed their day. Fiona enjoyed talking to Mr. Adamson like this. He was usually so formal.

"Did the girls tell you that Isaac Smith had been in Mount Alto?" he asked.

"Yes, and that he was well thought of there."

"He has a way of ingratiating himself, doesn't he?"

"Yes he does," she replied.

"Well, thank you for the cake. Goodnight, Fiona."

"Goodnight sir."

The next morning, after cleaning up from breakfast, Fiona left for mass. After mass, she met Mrs. Gormley and she invited Fiona to stop for a while.

"Sorry, I have to get right back. Helga isn't there until this evening," she answered.

Kate Gormley took her hand and asked, "Are you all right my girl? Sometimes you look like you have the world on your shoulders. They are such slender shoulders. Please come to me if you ever want to talk."

"I will, dear Mrs. Gormley. I will."

Fiona walked back to the Ritners thinking. *I don't know what I would talk about. Those silly fears that come over me sometimes; I don't even know what they are.* As she walked up the garden path, she could here Mr. Henry's voice in the kitchen and her spirits rose. He greeted her and suggested that they go for a stroll after Sunday dinner. Mrs. Ritner had started the roast beef and Fiona put on her apron and started peeling the potatoes. After dinner, Mr. Henry helped her clean up the kitchen and do the dishes. When they finished, they followed their usual path down by the creek in silence.

"I hear you had a nice day at the Meyers farm," he finally spoke.

"Oh yes, It was so nice."

"Would you like to live on a farm?'

"I don't know. Helga says farming is very hard work. What I really liked was her family. It would be wonderful to have a large family. It was always just Da and me. When you have a big family, you're never lonely. That's what I like about living here. There's always people to talk to about so many different thing. "

"There is so much you want to learn, isn't there, Fiona?"

"Oh, yes and see different things and travel. I love to hear about your travels to so many places."

"I have a feeling you will learn much and travel to many places, Fiona McKenna." He stopped. "Let's sit down here on the bank."

They sat in companionable silence for a while as they watched the flowing stream. He turned to her and said,

"Fiona, we are going to be leaving soon."

She suddenly realized that these were the words she had been dreading to hear. She only nodded and he continued.

"We have received all of the supplies that we need, so it is no longer necessary to stay in Chambersburg. Our headquarters will now be at the Kennedy Farm in Maryland and we will begin our mining operations from there. We're leaving the day after tomorrow. We don't plan on coming back here, but I will try to get back to see you if it is at all possible."

"That would be nice," she replied. "I will miss you very much," she said as she bit her lip. She jumped up and said, "I must get back."

He grabbed her and kissed her. Fiona found herself kissing him back and her heart surged with joy.

He let her go and said, "I'm sorry I had no right to do that. Goodbye dear Fiona."

She watched him walk back to the house with tears in her eyes. Fiona was glad to see that Helga was there when they returned. Mr. Henry went into his room and Helga eyed them both.

"What was that about?"

"There're all leaving the day after tomorrow."

Helga gave her shoulder a squeeze and said, "Did you see that new dog that Mr. Gross got?  Blood hound indeed. He came right up to the fence and licked my hand. If you say boo, he runs away. Ralph says his father is furious and is going to return the dog and demand his money back."

Fiona smiled in spite of herself and thanked God for Helga. They talked for a while, and then went up to bed. All she could think about was that Mr. Henry was going to be in some kind of danger. She got into bed and fingered her rosary as she prayed for Mr. Henry.

# Chapter Five

The next day dawned bright and clear. It was a beautiful crisp October morning. Mr. Smith and his men were up early. Mrs. Ritner and the girls made them a hearty breakfast. The men worked all day moving all of their supplies out of the house. Fiona was amazed at how much they had accumulated in the few months they had been there. Many boxes were carried out to the waiting wagons. When the wagons were loaded, they left for the Kennedy farm and said they would be back in the evening to finish up.

"I can't imagine what they have to finish," Helga said, "There's nothing left in their rooms."

Fiona walked into Mr. Henry's room and looked around. His desk, usually piled high with papers, was bare. The room already had a sense of emptiness, while Fiona had a sense of despair. Mr. Henry and Mr. Merriam were the only ones who returned in the evening. The others stayed at the farm. They did not join them for supper, but stayed up in the back room talking. Mr. Henry came down later in the evening and spoke to Mrs. Ritner when they were all gathered in the parlor.

Thank you ma'am for your gracious hospitality. I will say goodbye now as we will be leaving before dawn."

"You are welcome, sir, it was my pleasure."

"Goodbye all," he said as he left the parlor. He looked at Fiona and smiled warmly as he had on that first day.

She felt a profound sense of sadness and loss. She soon excused herself and said she had a headache and was going to bed. Mr. Henry's door was closed when she passed his room. She went up to bed, but sleep did not come. Later, she heard Helga come up and pretended to be asleep. She did not want to talk to her. It was still dark when she heard the horse and wagon in the alley. She got up and looked out the window, but all she could see was two dim figures on the wagon seat as they drove away.

The next few days were very busy and Fiona was grateful for that. The rooms had to be thoroughly cleaned. They took the beds apart and wiped everything down. They scrubbed the floors and washed the windows. They washed the curtains and the rag rugs. When they were finished the rental rooms were gleaming and Mrs. Ritner was pleased. The next morning she wrote an ad to be placed in the newspaper:

> Rooms Available for Rent
> Inquire at Ritner's Boarding House
> 225 E. King Street

Mrs. Ritner came into the kitchen and said, "Helga, would you please take this to the office of the *Sentinel* and give it to the editor, Mr. May?"

"Yes Ma'am," Helga jumped up and left, happy to be out of the house for a while.

Mrs. Ritner looked at Fiona and said, "You rest for a while dear, you've been working so hard. You look a bit peaked."

"Thank you Ma'am, but I'm fine. I'll just finish up these dishes and then I'll sit down."

Fiona had just finished her work when Helga burst through the back door shouting.

"Mrs. Ritner, Mrs. Ritner, at the newspaper office, news came over the telegraph."

"What is it?" Fiona cried, as Mrs. Ritner entered the kitchen.

"There's been a raid at the Federal Arsenal in Harpers Ferry, Virginia. It was a band of abolitionists trying to free slaves. People were killed. There're sayin' the leader was John Brown and that John Brown is Isaac Smith."

When Helga had finished, they all stood there in silent and total shock. Then they shouted questions at Helga.

"When did it happen?'

"Who was killed?"

"How do they know it was Mr. Smith?"

Helga replied, "I don't know, it was still comin' over the telegraph. They said it will all be in the newspaper when it comes out later."

The three women sat at the kitchen table, each in her own thoughts. All Fiona could think about was Mr. Henry and the news that people were killed. She also thought of her Da and wished that she could be home with him.

Finally, Helga spoke, "Mrs. Ritner, who is this John Brown?"

She sighed and replied, "He's a militant anti-slavery leader, but he went too far. He was involved in attacks in Kansas against pro-slavery homesteaders. He and his band murdered people out there." She dropped her head and began to weep.

Helga and Fiona sat in stunned silence. The three were still seated at the table when Mr. Adamson came in carrying several newspapers.

"Oh Charles, is it true?" Mrs. Ritner cried.

"Yes, I'm afraid it is Mary, and you could be implicated. They could say you knew who they were."

"Oh dear God, how could anyone believe that I would let a murderer stay in my home with my children?"

Mr. Adamson took her hand and said, "I know dear, no one will believe that. Please, everyone sit down and I'll read the papers so we know exactly what happened."

Mr. Adamson read all of the newspaper articles to them. In one paper, there was a sketch of John Brown; it was the man they knew as Isaac Smith. The papers revealed that Brown and his men had been receiving weapons in Chambersburg and stockpiling them in the Oakes and Caufman Warehouse before transporting them to the Kennedy Farm. They were also purchasing picks, axes, and other tools from the Edge Tool Factory in town. They had represented themselves as mineralogists. His plan was to raid the arsenal and spark a slave uprising.

The paper stated that Brown and his men seized the arsenal, killed seven men and injured a dozen more. His plan was to arm the slaves and strike terror in the hearts of the slaveholders of Virginia.

Brown detached a party under John Cook to Capture Colonel Lewis Washington at his nearby Bell Air estate. The article stated that Washington was the great grandnephew of George Washington. Some of Washington's slaves as well as several Harpers Ferry townspeople were also captured and held as hostages in the armory.

Brown's men cut the telegraph wires and seized a Baltimore and Ohio train passing through. A baggage handler on the train named Howard Shepherd confronted the raiders only to be shot and killed. The editor commented on the irony of a freed slave being the first casualty of the raid.

The local militia was called up and surrounded the armory. They also held the bridge over the Potomac River, so any escape route was cut off.

When news of the attack reached Richmond, the U.S. Marines, under the command of Colonel Robert E. Lee, rushed to Harpers Ferry. Brown and his men were barricaded in the small brick building and refused to surrender. Finally a company of Marines stormed the building and captured Brown and his men. The slave uprising never happened.

Governor Wise of Virginia announced that ten of the raiders were dead, seven had escaped, and five had been captured including Brown. The captured were A.D. Stevens, Edwin Coppoc, Shields Green, and John A. Copeland. The editor of the paper speculated that they would all be hung.

The escapees were Owen Brown, Barclay Coppoc, Francis Merriam, Charles P. Tidd, John Edwin Cook, Osborne P. Anderson and Albert Hazlet. Among the dead were Oliver and Watson Brown, Gerald Anderson, William Thompson, Dauphin Thompson, William Leeman, Lewis Leary, Dangerfield Newby, Stewart Taylor, and John Henry Kagi.

Fiona sat as if in a trance as the names were read. Her head jerked up when she heard a familiar one like Tidd and Merriam who had escaped.

What of Mr. Henry? She never knew his first name. Who was John Henry Kagi? She looked to Mr. Adamson for help.

He looked at her kindly and said, "I think our Mr. Henry was John Henry Kagi. He was among those killed."

*Yes, that was him,* she thought to herself. *I knew he was dead. I knew it when we first heard the news.* She felt the need to get out of the house. She started to say something to Mrs. Ritner, when Mrs. Knight appeared at the kitchen door.

"Is luncheon not being served today?"

"I'm sorry Agnes, there has been much excitement. Something has happened."

Mr. Adamson stood up and gave her the news of the raid and their former boarders' involvement.

Her face red with anger, Mrs. Knight shouted, "How dare they involve innocent people in their evil schemes! I will not tolerate it. I can no longer stay in this house," she fumed.

The red faced Mrs. Knight provided comic relief after the somber tales they had been listening to.

"I'm sorry to hear that Agnes, but where will you go?" Mrs. Ritner asked.

"I do have friends in town. Fiona, I will write a note and I want you to deliver it to Judge Flood's town house," she pronounced as she left the room.

"You don't have to do that, Fiona dear. I know you're upset," Mrs. Ritner said.

"Oh please, I need to get out. I was just going to ask you if I could go and see my friend Mrs. Gormley."

Mrs. Ritner told her to go and stay as long as she wanted. Mrs. Knight returned with the note. Fiona put on her bonnet and headed for the door.

Helga hugged her and said, "Take care little friend."

"I will. Thank you."

Fiona gave the note to the Judge's housekeeper without comment and ran to Mrs. Gormley's. As soon as she got in the door, she fell into her friend's arms and began to sob.

"He's dead. He's dead. My Mr. Henry is dead." She spoke through great gulping sobs and told Mrs. Gormley what had happened.

They sat on the sofa and the older woman held Fiona in her arms.

"Yes dear, I heard. It's all over town, but what about you and Mr. Henry?"

"Oh, I loved him. He was so kind and gentle. He made me feel so, so...."

"Yes I know dear, that's what love does."

"How could he have gotten involved in such a scheme with that horrible John Brown?"

"Well to many people, John Brown is a hero, Fiona."

"Do you think he's a hero?"

"No, but people who believe in his cause do. I guess Mr. Henry was one of them. He believed enough to die for the cause."

"He knew he was going to die. I can see that now, some of the things he said. I know he cared for me, but he never said anything. He knew there was no future for us."

"Just to know that he cared for you can be a comfort, dear."

"Oh yes, and I'll never forget him."

"You're young Fiona. There will be other loves, but you will always carry the first one in your heart."

"I can't think about anything now. I don't know if I can go back to that house. I want to go home to my Da."

"Of course you do, dear. I'm sure he'll be here to get you when he hears what happened. I'll make some coffee. Hattie's off today. You should eat something."

Mrs. Gormley set out coffee and cake. Fiona started to sip the coffee, but didn't really taste it. Suddenly they heard a knock and were surprised to see Helga at the door.

"I'm sorry, Fiona, but Mrs. Ritner sent me to fetch you. Federal marshals are coming to the house tonight and they want to talk to everybody about what they knew about John Brown and his men."

"But none of us knew who they were."

"No, but Mrs. Ritner says that's what the marshals will find out. Mr. Adamson says to just tell the truth and not to worry."

Mrs. Gormley invited Helga to sit down and have coffee with them and asked her about the happenings at the house.

"Judge Flood came right away and escorted Mrs. Knight out of the house in much grandeur. He said if the marshals wanted to talk to her, they were to do so at his house in the presence of his lawyer. He also added that his housekeeper would be there at all times and it was proper for Mrs. Knight to stay there."

This caused Fiona to smile for the first time that day. Helga went on.

"When the Ritner girls came home from school they were all excited. They had heard the news and weren't sure what to make of it. Little Ella asked, "Mama who is this John Brown that everybody is talking about?"

And she told her very calmly. "He is Mr. Smith."

Mrs. Gormley said, "Mary Ritner is a fine woman. I don't believe for a minute that she knew he was John Brown. I have seen her daughters riding in the wagon with him. She never would have permitted that if she knew who he was."

Helga said, "We better get going. I'm sorry to have to bring you back, Fiona. Will you be all right?"

"I'm fine. I just needed to get away for a while. It really helped talking to you, Mrs. Gormley. Thank you."

"Any time dear. You take care and come back as soon as you can. I'll get word to your father."

Helga and Fiona walked back hand in hand. Just the touch of her friend's hand gave Fiona the courage she needed.

The federal marshals arrived soon after the girls returned to the house. Mrs. Ritner had sent her girls to stay with a neighbor. There were three men, all very tall and intimidating looking. All of the occupants of the house were asked to gather in the parlor while the marshals searched the house. They heard them upstairs going through the rooms that Brown's men had occupied. They came down and went into Mr. Henry's room and rattled around in there for a while. They returned to the parlor and asked everyone to be seated. One of them, who appeared to be the leader, started asking questions.

"Mrs. Ritner, we are very sorry for the intrusion. I am Marshal Connor. I know this is difficult, but it is necessary. Did you ever meet the man called Isaac Smith before he came here last May?"

She replied in a strong voice, "No sir, I did not."

"Did you know that he was John Brown?"

"No."

"Did you know that he was plotting to raid the arsenal in Harpers Ferry?"

"I did not."

The marshal seemed satisfied with her answers. He then went around the room and questioned everyone in the same manner.

He looked around and said. "Isn't there another roomer, a lady?"

"Yes," Mr. Adamson volunteered. "That would be Mrs. Knight. She is currently residing at the home of Judge Flood. You may question her there."

"Good luck with that," Helga whispered to Fiona.

Marshall Connor said "That will be all. You may leave, but I would like to speak to Miss McKenna."

Two marshals escorted the others out and Marshal Connor remained.

He held up a package and said, "Miss McKenna, we found this package in a drawer in the room that John Kagi occupied. It has your name on it. Do you know what it is?"

Fiona's mouth fell open and she was barely able to reply, "No."

The marshal looked at her. "Would you please open it in my presence."

He handed her the package. It was wrapped in brown paper and tied with a string. She untied the string and when she saw what was inside, her eyes filled with tears. Three brand new books spilled out on the floor. Fiona picked up each one and looked at it lovingly. "Leaves of Grass" by Walt Whitman, "The Essays of Ralph Waldo Emerson," and "Walden a Life in the Woods" by Henry David Thoreau were all beautifully bounded. She opened the first one to the flyleaf and saw an inscription.

October 15, 1859
To Fiona, my Rhodora,
With love, John

Fiona's tears were flowing now and Marshal Connor cleared his throat and waited. He picked up an envelope that had fallen out. It had her name on it.

He handed it to her and said, "Please and open this miss.

She wiped her eyes and opened the envelope. Inside was a folded note.

> Dear Fiona,
>
> When you read this you will know that my real name was John Henry Kagi. I'm so sorry to have deceived you, but now you will understand that it was necessary. I believed in a cause and that was the most important thing in my life. Perhaps if I were a different man, other things would have been more important. Please know that I did care for you.
>
> I believe that you are going to be an exceptional woman and somehow I will know and be proud of you.
> Have a wondrous life,
> John

Fiona gulped and handed the note to Marshal Conner. He read it quickly and handed it back.

"I'm sorry to intrude on your privacy, miss, but it is necessary. This note does prove that you did not know who he was. I think our investigation is finished here."

After the marshals left, they were all gathered in the kitchen. No one asked why Fiona was question separately. She sat there quietly for a while before speaking. She explained what had happened and showed them the books. She told them some of the contents of the note, but did not show it to them. It was something that was hers alone and she would always keep it close to her heart.

Mr. Adamson said, "I think the marshals were assured that none of us had any knowledge of Brown or his activities. However, I think they will be watching the house. Some of Brown's men have escaped and they may be close by."

The Ritner girls returned full of questions. Emma came up to Fiona and said, "There's a funny looking man waiting out back for you."

*God, what now,* Fiona thought. She went out and was relieved to see Barney Carney waiting there.

"Good evening, Miss Fiona, I come with a message from your esteemed father. He will be here on the morn to take you home."

"Thank you Barney. Why didn't you come to the door?"

"I make it a practice never to enter an abode where officers of the law are present," he replied with a tip of his hat and was off.

Fiona went inside and told Mrs. Ritner that she was going home.

"I just need some time away from here after everything that has happened."

"Of course," Mrs. Ritner replied, "You and Helga may go home and take as much time as you need. It certainly looks like we're not going to have any boarders here for a while."

Helga and Fiona went up to their room and sat on the bed. Helga put her arm around her and said,

"How ya doin, friend?'

"I think I'm all right. Just knowing that he cared for me helps. I'll never forget him, but I'll never understand him."

"You will come back here won't you?" Helga asked with concern.

"I don't know right now. I need to go home and think about it."

Climbing into bed, they said goodnight and immediately fell into an exhausted sleep.

It seemed that they had just gotten to sleep when they heard a tapping on the window.

"What was that?" Helga cried.

"Probably a bird. Go back to sleep," Fiona answered.

Again a tap, tap. Helga jumped up and looked out the window.

"My God, there's two men down there tapping on the window with the bean polls." She opened the window and called, "What is it?"

They heard the reply, "Its Tidd and Coppoc, we need help."

"Dear God, Brown's men. Helga, go get Mrs. Ritner. I'll go down stairs," Fiona said as she put on her robe.

Fiona looked out the back door at the two bedraggled men. They looked at her pleadingly.

"We're hungry; please give us something to eat."

Fiona hesitated for a moment, then grabbed some bread and cheese from the larder and handed it out the door to them. Mrs. Ritner, looking concerned, entered the kitchen and saw the men at the door.

"You can't come in," she whispered. "The house is being watched. Go away. You're putting us in danger."

They watched as Tidd and Coppoc slinked away. Probably to their death, but there was nothing to be done.

The next morning, Da arrived early. He folded Fiona in his embrace and she sobbed in his arms. She felt she was home already. She wished everyone good bye. Helga was getting ready to go home too. She walked them to the wagon. When they pulled away, Fiona turned and saw Helga waving goodbye.

"Make sure you come back," she called.

# Chapter Six

For the first few days at home, all Fiona wanted to do was sleep. It was so good to be in her own bed in her own room. It was so quiet and peaceful. There were no street noises, no roomers coming and going, no one telling her to get up. She would wrap herself in the cocoon of her old quilt and sink down into oblivion. Da left for work each morning and let her sleep. After a few days, she felt guilty.

The next day, she woke up early to make Da's breakfast and see him off to work. She looked around and decided to give the house a good fall cleaning. She moved some of the furniture outside and took up the rugs, hung them out on the clothes line and beat out the dust. She scrubbed the floors, washed the curtains, and polished the furniture. When Da came home, she was still at it.

"What's all this, is Christmas comin' early?  Me ma used to turn the house upside down like this before Christmas. Then she would send us all outside to whitewash the cottage. Everything had to be clean and new for the Christ Child"

"I just wanted to make the house nice for you Da. Now that I'm home, I'm going to take better care of you."

"That's nice, love, but you won't be home forever."

"I'm not sure about that Da, not sure at all."

He just smiled, "We'll see."

Fiona saw he had brought home the newspapers. She told him to sit down and read to her while she made supper. He picked up the papers and read from the *Franklin Repository*

> From what we have heard, it appears our Southern neigh-
> bors of Maryland and Virginia, bordering on Pennsylvania,

are very indignant at the citizens of Chambersburg-regarding them as the most fanatical abolitionists with which the country is troubled, and as thoroughly identified with "Old John Brown" and his crazy followers, in their late foolhardy attempt at stirring up insurrection among the slaves in Harpers Ferry.

In the various accounts published, Chambersburg figures very conspicuously as having been the headquarters of these deluded men. Here is where they had their implements of war consigned, and from which it also appears; some of their correspondence was directed. That all of this is true, will not admit of a doubt; but that any of our citizens "aided or abetted" them or had the remotest idea of their design, we do not for one moment believe.

Several strange men, for some time past, were stopping in Chambersburg, boarding at different places: who they were or what their legitimate business was, nobody knew, and the strangers themselves did not see proper to tell. They purchased a number of articles at our Edge Tool Factory, such as picks, axes and such. They had a variety of boxes of heavy merchandise of some kind sent to one of our forwarding houses, directed to I. Smith & Sons. They represented themselves as mineralogists, but who they were and what they were after nobody knew.

The heavy boxes that passed through the forwarding houses contained war judging from what has lately been revealed. That our "southern brethren" should therefore be incensed at the citizens of Chambersburg, stigmatizing them as a "nest of vile abolitionist," to say the least is simply silly-as foolish as to assert that the citizens of Harper Ferry or Hagerstown were privy to the plot because the Sharp's rifles, revolvers, and picks were transmitted through their midst.

The Citizens of Chambersburg are an order loving, law-abiding people, and in these respects, or in any other moral virtues that goes to make a good American citizen and lover of the Union, are the superiors of our "Southern brethren" located on the border. But, because our people love liberty more than slavery, is no reason why they should be charged with a knowledge of the Harpers Ferry insurrection, or that in any way, even one of our citizens, was in the secret; and to suppose that they would, in the most remote degree, countenance or favor, or "aid and abet" such a ruthless and murderous plot, or anything even slightly approximating to it, with a view of wiping out of their "peculiar institution," is ungenerous, nay it is cowardly.

"Well they certainly covered all bases in extracting Chambersburg from all guilt," Da said with a laugh. His smile faded and he said almost to himself "Chambersburg may pay a great price for this someday."

Another article blamed the Buchanan administration "for the encouragement given to freebooters in Kansas for appointing murderers to office with full knowledge that their hands were reeking with blood, led the foolish participant of Harpers Ferry that they too would be rewarded for their deeds."

He went on to read that Brown and the others were being held in Charlestown, Virginia and were to be charged with murder. Albert Hazlett had been captured near Chambersburg. Fiona wondered if he had been trying to get to the Ritner house. There was no mention of Tidd or Coppoc being captured. *They must have gotten away. I helped them by giving them food. Does that make me an accessory? I don't approve of what they did, but I hate the thought of anyone being hanged. The thought of it made* her *shutter.* There was another article about the capture of John Cook.

"I don't know that name," Fiona mused, "He never stayed at the house." After listening to all those familiar names, it was a comfort to hear a name she didn't know.

"No," Da said, "he was the advance man and stayed in Harpers Ferry."

The article went on to state that Cook had been hiding in the mountains and came into Mount Alto looking for food and was captured by two men. His description had been published in newspapers and a one thousand dollar reward was offered. They took him to Chambersburg where he was turned over to Justice Reisher. He was being held in the King Street Jail.

Da looked at Fiona and said, "I know that there's one name you're waitin' ta here, but there's no mention of John Kagi."

"I would just like to know what happend to him and where he is buried," Fiona answered quietly. "Thank God I don't have to think of him being hung."

The next day Fiona went for a long walk. She loved these walks in the country. The road wandered through the pine woods and over streams. The October sky was bright blue with fluffy white clouds. She inhaled the fresh air and felt a great contentment fill her spirit. Her thoughts for the first time in days were rational and calm. In her heart she spoke to Mr. Henry. She still thought of him by that name. *I prayed to the Blessed Mother that you would be safe and I thought that she didn't answer my prayers, but she did. She answered in the only way she could. She sent you straight into the arms of God. That was the only safe place from the troubles of this world. You died for something you believed in. You would not have run away like some of the others.*

Fiona came to a small flowing stream. It reminded her of the creek they used to walk by. She picked a wild flower and tossed it into the stream. As she watched it float away she said, "Goodbye John, I can call you John now, thank you for coming into my life."

Fiona walked all the way to the Judge's farm that day. She gazed over the acres of orchards and fields that went on forever. There were many barns and farm buildings and way up on the hill stood his mansion. She thought of Helga's beautiful family farm. That was a real farm. This place was more like a corporation. Suddenly she missed Helga very much.

On the way home, she stopped into visit Annie Kelly. The Kellys were their nearest neighbors down the road. Mike Kelly also worked for the Judge. He was a mechanic and kept all the farm tools sharpened and repaired. Like Fiona, they were American born. Both of their parents had come from Ireland in the 1840s. Annie was more Irish then American. She kept the old traditions and ways of her parents. She was a no nonsense hard working woman. She wore a cotton house dress and her beautiful auburn hair was covered with a mop cap.

The Kellys had a new baby girl, the first girl after three boys. Fiona sat and cradled her in her arms while Annie fixed them tea. She gazed down at the perfect little face and thought how wise she looked. She remembered reading somewhere that the Indians believed that the soft spot on an infant's head was an opening to all of the wisdom of the world. But when the opening closed up, the knowledge was forgotten. *I wish you could pass on some of your wisdom to me*, she thought.

"Well Fiona, it's good to have you amongst us again," Annie said as she put the tea things on the table. "Aye, you got little Maureen to sleep. Here, I'll put her in the cradle."

They sat and had their tea and talked of the recent events in Chambersburg and of happenings in the neighborhood.

"My Mike says the Judge has been mighty happy lately, what with the bumper crop this year and his new lady friend."

"Oh, Mrs. Knight," Fiona laughed. She had forgotten about the courtship with all that had been going on. "I guess she's still staying at his townhouse."

"And the judge has proclaimed that the proprieties will be observed at all time, "

Annie solemnly declared. They both collapsed in laughter.

Fiona relaxed in the cozy little kitchen. She always enjoyed visits with Annie.

She and Mike were good neighbors. Suddenly, the peaceful quiet was broken, when the arrival of three Kelly boys from school. They were all redheaded like their father and full of energy.

"Ma, what's to eat? We're starving. Afternoon Miss Fiona," they all shouted practically in unison.

"Afternoon, boys," she replied. Their names were Michael Jr., Tim, and Kevin, but they looked so much alike, she could never remember who was who.

Annie gave the boys some biscuits and sent them out to play. The baby woke up just as Fiona was leaving and Annie picked her up and unbuttoned her dress to nurse her.

"Don't forget you and your Da are coming here on All Hallows Eve."

"We wouldn't miss it, Annie."

A few days later Da brought in the mail and handed Fiona two letters. One was from Helga and one was from Mr. Adamson. She was surprised to get a letter from him and wondered what it was about. But she had to open Helga's first.

October 24, 1859

Dear Fiona,

Well here I am, back on the farm. It was nice to be with the family again, but I'm all ready tired and bored. Ma is working me to death and life on the farm is boring. I miss you very much.

How is it for you? Are you glad to be home with you Da? What have you been doing? When are you going back to Mrs. Ritners?

Sorry for so many questions. I sent a note to Mrs. Ritner asking if I can come back next week. I hope she has some boarders by then. I hope that you can come back by then. Please let me know. I hope I can see you soon.

Your friend,
Helga

Fiona quickly opened Mr. Adamson's letter.

October 25, 1859

Dear Miss McKenna,

I am sorry to intrude on your visit with your father, but I wanted to convey some news to you. I know that you had a friendship with John Kagi and would like to know what happened to him. I have found the following information in a NY newspaper:

On the night of October 16, 1859, the duty was assigned to John Kagi, to capture and hold the Government Rifle Works situated on the Shenandoah River, about half a mile above its confluence with the Potomac. The next day these works were attacked by the Virginia Militia, and Kaigi and his men were driven out. In attempting to cross the river, they were all killed. The bodies of the slain were buried in a grave on the southern bank of Shenandoah about a half mile above Harpers Ferry.

He died in obedience to his ideals. He fell a martyr to the cause of human freedom and gave his young life as a sacrifice to a downtrodden and oppressed race, the most complete measure of devotion that can be given.

I hope that this information has not been too distressful to you, but I thought you would like to know the circumstances of his death. He did die a hero.

Also, I would like to inform you that Mrs. Ritner would welcome you back anytime that you should feel ready. Mrs. Virginia Cook, the wife of John Cook, is staying with us. She has an infant son and is under great distress with her husband recently captured and in jail. I feel that your help here would be appreciated.

The trial for John Brown starts tomorrow in Charlestown and I feel it will be a stressful time for all of us.

Your Obedient Servant,
Charles H. Adamson

Da sat and watched her as she read his letter with tears streaming down her face.

When she was finished, she silently handed the letter to her father.

"Well, now you know what happened. Does it help?"

"Yes, it's painful, but it does help. It was so kind of him to let me know what happened."

"Fiona, do you want to go back?"

She suddenly realized that she did. "Yes, Da, I do. I'll go after All Hallows Eve."

He patted her cheek and said, "I have to go into town for supplies tomorrow. I'll drop a note off to Mrs. Ritner for you."

"Da, what do you think will happen to John Brown and his men at trial?"

"They'll be charged with murder, maybe treason. I think people will come from far and wide. Abolitionist supporters of Brown will hail him as a hero. Others will condemn him as a killer."

"Do you think they will be found guilty and hung?"

"Most likely, most likely. The tenor of the times will condemn them. People are afraid of the slavery issue. They don't want anybody stirrin' things up. They want it to go away, but it won't go away. God help us, it won't go away."

"Oh Da, that sounds frightening. What will happen?"

"I don't mean to frighten you darling,' but somethin' will happen. The country could split in two. There could be a war."

All Hallows Eve was crisp and clear. It was still daylight when Fiona and Tom walked up the road to the Kelly's house full of happy anticipation.

Fiona carried the traditional barnbrack cake she had baked. They joined others on the road; all of the neighbors had been invited, Irish or not.

Young Josh Miller walked beside Fiona and asked, "What exactly is this All Hallows Eve?"

"In ancient Ireland, it was the night when the dead walked the earth. It was called Samhain, the end of summer, harvest time and the beginning of winter. The whole village would gather together and light bonfires to ward off the spirits. With Christianity, it became All Hallows Eve or the night before All Saints Day. Some now call it Halloween."

"Do you still believe that the dead will walk the earth tonight, Fiona?"

She looked at him with a wide eyed expression and said, "Nobody really knows."

The Kellys had long plank tables and benches set up outside. Annie was bringing the food out from the kitchen and Mike was dispensing whiskey from a jug. They all sat down to a meal of colcannon, lamb stew, applesauce and brown bread. In the colcannon, creamy mashed potatoes and cabbage, Annie had buried several coins wrapped in gold paper. Whoever found one would have good luck for a year. Several of the children squealed with delight when they found the coins.

After the ladies cleared the supper dishes, Fiona brought out her barnbrack cake. It was her mother's recipe, a rich dark cake laden with fruit. Before it went in the oven, she had carefully placed in the batter, a small clean piece of rag, a coin, and a ring.

As Annie cut the cake and handed it around, she explained to the non-Irish, "whoever gets the rag, will not have good finances this year, whoever gets the coin, will have a prosperous year, and whoever gets the ring, will soon have a romance."

Fiona hesitated before putting a fork in her cake. She was relieved when she heard Mary O'Brien exclaim that she had gotten the ring.

Mike unfortunately got the rag and said, "Well, it won't be different than any other year."

From across the table, Tom held up the coin and winked at Fiona, "Aha, Maybe a different year for me."

Mike hung an apple on a string from a tree limb. The children, some in makeshift costumes, were blindfolded and tried to bite the apple. Mike Kelly Jr. was the first to get a bite and got the prize of a bag of penny candy.

Darkness was descending fast and the tables were pushed back and the bonfire was lit. They all sat around and watched the flames. The unmarried girls were told if they would pull out a hair and throw it in the fire, they would dream of their future husband that night. As some of the girls threw theirs in the fire, Fiona sat with her hands folded.

Mike brought out pumpkins that the children had carved. They lighted candles and placed them inside. The children formed a procession and carried the pumpkins around the bonfire as the adults clapped.

When they all sat down, Mike said, "Give us a story, Tom."

Tom sat up and began his story:

"Long ago in Ireland, a blacksmith named Jack colluded with the Devil and was denied entry into Heaven. He was condemned to wander the earth, but asked the Devil for something to light his way. He was given a burning coal ember which he placed in a gorged out turnip. He wanders the earth to this day with his Jack- o- Lantern. So on All Hallows Eve we commemorate Jack's wandering. When the Irish came to America, they found the pumpkin was better than a turnip for holding a light."

Many more tales were told around the fire until the embers were low. Sleeping children were picked up and good byes were said. Fiona and Tom headed back to their cottage. When they got to the gate, they stood for a while and looked at the beautiful harvest moon.

Tom put his hand on Fiona's shoulder and said, "We'll head into town tomorrow and go to the All Saint's Day mass. Then I'll drop you off at Mrs. Ritner's."

They stood for a while in the moonlight and Fiona thought of Samhain and the end of summer and the beginning of winter. She wished that for her it would be a new beginning.

# Chapter Seven

The church was full for the All Saints Day mass. Even Barney, who was anything but a frequent church goer, was there.

"I always go to mass on this day for me sainted mother," he explained to Fiona after church. "Are you back in our fair city for good?"

"I don't know about for good, but I'm here for now."

"Do not fail to call on me if you are ever in need for goods or otherwise," he said as he tipped his hat and went on his way.

Mrs. Gormley soon joined them and invited Fiona and Tom to stop for a while. "I know you're anxious to get back to the Ritners, but have a cup of coffee with me so we can catch up."

They sat in Kate Gormley's parlor and she gazed fondly at Fiona. "The time at home has done you much good. You look a great deal better."

"I feel better and I'm glad to be back here."

Kate wanted to know all about the All Hallows Eve celebration at the Kelly's and the happenings in the neighborhood. Fiona described the Halloween party and told her about all the neighbors who attended. Hattie came in with the coffee.

"Hello Mr. Tom. Welcome back Mis' Fiona. How you bin?"

"I'm doing all right. How are you and Enoch?"

"We doin fine. The whole town buzzin bout that John Brown's trial. Do you think all them mens gonna hang, Mr. Tom?"

"I'm afraid they will, Hattie."

She left the room shaking her head muttering, "Lord a Mercy."

"Lord a Mercy is right." Kate said as she sipped her coffee. "Did you hear about the capture of John Cook?"

"Only what we read in the paper," Tom replied.

"Well, it was sometin," Kate sighed

Tom and Fiona sat back for a long story.

"He left the rest of the men he was travelin' with to search for food. Daniel Logan and Clegget Fitzhugh spotted him near Mt. Alto They recognized him right off. The Governor of Virginia had circulated his description and offered a thousand dollar reward. They were keen on getting that money. They jumped him and took his gun away. They brought him back here in an open buggy." Mrs. Gormley took a sip of coffee and went on.

"On the way, Cook said that if all they wanted was the reward, he could get them a thousand dollars or more from his brother- in-law, Governor Willard of Indiana. Now Logan and Fitzhugh, they weren't sure if they could trust him," she said with a smile.

"Cook then asked if there was anyone in town who could serve as his lawyer and they suggested Colonel McClure. They agreed that McClure would seek the payment from Governor Willard in exchange for Cook's release. Well when they got to Chambersburg, they couldn't find McClure. They gave up on McClure and wanted to make sure they got their money. So they took him to the Franklin Hotel." Kate took a breath and said.

"Albert Johnson was at the hotel and told me the rest. They put him in room nine and Albert saw him sittin' on the bed. He described him as 'a ragged, tattered and dirty creature.' His heart went out to him. He got him somethin' to eat from the hotel kitchen. Logan went to fetch Justice Reisher to get a warrant for his arrest. They gave him a hearing in Reisher's office and sent him to the jail on King Street.

"I hear many people in town were plotting his escape, but the next day, he was taken to Charlestown and imprisoned with Brown and the others. And that was the end of that."

"Well it's a good thing they dinna find McClure," Tom said. "They wouda got themselves in a mess of trouble."

"Yes that's for sure," Kate replied. Oh and Cook's poor wife is and baby were stayin' at the Kennedy farm. Now that good Mrs. Ritner has taken them in."

Fiona stood up and said, "Yes, I know and now it's time for me to get back there."

They said their goodbyes and headed for King Street. They walked past the jail and Fiona's thoughts were of the jailed men and the price they would have to pay. As they got closer to the house, her spirits rose at the thought of seeing Helga and the others. They had no sooner started up the garden path when Helga came flying out the back door.

"Fiona, Fiona, it's about time. I thought you'd never get here. Hello, Mr. McKenna. Good to see you too. Come on in."

"Good to see you, Lass, but I have to be goin'. It's a work day for me. He hugged Fiona "God bless."

When they entered the house, Fiona could feel the difference. The door to the room off the kitchen was closed and she briefly felt a sense of loss. Helga went to tell Mrs. Ritner that Fiona was back and she stood there waiting just as she had that first day. Suddenly, the door to the bedroom opened and a young woman emerged.

"Shush," she whispered with a finger on her lips. "I just got the baby to sleep."

Fiona stared at her. She had never seen such a pitiful creature. She was very slender with wispy blond hair and pale eyes, red from crying. Her entire manner was one of defeat and sorrow. Mrs. Ritner appeared in the doorway and motioned them into the parlor.

"Fiona, this is Virginia Cook. She and her five month old son Johnny will be staying with us for a while. Please do everything you can to make them comfortable."

Fiona smiled at the poor creature and said, "Of course I will. Just let us know what you need."

Helga came in with tea for the ladies and the girls went back to the kitchen. They went outside and sat on the garden bench so as to not wake the baby.

"Tell me everything you been doin' since you left," Helga began.

"Not much, just taking care of Da and visiting the neighbors."

"You look better. Are ya feelin' better?"

"I am," she said and smiled, "and what about you? Did you see Fritz when you were home?"

"He came to call a few times."

"And?"

"And nothing. He's still Fritz; nice but not exciting."

"Well exciting isn't always good," Fiona replied wistfully. Helga squeezed her hand.

"Hello ladies," the familiar and annoying voice of Ralph was heard.

Helga stood up and went to the fence. "Hey Ralph, I thought it was your job to watch this house. You had no idea what was goin' on here. You didn't do a very good job. You're no better than that useless blood hound your Pa bought."

"Oh Ya, well he has a new dog now and he's a killer and you better watch out."

He ran back in the house looking like he was going to cry. Fiona almost felt sorry for him.

That evening after dinner they were all gathered in the parlor. Fiona was glad to see the Ritner girls and Mr. Adamson again. Mrs. Cook sat in the rocker with little Johnny on her lap. He was a beautiful little fellow with curly blond hair and a sweet smile. Mrs. Ritner played a waltz on the piano and Fiona found herself humming along. She felt very peaceful. When the music finished, Mr. Adamson went to the bible and read Psalm 4:7

> "Many say, May we see better times!
> Lord, show us the light of your
> 　　Face!
> But you have given my heart more
> 　　Joy
> than they have when grain and
> 　　wine abound.
> In peace I shall both lie down and
> 　　sleep,
> for you alone, Lord, make me secure."

They all sat quietly for a while. Then they slowly got up and wished each other good night. Fiona went up to bed and slept very well.

The next few days were very busy. New boarders were expected and the rooms had to be readied. Mrs. Cook stayed in her room most of the time. Helga and Fiona took turns caring for the baby so she could rest. They bounced him on their knees and made him laugh. Sometimes Mr. Adamson came in and picked him up and walked him around.

"Babies like to be walked," he would tell them. "I used to do this with my sister's children."

One afternoon, he sat in the kitchen with Fiona over coffee and told her about Virginia Cook. "Her husband brought her down here and told her that they were going to join a party going west. They had not been doing very well financially and he felt there would be better opportunities out there." He sipped his coffee and continued.

"She stayed at the Kennedy Farm with the baby. He made several trips to make arrangements for their journey west. That's what he told her. When she learned of the raid at Harpers Ferry and her husband's connection to it, she was terrified. She was a total stranger here with a small baby and no money." Mr. Adamson frowned.

"When I heard of her plight, I asked Mrs. Ritner if I could bring her here. She is devastated and fearful for her husband, but she just wants to go home. She has family in New York and wishes to go there. We are trying to raise funds for her transportation."

Fiona looked at him and said. "Charles Adamson, you are the finest gentleman I have ever known. Thank you for all of your many kindnesses to everyone and especially to me. Thank you for your letter about John Kagi. You were right; I needed to know what happened. It was so thoughtful of you to realize that. You are like the knights of old in your kindness and chivalry to all."

He laughed and replied, "Fiona I must say, that's the finest compliment I have ever received, but I just do what is necessary."

In a few days, Mr. Adamson announced that, thanks to several businessmen in town sympathetic to her cause, he had raised the needed funds for Mrs. Cook. They all saw her and little Johnny off at the depot. She thanked everyone for their kindness with tears in her eyes. *At least she would be with her family while she awaits the fate of her husband,*

Fiona thought. The house was quiet when they returned. They would all miss little Johnny.

Every day the papers were full of stories about the Brown trial. Militant abolitionists called it a travesty. The presiding judge, Richard Parker, charged Brown with "invading by force a peaceful, unsuspecting portion of our country, raising the standard of insurrection amongst us, and shooting down without mercy Virginia citizens defending Virginia soil against invasion."

The defense council was appointed by the court and expressed strong misgivings. The trial was rushed due to the hysteria in the community. Brown was brought into court on a cot, still recovering from his wounds. Colonel Lewis Washington was the chief witness. He testified how he had been kidnapped out of his home and held hostage.

Many documents were found at the Kennedy farm in Maryland. They included a provisional constitution, which Brown and his officers had signed. The documents proved the treason and pre-meditation charges against John Brown.

On Wednesday, the eleventh of November, Mr. Adamson came home with the newspaper and announced that the trial was over. They all joined him in the kitchen. He spread the paper out on the table and began to read. The headline screamed that John Brown was found guilty and condemned to hang by the neck until dead. The jury had taken only forty-five minutes to deliberate. The execution would be carried out on December second. The paper commented that Brown was unrepentant and gloried in his martyrdom and that the trials of his co-conspirators would proceed without delay.

The mood around the table was somber. Thoughts of the strange man who had lived under their very roof and would die in such an awful way was on everyone's mind.

On the day of the hanging, Fiona woke with a start, realizing what day it was. She went downstairs and out to the pump to fetch water for breakfast. She looked up at the overcast sky and felt a shiver pass through her body. All through the day, the women went through their household chores, but the events in Charlestown were never far from their minds.

Mr. Adamson came home with the evening papers and they all gathered in the parlor. He read of how the hanging had gone off as scheduled and of the vast crowds that had gathered there. John Brown had passed a note to one of his supporters as he was led to the gallows. The supporter gave the note to the newspapers to be published. Mr. Adamson read:

> *I John Brown am quite certain that the crimes of this guilty land will never be purged away, but with blood. I had, as I now think, vainly flattered myself that without very much blood; it might be done.*

"Indeed, indeed," was all Mr. Adamson could say.

Mrs. Ritner asked the girls to serve supper, but no one was able to eat much.

The following day was brightened by the arrival of the new boarders. Mr. Edward Butler was a carpenter who worked for Mr. Adamson. He was a quiet gentleman in his mid-thirtys. Joseph Leiss was a machinist who worked at the tool factory. He was only in his twenties. He was a bit plump, but had a ready smile and thick dark hair. Helga thought he was handsome. The two men would share the large upstairs room in the back. They didn't seem to mind that it was the notorious room where John Brown stayed. Another gentleman was expected. He had written ahead for a room. He wrote that he was passing through town and would only be there for two weeks. Mr. Leopold Monteith would be a boarder they would never forget.

He arrived in a painted wagon. The sides were emblazoned with colorful pictures of Indians and snakes and Leopold Monteith Medicine Man was printed in bold letters. Mr. Monteith entered the house like a force of nature. He removed his hat with a sweeping gesture and revealed a face with a hook nose and a large drooping mustache.

"Hello, Hello, I'm Leopold Monteith, call me Leo. I sell patent medicine. I have the cure for whatever ails you. I'll be putting on a show in town tomorrow evenin' and you're all invited. Come one, come all. I'm expecting a large crowd with all of the folks in the area for the hanging."

Mrs. Ritner asked him to park his wagon around back. Helga and Fiona giggled and said they would like to go to the show. The others just smiled and shook their heads. Mr. Monteith didn't want the small room adjoining the other gentlemen's room. They put him in the room off the kitchen and Helga and Fiona got to know him. He told them many stories of his exploits out west.

"Many of my medicines were obtained from my Indian friends. They are ancient remedies known only to them. The Kickapoo Liver and Kidney Renovator and the Kickapoo Cough Cure are some of their finest. Come to the show young ladies and you will hear all about it."

They noticed that he took frequent sips from his medicine bottles. The next morning, he took his wagon into town to prepare for the show. Mrs. Ritner gave Helga and Fiona permission to go to the show and Joe Leiss offered to accompany them. They discovered that the show was not actually in town, but out by the quarry.

"I guess, he couldn't get permission to have it in town," Joe commented. "We have a long walk ladies, but it's a nice evening, and not too cold yet."

There was a large crowd of people when they arrived at the sight. Leo was just getting into his performance. He stood on the back of the wagon. On either side of him on the ground were two Indians in full battle dress. They beat their drums and did a war dance until Leo raised his arms for silence.

"Ladies and Gentlemen, you have seen the native dance of my Indian friends. Their ancient medicines have been secret for many years, but they have entrusted me with their secrets. I, therefore, have the privilege of offering their miraculous medicines and many others to you at a nominal cost. But first hear the Indian's song."

He raised his hands and the Indians began to chant to a slow drum beat.

>"At the center of the earth
>I stand,
>Behold me!
>At the wind center
>I stand,
>Behold me!
>A root of medicine
>Therefore I stand,
>At the wind center
>I stand"

How beautiful, Fiona thought. They are magnificent. I wonder where they came from. The Indians disappeared inside the wagon and Leo started his spiel.

"The body is made up of four humors: blood, phlegm, black bile and yellow bile. The amount of humors in the body determines the state of health and temperament. They must be kept in balance. This is what these magnificent medicines do. They keep the body in balance."

He went on to proclaim the restorative powers of the remedies he had for sale. The Kickapoo Liver and Kidney Renovator were good for many ailments of the elderly as was Babcock's Rheumatic Tincture, Blood Purifier and Cancer Cure. Many other liquid medications and healing salves were offered. People started coming forward to purchase the products. Governor's Blood Root Elixir was selling well. It was good for everything. Snake Oil Salve that cured all kinds of skin rashes was also doing well. Helga and Fiona both brought the Kickapoo Liver Restorer for their fathers. Joe just laughed. The show ended with another war dance and Leo thanked everyone and said goodnight.

"We will be here every night for the next two weeks. Tell your friends," he proclaimed.

As they walked home, Joe said, "I'm sure your fathers will enjoy the medicine. It won't do them any harm, but it won't do them any good. It's mostly alcohol."

"Oh, they couldn't sell it as medicine if it was," Helga replied indignantly.

"Yes they can. There's no law against it." Joe replied

Fiona wasn't sure what to believe.

Leopold Monteith stayed for two weeks and put on a show every night. He was pleased with the crowds and the sales he made.

"This is a good town," he said to Fiona one day as she served him breakfast in the kitchen.

"Mr. Leo, please tell me about the Indians. Where are they staying?"

"Oh they put up teepees out by the quarry. They're used to sleeping in the open."

"Where are they from?"

"Out west somewhere, I don't know what tribe. They were working for another medicine show in Virginia when I picked them up."

Fiona felt that he didn't care much about the Indians and hoped that they weren't badly treated. "Do you think your medicine will do my father good?" she asked.

He smiled, "I do. I do, my dear. All of my medicines are guaranteed."

The day Mr. Leo was getting ready to leave; Da came to pick her up for her week-end off. He met Mr. Leo and Fiona gave him the medicine. He said thanks, but looked a bit skeptical. They said goodbye and wished Mr. Leo luck.

Da had to stop at the feed store and pick up supplies. Before they started home, Fiona asked him to go by the quarry. She wanted to see the Indians, but they were gone. Fiona could not stop thinking about them. She said a little prayer for them.

The weekend at home passed quickly and soon she was back in Chambersburg. Helga started telling her that she probably wouldn't be able to go home the following weekend.

"It's hog slaughtering time and Pa and the boys will be too busy to come and pick me up."

Fiona looked at her and felt that she didn't look too disappointed. *I think she would like to stay here with Joe Leiss*, she thought. Just then, Mr. Adamson came into the kitchen.

"Helga dear, Mrs. Ritner told me of your plight. It so happens I have to go into Gettysburg on Saturday and will be staying over and coming back on Sunday. I am going to hire a horse and buggy and will be going right by your farm. I will be happy to take you and pick you up on Sunday."

Fiona noticed a slight flicker of disappointment on Helga's face, but she quickly replied, "Thank you Mr. Adamson, that's very kind of you."

That Saturday night, Fiona fell asleep quickly. It was nice having the big bed to herself. It felt like she had just fallen asleep when she woke with a start to a presence in the room. Mrs. Ritner was standing by the bed.

"Fiona wake up, I need your help. Get dressed and come down to the kitchen. Please hurry and don't light a candle."

Fiona dressed quickly and felt her way down the narrow stair case. It reminded her of the night when Tidd and Coppoc came. For one brief moment she thought *maybe it's John Kagi; maybe he's not dead*. But when she got to the kitchen there was only a young black girl sitting at the table. The only light was a small fire in the grate.

Mrs. Ritner spoke in a voice full of distress. "She's an escaped slave. I don't know why she came here. Someone must have told her we would take her in, but we haven't been able to do that for a long time. I came down stairs because I heard a noise. She was scratching at the back door. I gave her some bread and porridge."

The girl was hungrily shoving in the food. When she looked up, her eyes were frightened and watchful. He dress was in rags and her feet were bare.

Mrs. Ritner appealed to Fiona, "I have to go and contact someone who can help to get her farther north. Please stay with her and help her get cleaned up. I brought down some clothes and shoes of Laura's that should fit her."

"Of course, Mrs. Ritner. Is there anything else I can do?"

"Just keep things very quiet. I know Mr. Gross nextdoor is away and has the hound with him, but Ralph is there and he's been keeping an extra watchful eye on the house since Harpers Ferry. My biggest fear is that we won't be able to get her out before daybreak. He'll be watching."

"Don't worry Ma'am, just get going. I'll take care of her and we'll think of some way to get her out."

Mary Ritner hugged her and slipped out the door. Fiona looked at the girl. She had finished eating. She asked if she wanted more and she shook her head. There was a pan of water on the stove and Fiona brought it over to the girl with a rag.

"Would you like to wash up and change clothes?" she asked.

Again the girl just nodded. Fiona set the water and rag in front of her and turned away while she changed clothes. When she turned back the girl looked much better. Her face and hands were clean and she had slicked her hair back. Fiona indicated the shoes and she slipped them on. She almost smiled.

"What's your name?" Fiona asked

"Sadie," she replied

"Where did you come from?"

"South a here."

Fiona could see that Sadie was exhausted and stopped asking her questions. Soon the girl put her head down on the table and slept. Fiona sat there in the dim glow of the firelight and thought. How can we get her out of here without Ralph seeing her? Slowly a plan was forming in her mind. It seemed like hours before Mrs. Ritner got back. But it was still dark.

"I was able to contact someone who can get her north, but it will take a while to make the arrangements. I'm afraid they won't be here before dawn. Fiona quickly told her of her plan.

She looked at her and whispered, "Are you sure?"

"No, but I know he's always asking what he can do for me. I'll put him to the test. There's no time to waste. I'll get going."

Mary Ritner took off her shawl and wrapped it about Fiona, "It's cold out there. Please be careful and God bless you."

Fiona slipped out the door and went up the back walk to the Gross house and banged on the door several times. A sleepy Ralph finally came to the door.

"What's all the racquet?" he yelled. His voice changed when he saw her. "Fiona, what is it?"

Fiona sucked in her breath and started, "Oh Ralph, I'm so sorry to wake you, but I need your help. Mrs. Ritner got word that several guests will be arriving this morning and we don't have enough sheets. Old Molly is ailing and can't bring them. They are too heavy for me to carry and I need your help."

"Do you have to get them in the middle of the night?"

"Well it will soon be morning and Mrs. Ritner wants the beds ready when they get here. Well if you don't want to help me I can get someone else...."

"Oh no, I can help. Just give me a minute to get dressed." True to his word, Ralph was back in minutes and they were on their way. Fiona was trembling inside and her mind was racing. She wasn't sure what she would do when they got to Molly's.

Ralph was all smiles. "You know I'm always willing to help you Fiona."

She smiled at him and said, "Yes, you are so kind."

Daylight was just breaking and she could see the silly grin on his face. They were almost to Third Street and Fiona knew she had to stall for time.

"Please wait here a moment, Ralph. I want to run into Enoch's first. Old Molly's ailing and might not be up. We'll send Hattie over to wake her so she won't be frightened."

Ralph started to say who cares, but stopped himself. "Sure, I'll wait for you Fiona."

She started to knock on the door, but Enoch had seen her and quickly let her in. He was up early expecting customers before they went to work.

"Is something wrong, Fiona?" he asked, looking over her shoulder at Ralph.

"Yes there is," she almost sobbed and quickly explained the situation and her plan.

Hattie came in while she was explaining and said, "Don't worry, we'll take care of everything."

Fiona took her time returning to Ralph and said, "There're going in to wake old Molly up and see if the sheets are ready." In a little while, Hattie came out.

"It will be awhile, Mis' Fiona, some of them ain't ironed yet. I'm helping Molly."

Hattie waited as long as she could before she announced that the sheets were ready. Enoch loaded them onto the cart.

"Take your time now, this old cart can't move too fast."

Fiona saw Molly in the doorway smiling and waving. Ralph and Fiona began pushing the cart down the street. The two of them could barely move it. God Lord, Fiona thought, Enoch must have put rocks in this cart. Suddenly, her nerves gave way and she began to laugh hysterically. She had to stop and sit down on the ground for a minute.

"What's so funny?" Ralph said in his old sneering way.

"Oh, I'm just giddy from getting up so early and isn't it funny, you and me pushing this cart?"

"Anything I do with you is fun, Fiona."

They were getting near to King Street and she was starting to panic. What if the girl was still there? What could she do to stall for more time? Suddenly she saw a familiar figure ahead. What was Barney doing up so early or was he still out from an evening of drinking? She was never so glad to see him.

Barney looked over the situation and asked, "What's up Fiona?"

Fiona looked him straight in the eye and prayed he would understand. "Mrs. Ritner is waiting for these sheets. It's very important," she emphasized. "Barney, could you please run ahead and tell her we're on our way and ask her if everything is all right?"

"I'm already on me way," he replied.

"Why do you bother with that old drunk?" Ralph sneered.

"Oh, he's not so bad," she answered and prayed that she was right.

They were almost to the house when they saw Barney coming back.

"The esteemed Mrs. Ritner says that all is well and to thank you both for bringing the sheets and most especially you, Mr. Gross. Top of the mornin' all," he said as he walked away.

At that moment, Fiona loved Barney Carney with all her heart.

# Chapter Eight

Fiona thanked Ralph and told him to leave the cart by the door. Everyone was up and about when she entered the house. Mrs. Ritner, busy serving breakfast, said nothing to her. But, her smile conveyed her thankfulness. Later they spoke in the parlor.

"Fiona, I don't know what I would have done without you. Your plan was brilliant. Sadie was only gone for about half an hour before Mr. Carney came with your message. He was so kind. He didn't ask any questions."

Fiona sighed and felt relief flood over her. "I'm so glad she got away. Who came for her? Where did they take her?"

"Fiona, you must understand, I cannot tell you any names for your sake and theirs. And you must tell no one what happened. It is not safe. I understand you had to tell the friends who helped you, but I'm sure they will be discreet. Please thank them for me."

"I will and I understand the need for secrecy. After I finish the breakfast dishes, I would like to go back and let them know that Sadie got away."

"Of course you may," she answered. Then Mary Ritner took her hand and said, "I will never forget what you did for me. You are an extraordinary woman Fiona McKenna."

Fiona left the room blushing. No one had ever called her a woman before.

Fiona took the sheets out of Molly's cart. She laughed when she saw several large rocks in the bottom. After putting the sheets away, she pushed the cart back to Molly's. It was a leisurely trip this time. Hattie ran out to greet her when she saw her coming.

"What happen to the girl? Did her get away?"

"She did, she did," Fiona shouted

They ran over to Molly's and she was already at the door.

"Thank you Jesus," she said when she saw their faces. "A lamb has been rescued from the lion's den."

The three women sat around Molly's table as Fiona told them about Sadie's escape.

"Mrs. Ritner sends you her thanks. She can't thank you in person. These are dangerous times. There is a great need for secrecy."

Hattie and Molly nodded in agreement. Hattie got up and said she had to get to Mrs. Gormley's, but Molly asked Fiona to stay awhile.

"Chile, you is always askin for your fortune. I think it time," she began. She took Fiona's hand and gazed into her eyes.

"You dun had a great sorrow, but you'll survive and find love again. You'll have more sorrows, but that what life is. It's how you learn to bear them. That's the secret. There be big trouble comin' to this town. I feel it in my bones. You will survive, but some won't. You will have a long life. You carry many wishes in your heart. Some will come true. You will go away, but you will come back."

Fiona thanked Molly for her fortune and pondered it on the way back to the house Some of it frightened her, but she asked for it. She felt that it was not always a good thing to know your future.

As Fiona drew near to the house, she wondered how she could keep the events of the night from Helga. She would certainly notice if she started being nicer to Ralph. *And I will have to be nicer to him. Oh well, I'll work it out somehow.* Fiona needn't have worried. When Helga returned, all she wanted to talk about was Joe Leiss.

They sat on their bed and Helga sighed, "I was so bored at home. I missed being around Joe. He is so much fun. Remember the night he took us to the Medicine Show? He took hold of my hand on the way home. Do you think he likes me?'

Fiona looked at her and said, "Of course he likes you. Who wouldn't like you?"

"I mean in the way a boy likes a girl."

Fiona laughed, "Yes, in that way. He's always hanging around and teasing you and calling you a Dutch dumpling. He surely likes you as a boy likes a girl."

"Me too," proclaimed Helga.

"But what about Fritz?" Fiona asked.

"What about him!" was her reply.

Helga and Joe were not the only couple being discussed. That evening in the parlor, Mrs. Ritner announced that she had received an invitation. She opened it and read it to those gathered there.

His Honor Howard J. Flood
Request the Honor of Your Presence
At His Marriage to Mrs. Agnes Knight
December 10, 1859, 12:00 noon
At the Episcopal Church on South Second Street
You are cordially invited to a reception to follow
At the home of Judge Flood on East Market Street

Helga whispered to Fiona, "The old gal got herself a rich man. She'll be the queen of the town now."

Mrs. Ritner said kindly, "I wish them much happiness. I will be attending the wedding and Mr. Adamson will be my escort." She smiled and added, "I'll be sure to tell you all about it when we get home."

"Oh Mama," Laura chimed in, "Can't I go? I've never been to a wedding."

"No, I'm sorry dear, it will be a small affair. It is a second marriage for both. Just Mr. Adamson and I are invited. And I will need you to look after your sisters on that day. Now, how about playing us a nice tune before we retire?"

Laura went to the piano and played one of her practice tunes, but her heart wasn't in it.

The next day Da appeared at the back door with a basket of apples. "Complements of Judge Flood," he explained. "We had a bumper crop this year. Fiona, I'll pick you up early on Saturday morning. Can't wait to get you home."

The way he looked at her, made Fiona suspect that he knew something. He must have been talking to Barney. She wished him goodbye and said she would see him soon.

When Mrs. Ritner saw the apples, she decided to make apple pies. Their delicious smell filled the house. When they were cool, she took Fiona aside.

"Fiona, I want you to take one of these pies over to Ralph to thank him for what he did. I'll send Helga on an errand, so she won't suspect anything."

Later that day, Fiona went next door and knocked at the door. She heard a great commotion of barking and yelping from within.

"What do you want?" she heard Mr. Gross yell through the door.

"It's Fiona from next-door. I'm here to see Ralph," she timidly replied.

The door opened and Mr. Gross stood there holding the snarling new hound by the collar.

"This is Devil. He doesn't like people," he snarled, sounding somewhat like the dog. "Stay there, I'll send him out. Hey Ralph," he called, "your lady friend is here."

Fiona just rolled her eyes and waited. Ralph came out and closed the door.

"Hello Fiona, I haven't seen you for a few days."

"I've been very busy." She handed him the pie and said, "Mrs. Ritner made this for you to thank you for helping me get the sheets."

"Tell her thanks," he replied. "Hey what happened to all of them new guests that were comin'? I didn't see anybody."

"Can you believe, they sent a note and canceled at the last moment? After all that work we did, it was a disappointment. I'm sorry I had to put you to so much trouble."

"It was no trouble, Fiona. I'll help you anytime."

"Thanks Ralph, you are kind. Enjoy the pie. I have to go."

She hurried back next-door and looked back and waved at Ralph. He gave her a foolish smile. She just shook her head. Poor boy he never had a chance being raised by such a father.

The weather on the day of Mrs. Knight's wedding was cold, but bright and clear. Laura and Fiona helped Mr. Ritner to dress.

"Oh Mama, you look beautiful," Laura sighed.

Emma Jane, Ella, and Helga all came in to inspect her. She wore a rose colored dress with a hoop skirt. She had added her best white lace collar and cuffs. Her hair was swept up with two silver combs.

"Oh you are beautiful," Helga exclaimed. "Mr. Adamson is here with the carriage."

They all descended the front staircase where Mr. Adamson was waiting resplendent in a grey morning coat. He took her arm and led her out to the carriage.

After they left, Laura, Ella, and Emma looked dejected. Joe Leiss came down stairs and asked them what was wrong.

"They feel left out because they can't go to the wedding," Helga explained. "Wait a minute," she suddenly burst out. "We can have our own wedding here."

She explained her plan and asked Joe to help. He readily agreed.

Helga began giving instructions right and left. "Joe, you have to be the groom. Go and put on your best clothes. Laura will be the bride. Fiona, Emma Jane, and Ella will be the bridesmaids, and I'll be the preacher. Come on girls, we'll go upstairs and find some outfits to wear."

A half hour later they took turns inspecting themselves in the mirror in Mrs. Ritner's room. Helga was wearing an old pair of men's trousers they had found in a trunk. She had added a shirt and tied a scarf around her neck as a necktie. Laura had on her best dress and wore an old lace curtain over her head as a veil. The other girls were all in their best dresses.

"I need some lace on my dress," Ella complained.

Fiona pulled some crocheted doilies from the trunk and pinned them to her dress.

Helga looked them over and said, "You all look splendid. Let's go down."

Joe was standing in the hall in his suit, shirt and tie.

"Oh Joe, you look fine" she almost gushed. "Thank you for doing this."

"Hey, it's fun," He said with a smile.

Helga grabbed the bouquet of Mrs. Ritner's wax roses from a vase and handed them to Laura. She instructed the girls to wait in the hall. She took Joe into the parlor and asked him to move a table to the front of the room.

"You stand here, Joe, this will be the altar."

"Whatever you say, preacher, you do look fetching in those pants."

Helga blushed as she turned around and called to the girls, "When I give the signal, walk in slowly in a straight single line singing 'Here Comes the Bride.' Laura, then you come in last and walk up and stand next to Joe." "What's the signal?" Emma called back.

"The signal is now. Now!"

All went well until Emma tripped on the rug and Ella had a fit of giggling. They soon recovered and the ceremony went on. Joe and Laura stood before Helga.

She held an opened book in front of her and said, "Do you Joseph Leiss take this woman to be your lawfully wedded wife?"

He answered dutifully, "I do"

"Do you Laura Ritner take this man to be your lawfully wedded husband?'

"I do," Laura answered, trying to suppress a giggle.

With great solemnity Helga said, "I now pronounce you man and wife."

Then they all retired to the kitchen for a party. They sat around the table sipping cider and eating apple pie.

Little Ella said, "This was the best wedding I ever been to"

"It's the only wedding you have ever been to," Laura said. "Thank you everyone. It was great fun."

Later Fiona whispered to Helga, "How come you didn't make yourself the bride?'

Helga laughed and said, "I didn't want to be too obvious."

When Mrs. Ritner and Mr. Adamson returned that evening, they told everyone they about splendid wedding.

"Agnes wore the most beautiful gown," Mrs. Ritner exclaimed. "It was the color of pale gold and she told me it came from Paris, France."

Mr. Adamson told them about the reception, "There were several flavors of ices and a cake that was three tiers tall. We brought you each a piece."

They all thanked him for the cake. Laura and the girls smiled and thought that their wedding was probably more fun

The next Saturday, Fiona was a little anxious about going home. She had never in her life kept anything from her Da. She could never deceive him if she tried. Since the day he dropped the apples off, she had a feeling he knew something was up. She couldn't tell him about the slave girl. She had promised Mrs. Ritner.

She found herself talking constantly on the ride home. "Mrs. Ritner went to the Judge's wedding and told us all about it. It was quite an elegant affair. I can't imagine him with a wife. Do you think she will try to change him?"

"Probably," he answered. "Most women do and most men need to be changed."

"Christmas is coming," Fiona sighed. "The Ritners are going to have a Christmas tree. Could we have a Christmas tree, Da?"

"Aye, if you want one. There's plenty of pine trees around our property. I'll cut a small one down. You know the tradition of the Christmas tree started in Germany. The Germans brought it to America."

"Oh Da, I forgot to ask you did you finish taking the medicine I bought for you at Mr. Montieth's show?"

"I did, I did," he said with a laugh. "I took a draft every night and slept very well."

For the rest of the ride home, Fiona rambled on about the play wedding they had for the girls, when they would have the first snow, how their old horse Roisin was looking and all of the talk in town about the coming trials and hangings of the rest of Brown's men. Da just listened and let her ramble.

She fixed tea when they arrived at the cottage and they sat down by the fire.

Da stared at her and said, "Barney told me he ran into you early one mornin.' He thinks you were on some kind of mission for Mrs. Ritner."

"Yes I was, Da, but I really can't tell you about it. It was just the one time. I was the only one there who could help her. I know you worry about me, but it was just the one time. It won't happen again."

"You are a lass who follows her heart. That can get you into trouble. I just want you to promise me to be careful. These are troubled times we are livin' in. I remember the troubles in Ireland. You have to be true to what you believe in, but don't go too far. It could cause you great harm. That's what happened to me brother Michael and now he's in a penal colony in Australia. Barney got in trouble too. He had to leave his family behind in Ireland and flee to America. He can never go back. He has a price on his head."

"Barney?" Fiona exclaimed. "I never knew."

"Don't speak of it to him," Tom replied, "He's not one to talk of it."

Fiona sipped her tea. *That's why he caught on so quickly the other morning. He's used to intrigue.* She felt a new respect for Barney.

Later Fiona went in to her room and opened the little chest where she kept John's books. The chest had belonged to her mother and she had kept her treasures there since she was a little girl. She lovingly picked up "Leaves of Grass" and carried it out to her father.

"Shall we read some of Mr. Whitman's poems, Da?"

"Indeed we shall, darlin." He turned to 'Song of Myself,' picked a verse, and read.

> "The big doors of the country barn stand open and ready,
> The dried grass of the harvest-time loads the slow-drawn wagon,
>     The clear light plays on the brown and gray and green intertinged,

The armfuls are pack'd to the sagging mow.
I am there, I help, I came stretch'd atop of the load,
I felt its soft jolts, one leg reclined on the other,
I jump from the cross-beams and seize the clover and timothy,
And roll head over heels and tangle my hair full of wisps."

"His poems are different without a doubt," Da said. "They don't rhyme but tis a certain rhythm there. As a farmer, I can understand this verse. He is a man who understands the work and the joy of the harvest."

"Yes, they are difficult but beautiful," Fiona replied. "I think he will be a great American poet. John Kagi thought highly of him."

At the thought of his name, a wave of melancholy swept over her. Her thoughts went to Virginia Cook. John Cook was due to hang the next day. How would she bear it?

"You're a million miles away," Da said.

"Sorry, what did you say?"

"Most of the papers condemn Brown's raid and approve of his bein' hanged, but here's a quote in the paper from an address that Henry Thoreau gave on the day of John Brown's hangin:"

"John Brown was a man of principle, of rare courage and devoted humanity, ready to sacrifice his life at any moment for the benefit of his fellow man.

I am here to plead his cause with you. I plead not for his life, but for his character, his immortal life, and so it becomes your cause wholly, and is not his in the least. Some eighteen hundred years ago Christ was crucified; this morning perchance, Captain Brown was hung. These are two of a chain which is not without its links.

He is not Old Brown any longer; he is an angel of light. I see that it was necessary that the bravest and humanist man in all the country should be hung. I foresee the time when the present form of slavery will no longer be here. We shall be at liberty to weep for Captain Brown. Then and not till then, we will take our revenge."

Tom put the paper down and gazed out the window as if looking into the future. "John Brown will be immortalized and his prediction that this guilty land will be purged with blood will come true. May God help us."

# Chapter Nine

The next morning Fiona and Tom were getting ready to leave for town when Clyde, one of Judge Flood's field hands, arrived with a note. Tom scanned it and turned to Fiona.

"The judge needs me darlin.' His favorite mare is ready to drop her foal and he's afraid the vet won't get there in time."

"But Da, you're not a vet. What can you do?"

"I know, I know, but I've had much experience with horses. Me Da was the unofficial vet in our town. People always called on him to help when their horses needed tendin.' I would go with him and help. Fiona, you take the wagon. It's too cold to walk. You can leave it at the livery. I'll get Mike Kelly to drive me in tomorrow ta fetch it."

Tom hitched up the wagon and helped Fiona up, "Mind yourself darlin', next time you come home, it will be Christmas."

Fiona waved as she turned the wagon into the road. She smiled to herself as the old horse Roisin trotted along. She loved driving the wagon and remembered the days when she would get the horse to race along the country roads. She loved the exhilaration of the wind in her face and the trees flying by. Roisin was too old to race now and Fiona held her to a trot. That was nice too. It gave her time to think.

*This is like that first day I walked into town to work at Mrs. Ritner's. That was only last April. It seems like a life time ago.* She pondered all that had happened. *I wanted to meet new people and have new experiences. I sure did,* she laughed. *I fell in love and lost him, but he taught me much about life. I made new friends and did have new experiences, some of them kind of scary. Most of all, I had fun and learned a great deal about life. I'm not the same scared little girl who walked into town that day.*

Today, Chambersburg looked busy for a Sunday morning. Fiona headed down Main Street and pulled into Reisher's livery stable. It was right next door to Granny Reisher's candy store. The candy store was closed on Sunday, but the stable was always open. She breathed in the pungent stable smells of horse dung, hay and leather. Mr. Reisher helped Fiona down from the wagon. He was a big man with large powerful hands used to handling horses.

"Pease take care of the horse and wagon, Mr. Reisher. My father will be here in the morning to pick them up."

"Of course, Miss. Be glad to. Lots of commotion in town today. You know they hung two more of them radical abolitionists in Charlestown yesterday. Good riddance I say."

"Yes, many people feel that way," Fiona replied.

"Not me," a voice proclaimed from the back of the stable.

"Granny, nobody cares what you think," Reisher replied, as his elderly mother made her way to the front of the stable.

"You hush boy. Let me talk to Fiona. How you doin' dear? I feel bad for those poor men that was hung. Cook was right here in jail. Didn't his wife and baby stay with Mrs. Ritner?"

"Yes they did," Fiona answered. "My heart goes out to her."

Mr. Reisher grunted, "Them abolitionists are causin' a heap of trouble in this country. I say let sleepin' dogs lie. If them folks down south want to keep slaves, it's their business."

"It's everybody's business," Grannie shot back. "It ain't decent for folks to own human beings and treat em like animals. The nigras are God's children too. Don't you think so, Fiona?"

"We're all God's children," Fiona replied as she walked away. "I have to go. I'll be late for mass."

Fiona smiled to herself as she hurried. *I'm not going to get in the middle of a family argument. A family argument! That's what it is in this town, abolitionist and pro-slave, an ongoing argument.*

In his sermon Father Mahoney prayed for those who had lost their lives yesterday in Charlestown, but did not mention the issue of slavery.

Fiona waited after mass and asked to speak to him. After the last parishioner had departed, they sat on a bench in the back of the church.

"Is something troubling you, Fiona?" He asked, looking concerned.

She paused a moment. "What is the church's position on slavery?"

Father Mahoney sighed and answered, "No position really, the Old Testament sanctioned slavery and the new testament gives no clear answers on slavery. Saint Augustine said that slavery was not justified under natural law, but was not forbidden by that law. Pope Gregory issued a Papal Bull in1839, condemning unjust types of slavery. Most American bishops interpreted it as condemning the slave trade but not slavery itself."

Fiona frowned and said, "I hear that some priests in the South have slaves."

"Yes, that's true," He answered as he took her hand. "As for myself, I agree with Daniel O'Connell. He achieved Irish Emancipation from the British in 1839. He believed in emancipation for all mankind and started an anti-slavery movement. He influenced many Irish immigrants like your father. My advice is to follow your conscience and believe in what you think is right."

Fiona smiled and said, "Thank you Father, I do believe slavery is wrong, but I don't always have the courage to speak out against it."

"Most of us don't, Fiona. Some sects of the Protestant Church are far ahead of us in speaking out. I admire them very much."

Fiona stood up. "Thank you father, you've been a great help."

He walked her to the door. "Goodbye dear. Take care, the time is coming soon when we shall all have to take a stand."

His words resounded in Fiona's head until she reached the Ritner house. She entered the kitchen to delicious smells and joyful noise. Helga, her little sister Gerti, and the young Ritner girls, were all covered with flour and smiling broadly.

Helga shouted, "Come on in Fiona, we're making gingerbread men to hang on the Christmas tree."

"It smells delicious in here. I'm glad to see everybody so happy. Hello Gertie, it's good to see you."

"Papa dropped me off while he did errands in town. I'm helping," Gertie said with glee.

Her little face shone with drops of gingerbread dough and Fiona laughed at the happy scene. She was glad to join in and helped with rolling the dough. The little girls pressed the cookie cutter and delighted in the shape of the ginger man. They worked all afternoon and when the last tray of cookies came out of the oven, they admired their handiwork. Tray after tray of little gingerbread men covered the table. Helga had inserted a string in each one before baking, so they could be hung on the tree. She told the girls they could each have one to eat after they washed up. They ran out to the pump and Helga put the rest of the cookies away. The girls returned and they all enjoyed their cookies. They went off to play as Helga and Fiona cleaned up the kitchen.

"How was your weekend at home?" Helga asked.

"It was fine. I always enjoy being with Da, but I had lots of heavy talk with him about slavery. The people in this town are so divided. I don't know what's to become of us. What do you think, Helga?"

"Me, I don't think about it. It's nothing to do with me. So why should I think about it. Guess what?"

Before Fiona could reply, Helga went on, "Joe asked me to go for a walk yesterday. We walked up town and he brought me a little sugar cake. We sat on a bench in The Diamond and talked for the longest time. We didn't even notice the cold. Oh, I do like him. Do you think he'll ask for my hand? I'm almost seventeen."

Fiona gulped and said, "Wow, you sure are moving fast. I'm sure Joe cares for you, but just give it some time. You're both young and what about your Pa? He wants you to marry Fritz."

"But I don't want to marry Fritz. I love Joe."

"Well as I said, give it some time. Just enjoy your time with Joe and see what happens."

"I will enjoy it," Helga giggled

Gertie wandered in. "Helga, remember Papa said for you to take me to the Wentz's house and he would pick me up there. Can we go now? Mrs. Wentz always gives me candy."

"You are a greedy child," Helga scolded. "We can go now. Mrs. Ritner wants me to get some things at the store. Come with us, Fiona. We don't have anything to do till supper time. "

They put on their capes and hats and headed out. Gertie skipped ahead of them, her pigtails flying about. *When was the last time I skipped?* Fiona wondered. *When does childhood and its joys end and grown up worries begin? Why can't I be more like Helga and not think about things.* She resolved, for the next few days, she would think about Christmas and not the worries of the world.

Soon Christmas Eve was upon them and Mrs. Ritner gave Helga and Fiona the week off. The boarders were all going to spend the holidays with their families. Before they left for home, Helga and Fiona had a lot of work to do. Mrs. Ritner's step-sons were expected home for the holidays and their rooms had to be ready. The girls spent the morning baking while Joe and Mr. Adamson went out to get a Christmas tree from a nearby farm. They returned and dragged it through the kitchen. The girls swept up the needles and breathed in their fresh fragrance. They finished cleaning up the kitchen and Mrs. Ritner called them in to the parlor where everyone was gathered. The Ritner boys had arrived and were introduced to Fiona.

Fiona gasped when she saw the tree standing in the corner, "Oh how beautiful! This is my first Christmas tree."

"Come and help us decorate it," Mrs. Ritner beckoned. They all carefully took the beautiful glass ornaments from a box and hung them on the tree.

Mrs. Ritner said, "My Grandmother brought these from Germany. I have always treasured them."

The girls then tied their gingerbread men to the branches and Mrs. Ritner placed candles in holders on the strongest boughs. Mr. Adamson lit the candles and they all stepped back to admire their handy work. They all explained "Beautiful" and clapped their hands.

Mrs. Ritner sat down at the piano and they all sang carols. John Ritner joined in a beautiful baritone voice. She asked Helga to come up and sing. "My family came from Germany generations ago, but we lost the language. Would you sing Silent Night in German for us?"

Helga hesitated for a moment, but soon broke into a surprisingly sweet alto voice.

"Stille nacht,
Heilge nacht
Alles schlaft, unson auch
Nur das traite hochheilige Paar,
Holder knabe in lochiger Haar,
Schlof in himmlesscher Ruhl!
Schlof in himmlesscher Ruhl!"

Joe came forward and took Helga by the hand and said "that was beautiful."

She was blushing when Fiona hugged her and said, "I never knew you had such a beautiful voice."

They sang a few more songs and finished the cookies and punch before gathering up their things to go their separate ways. As they left, Mrs. Ritner handed Helga and Fiona each a small wrapped gift.

"Merry Christmas and thank you for your loyal service," she said as she kissed each of them on the cheek.

Mr. Adamson, Mr. Butler, and Joe were headed for the livery stable. Mr. Adamson was giving them a ride to their destinations. He was off to his sister's house in Gettysburg, Joe to his aunt's and Mr. Butler to his mother's.

The Ritner girls wished them all a Merry Christmas and Mr. Adamson shook their hands and told them to enjoy their holidays with their families.

Joe took Helga aside for a few whispered words. Everyone was in a joyful mood.

Helga and Fiona walked arm and arm down the street. Fiona was going to Mrs. Gormley's where Da would pick her up and Helga had been invited to the Wentz's to wait for her Pa. They stopped at the corner before going their separate ways and chatted, their breath blowing up in billows in the cold air.

"Joe is coming to visit my family the day after Christmas. His Aunt's house is not far from ours," Helga said, her voice ringing with excitement.

Fiona hugged her. "I wish you all my love dear friend. May you have the best Christmas ever. Tell Gertie I hope Christkindl brings her many gifts."

Da was already enjoying a cup of cheer with Mrs. Gormley when Fiona arrived. Hattie beckoned her into the kitchen

"That nice Mrs. Ritner sent us a Christmas ham and one to Molly too and there was a note to thank us for helpin' when she needed it," Hattie whispered.

"Oh that was so nice of her," Fiona replied. "I wish you and Enoch a Merry Christmas and Molly too."

She returned to the parlor and Da was anxious to get started. Snow was in the air. Mrs. Gormley handed Tom a bottle of whiskey and Fiona a box of candy as they left.

"Merry Christmas my dear friends and safe home," she called from the door way.

When they pulled up to their cottage snowflakes were began to fall.

"I may have to hitch up the sleigh if this keeps up," Tom said as he helped Fiona down. "Go in and start the fire while I settle Roisin in the barn."

Fiona entered the cottage and looked around. Da had already spruced up the house for Christmas. He always told her about Christmas in Ireland and how they would white wash the cottage and get the house ready. She took off her cloak and lit the fire and started the dinner preparations.

The front door opened with a bang. She turned and saw Tom dragging a tree through the door.

"Oh Da, you cut down a tree! Where will we put it?"

"I built a little stand over there in the corner," he said pointing to the other side of the fireplace."

They set up the tree and stepped back to admire it. The pine fragrance filled the room and Fiona took her father's hand and kissed him.

"Thank you, Da. Our first Christmas tree! Oh, but we don't have any decorations."

"We do," he replied as he carried in a box from the doorstep. He pulled out pine cones, red holly berries and dried flowers. "It will be all natural."

They hung the decorations on the tree and put the candles in the windows just as Da had in Ireland. The candles were to light the way for the Holy Family or any poor traveler who is out on that night. They finished just in time as the neighbors began to arrive. The room was filled with the Kelly family, the O'Briens and other neighbors. They all gathered around the tree and clapped their hands in wonder. Tom passed around his whiskey punch and they all sang carols as Mike Kelly played his fiddle.

He stopped and asked, "Tom, please sing the Wexford Carol

Tom stood in front of the tree and began in his best tenor voice:

> "Good people all this Christmas time,
> Consider well and bear in mind
> What our good God for us has done
> In sending His beloved Son.
> With Mary holy we should pray
> To God with love this Christmas day.
> In Bethlehem upon this morn
> There was a blessed Messiah born."

"It brings a tear to my eye every time," Annie Kelly said as she wiped her eyes.

Fiona called everyone to the table where she had spread out the traditional Christmas Eve meal of fish with white sauce and potatoes. When they finished, Annie Kelly brought out her ca'ca Nollaig, the Christmas cake to ohs and awes from everyone. She had made it weeks ago and stored it in a cloth soaked in whisky. It was covered with white icing and decorated with candied cherries.

Talk around the table was of the Christmas dinner tomorrow at Judge Flood's mansion. It was the first time that the Judge's employees and all of the people of the surrounding cottages had been invited to the house.

"I think the new Mrs. Flood likes to play the lady of the manor, Mrs. Miller said as she enjoyed her cake.

"I heard that they held a ball at the town house last night for the important people in town," Annie Kelly chimed in.

"Well I think the really important people will be there tomorrow," Tom added, "and we will enjoy the hospitality."

After the feast the table and chairs were pushed aside and Mike played his fiddle while the dancing began. The reels and jigs shook the old floors of the cottage and the joy of Christmas filled their hearts.

Fiona noticed the children sneaking out. She knew they were going to the barn to spy on the animals and see if they would speak on Christmas Eve. She remembered doing the same as a child to test the old legend. She never heard them speak, but it was great fun to sit on the hay and pretend it was the stable of Bethlehem. The giggling children returned and the little ones cuddled up on the chairs and soon fell asleep. As the clock struck midnight, a final toast was drunk and sleeping children were picked up. They all wished each other Merry Christmas and, in Irish "Nollaig Shona Druit" as they bid good night.

Fiona stood in the doorway and watched the snow falling. The ground was covered and she sighed with contentment.

"Oh Da we will have a grand Christmas snow and a Christmas tree. "

# Chapter Ten

Christmas day dawned bright and clear. Da looked out and saw there was just enough snow on the ground to hitch up the sleigh. After breakfast they opened their gifts. Fiona was filled with anticipation. She had saved up enough money to have her likeness taken at Mr. Bishop's photography shop. She wasn't sure how she looked. It took so long for the picture to be taken and she had to sit very still. She felt that she looked rather stiff and stern. Mr. Bishop had put it in a frame for her and she wrapped it in silver paper.

She handed it to her father and said, "Here Da, please open this first. I hope you like it."

Tom opened the package and looked at it silently. Fiona held her breath and waited. She was surprised to see tears well up in his eyes.

He looked at her and said, "I always wanted a likeness of your mother and when I look at this lovely image of you, I can also see her in you. This is a treasure. Thank you my love."

Fiona opened her gift from Da. It was a beautiful set of silver combs in a satin lined box.

"Oh Da, they are beautiful, but too extravagant."

"Not atall, atall for my only daughter. The judge was very good to me in my Christmas bonus."

Fiona opened her gift from Mrs. Ritner. It was a little music box that played a lovely waltz. It reminded her of lovely evenings in the Ritner parlor.

"Oh Da, she is such a kind lady. I'm lucky to be working for her."

"She is that," he replied. "I admit I had some fears of you going off to work for her, but I'm glad you are happy there."

They both enjoyed the quiet of the remainder of the morning. All too soon it was time to get ready for the grand party at the Flood house. Da looked splendid in his best suit and Fiona in her best winter dress of dark green. Da brought the sleigh around and old Roisin was chomping at the bit. Fiona had barely climbed in, when she was off. She ran through the snow like a young filly with the sleigh bells ringing. They joined other neighbors on the road with shouts of "Merry Christmas."

When they arrived at the Flood house, they took the horse to the stable, and Da guided Fiona to the back door. She had never been in the house before. The Judge greeted them in the hall and invited them into the drawing room where many of the neighbors were already assembled.

Mrs. Flood stood in front of the fireplace in a red velvet gown and greeted one and all. "Merry Christmas and welcome to our home."

Fiona noticed that she looked happy. She was no longer the sad and mean Mrs. Knight she had known. Fiona looked around the room and was amazed at its grandeur. There were crystal chandeliers and velvet draperies that hung to the floor. Beautiful paintings in guilt frames lined the walls. The simple people gazed around in amazement.

It reminded Fiona of a scene from English novels she had read. It was like the people of the great manor house entertaining their tenants and showing off their splendors. There was a sumptuous buffet with ham and turkey, but also the guests had other dishes they had never seen before like fried oysters and aspics. After everyone had eaten their fill, the table was cleared and desserts were laid out. All kinds of cakes and jellies filled the table. It was more food that they had seen in their lives. Most of the ladies were too full to touch the desserts, but the men and children did their best.

After dessert, the tabled were pushed aside, a three piece ensemble was brought in and the dancing began. Fiona danced with some of the young men and was having a very good time. During a break in the music, Mrs. Flood came up to her and said she would like to speak with her in the hall. Fiona followed her out wondering what she wanted. She knew from experience that Mrs. Knight, now Mrs. Flood, always wanted something. She pointed Fiona to a bench and asked her to sit down.

"Are you enjoying the party dear," she asked.

"Oh yes, I'm having a wonderful time," she replied

Mrs. Flood went on to inquire about the well- being of all the residents of the Ritner household before getting to her point.

"How do you like working for Mrs. Ritner?" she asked.

"Oh, I like it there very much," Fiona said with enthusiasm.

"Yes I see, but I know she doesn't pay you very much. I am in need of a lady's maid. I could pay you twice as much. You would live here at the house and travel with me when needed. It would be a great opportunity for you"

Fiona was unable to speak for a moment. Visions of living in this great house swam through her head. Travels to big cities and foreign places sounded enticing.

All she could reply was, "Why me?"

"Well of course, you would require a great deal of training, but you do have some potential. None of the other backward country girls around here would do," Mrs. Flood said in her usual haughty tone.

This brought Fiona to her senses and she replied, "No, I don't think I could do it."

"What?" she exclaimed. "How could you turn down such an opportunity?"

"I'm loyal to Mrs. Ritner and I like living there and working for her. I have friends there."

"Well you are not the intelligent girl I thought you were then," she replied with an edge in her voice. "I will have to look elsewhere."

"Mary O'Brien is a nice hardworking girl. Maybe you should consider her," Fiona replied hopefully.

"I will not have Irish riffraff looking after me," she replied.

Fiona stood up and said in her most forceful voice, "You forget yourself, Mrs. Flood, I am Irish riffraff."

She returned to the parlor still seething. Da gave her a questioning look, but she just smiled and joined the dancing. The party went on for a few more hours and all exclaimed it had been a splendid affair. They thanked the Floods and were guided to the back door.

On the ride home, Fiona told Da about turning down Mrs. Floods offer.

"Are you sure darlin' girl? It would have been a great opportunity," he wondered.

"I'm sure Da. Oh it would have been exciting at first living in that fine house and traveling to new places, but I know I would not be happy there. Mrs. Flood once told me that she used to have slaves to wait on her. I could not be her slave."

"Well, I'm sure it would not be quite that bad. There are laws against it here now," he said with a laugh.

"I know, but you know I almost feel sorry for people like her."

"And why is that daughter?"

"There is a great insecurity about her that makes her look down on others. She never got over the loss of her great wealth down south. Now that she has wealth again, she has to show it off and prove that she is superior."

"Fiona, you are gifted with great insight. Use it well. I congratulate you on your wise decision."

By the time they reached the cottage, the wind was howling. Da drove the sleigh right into the barn and they got off to unhitch the horse. Suddenly, they were startled by a movement from the back of the barn. A tall man stepped forward and spoke.

"Sir, are you Thomas McKenna?"

"I am," Tom replied, as he pushed Fiona behind him and held up the buggy whip. "And who are you?"

"My name is Liam Healy. I am the son of your sister Annie."

"What are you doing here?" Tom shouted.

The man started to answer as the wind picked up and howled. Fiona suggested that they unhitch the horse and go inside. Liam helped them unhitch Roisin. He wiped her down with a cloth and gave her some hay and water as Tom stood in silence like a man in shock.

"Please, Liam let's go inside." Fiona said as she guided him to the house and Tom followed.

She lit some candles and started the fire. She motioned Liam to come and sit down by the fire. In the firelight she got a good look at him. No longer the menacing stranger in the barn, he looked poor and bedraggled. His black hair and beard were matted and dirty. His clothes were ragged and wet. *Now that's the look of Irish riffraff,* she thought, as she went to fetch some dry clothes for him from Da's room. When she returned, Da had regained his composure and was talking to Liam.

"I'm sorry, I didn't know Annie had a living son."

"My poor mother died giving birth to me. Her parents were dead and there was no one to care for me. I was sent to live with my father's aunt in Roscommon. My father took to drink and we lost touch with him. We heard that he died some time ago. When I was old enough, me auntie gave me some letters and things of my mother's. Among them were letters from you in America. Mr. Grady in the village read them to me and I made up me mind to come here as soon as I could."

"Why didn't you write to me?" Tom asked.

"Sorry sir, I never learned how." Liam replied. "I was a thinkin of askin Mr. Grady to write to you, but I never did. Me old Antie died and I had to hit the road and fend for meself."

"That's enough with the questions, Da. Let's get this boy cleaned up and fed. She heated up some water in a basin and sent him into Da's room to clean up and change his clothes. When he returned, she had the rest of the Christmas soup heating on the stove. Liam sat at the table and she set the soup and some bread before him. As he ate she studied his face and saw the resemblance to her father. He was his nephew all right and a very handsome man. His thick black hair was combed back to reveal a high forehead and broad cheek bones. He looked up and smiled at her. It was a smile that lit up the room.

After Liam had finished eating, he entertained them with the story of how he came to America.

"As long as I can remember, my goal was to go to America. I was inspired by your story, Uncle Thomas. I landed on the estate of Lord d'Arcy where I tended the horses. I always had a way with horses and the ladies. I saw these talents as God given. Lady d'Arcy took a likin ta me and paid me extra for tending her horse and other favors. That's how I got the passage money for the trip."

Tom shook his head at his nephew's story and gestured to him to continue.

"I took passage on the good ship Bristol out of Liverpool and landed in Philadelphia three months ago. I found work with a lady who runs a boarding house on Second Street. Mrs. Leary was very good to me. I did odd jobs for her and tended her horses. As I said, the good Lord gave me the gift of being favored by the ladies. She was generous and I saved enough to take the train to Chambersburg."

"When did you arrive here?" Fiona asked

"Well, dear cousin Fiona, it was yesterday on Christmas mornin'. I had a vision of spendin' Christmas wid me relatives. But when I got off the train, I asked the first person I see to point the way to Thomas Mc Kenna's house. He said he didn't know. I was shocked. You're not very well known in this town are ye uncle?"

Tom had to laugh. "Not by one and all that's for sure."

"Well," Liam continued, "it took me awhile to find somebody who knew of you and I find you are not in the town, but way out here. I finally procured a ride with a fellow who was going this way. He dropped me off, and not finding you ta home, sought shelter in the barn."

"That's quite a story," Tom got up and poured a drink for each of them. "I lift my glass to my dear sister Annie's son and welcome him to America."

They talked for hours of family and forgotten friends. When the hour grew late, Fiona set up a pallet for Liam by the fire and they bid each other goodnight.

Neighbors stopped in the next day and were introduced to Liam. Mike Kelly suggested that he speak to Judge Flood if he needed work. The Judge was looking for someone to tend the horses. Liam grew eager to talk to him.

"I'll take you up there after the New Year," Tom told him.

Liam was very interested in the political situation in the country and asked many questions.

"In Philadelphia there was much talk in the pubs of what would happen if the south left the union. Some said it would never happen and some said there would be war if they did."

"No one knows what will happen," Tom answered. "A lot depends on who wins the coming election for president."

"Most of the Irish I talked to were against the blacks. They didn't like them comin' up north and takin' their jobs. Let them stay down there as slaves. Didn't bother them. What do you think Uncle Thomas?"

"I am against slavery. It is an inhuman condition. Blacks are human just as we are. In Ireland, the British treated us as sub-humans and we were their slaves. All men are equal and must be treated as equals," Thomas answered.

"Never thought of it that way," Liam said. "I will surely think on that."

The rest of the week passed quickly and the last day of the year was upon them. Tom announced he was driving into town to pick up his friend Barney for their annual New Years Eve get together. Fiona was never fond of these encounters. Barney usually got her father drunk and she didn't like seeing him in that condition. However, Da enjoyed it so she couldn't object.

He took Liam with him and said he would introduce him around to the people who did know Thomas McKenna. Hours later they were back looking like they had already started the celebration.

"Cousin Fiona," Liam exclaimed, "What a grand time we had. First we met at the pub with my new friend Barney and then at the home of the lovely Mrs. Gormley. She is a great lady indeed."

"Yes she is," Fiona laughed, "But don't you be putting any of your designs on her. She is a dear friend and has been like a mother to me."

"I am always respectful to great ladies," was his reply.

They settled down for the evening and it turned out to be a New Year's Eve that Fiona would never forget. She set out the drinks and snacks on the table for the gentlemen. She sat over in the corner and took up a book.

Barney asked Liam about how things were in Ireland.

"Poor. The people are still poor and emigratin' in droves. A man once said that young people are our greatest export. The bright ones are the ones who leave. It's our great loss. Potatoes are growing again, but most of the land is still in the hands of the British. There has been a rise in the Fenians and there's a new one called the Irish Republican Brotherhood. Ireland will never give up her fight for independence."

"Aye," Barney replied. "I got involved meself over there in some trouble. It was in Graiguenamanagh, Kilkenny in the time of the Tithe War."

Fiona was listening with interest and had to ask, "What was the Tithe War?"

Barney looked up and answered, "That is just another one of the lovely taxes the British impose on us. We have to pay ten percent of the value of our produce for the up-keep of the clergy and the church. Not our church but the so called Church of Ireland which is just the Church of England. The collection of the tithe payment was resisted and the revolt spread to Wexford. Many were killed and the revolt was put brutally down when the British army arrived. I was just a boyo, but I fought with the rest of them. Many of my friends were killed or captured. I was lucky; a neighbor hid me in her cottage. That night a farmer, heading for New Ross, hid me under the hay in his wagon. I signed on as a deck hand on a British ship in port and made it to New York. I jumped ship and said fair thee well to the British and to dear old Ireland."

Barney took another drink. "I never knew what happened to me friends who fought with me. They were likely hanged or transported and here I am, a worthless man."

Tom held up his glass to Barney. "You're not worthless at all, my friend. You fought the good fight and you can be proud."

"How did you wind up in Chambersburg?" Liam asked.

"I made my way to Philadelphia and heard about a job here in the mill. Well the job didn't last, but I stayed."

Liam went on to tell his tale of getting to America. By then, the men had forgotten Fiona's presence, and Liam went into more detail about his conquest of the ladies. He then suddenly remembered something. "Uncle Thomas, I almost forgot. I brought the packet of letters you sent to me mother."

He opened his small bag that stood in the corner and pulled out the letters. He handed them to Tom. Tom opened one letter and began to reads it to himself. Fiona could see a tear running down his cheek. "Oh what memories this brings back. This was written when I first met Kathleen."

He began to read out loud.

> "My dear sister Annie,
>
> I hope all is well with you. I was very happy to hear of your marriage to Hugh Healy. I wish you both many blessings and joys. I'm also thinking of getting married soon. I met a wonderful girl and I hope she will have me. She's from Mayo, but I don't hold that against her. Kathleen is working as a maid in a great house on Rittenhouse Square. I'm working in a malt house and saving me money. I look forward to a good future here.
>
> Love, your brother Tom"

He went on to read from other letters, telling of their happy times together and the birth of their daughter. He read aloud, but it was like he was reading them to himself. Sometimes he would pause and his tears would flow. Fiona listened enthralled. Her father had rarely talked of those days. He wrote of his pride in taking care of his little family. They rented a little house in South Philadelphia. He called it a Father, Son, and Holy Ghost House. It had three floors with one room on each floor. He started to read the letter that told of Kathleen's Tuberculosis and death.

Tom finally looked over and saw Fiona. "I loved her so. I could not save her. "

She went over and put her arms around him and said, "I know Da, I'm so glad to hear about my mother and your life together."

Barney stood up and pulled out his pocket watch. "Look here, my friends, it's almost midnight. Let's go outside and greet the New Year."

He poured them each a drink and one for the wee folks. They all went out and Barney poured a drink on the ground for the wee ones. They all joined him and lifted their glasses.

"Here's to 1860," Tom toasted. "God only knows what's in store for this country, but let's pray for her protection. God bless Liam in his new life here and God bless all of us."

# Part Two

# Chapter Eleven

**1861**

It was a soft April morning. Fiona could smell the sweet fragrance of spring in the air as she filled the water bucket at the pump in the Ritner's backyard. This morning the promise of spring did not invigorate her. She put the bucket down and sat on the bench. She felt an unease of spirit thinking over the events of the past few months.

Abraham Lincoln of Illinois had been elected in November and most of the people of the town had celebrated. They saw him as their best hope. However, to many his election was not a cause to celebrate. They feared that his opposition to the spread of slavery would tear the country apart. Before Lincoln was inaugurated, South Carolina had seceded from the union and other states followed. The country was, as Da put it, on the brink of war.

Fiona remembered the evening of Mr. Lincoln's inauguration in March. They were all gathered in the Ritner parlor as Mr. Adamson read from the papers the stirring words of Lincoln's inaugural address ending with:

> That every living heart and hearthstone all over this be-
> loved land will swell the chorus of the union when touched,
> as surely they will be, by the better angels of our nature.

There was silence for a while as everyone took in the words of the President's speech. Then they all began talking at once.

"He says he won't interfere with slavery in the states where it exists. That should satisfy the South," Mr. Adamson said as he put down the paper.

Mrs. Ritner clasped her hands and said, "I pray that all will be touched by the better angels of our nature."

Joe Leiss stood up and said, "He also said he made a solemn oath to defend the government and to defend all places belonging to the government."

Mr. Adamson looked up, "Union forces still occupy Fort Sumter in Charleston Harbor. The South is demanding that the fort be vacated. The Union troops are still there. If war comes it will start there."

Joe again jumped up with excitement, "Damn right and I'll be in it. Sorry, ladies," he apologized, "but I'm ready to fight for the Union."

Fiona saw a look of concern on Helga's face at Joe's outburst. She and Joe were engaged. He had won her father over. He was doing well at the tool factory and saving money. Mr. Meyers was impressed that Joe was a hard worker and able to care for his daughter. He came from farming stock and was willing to help out on the Meyers's farm. Fiona and Helga later talked about Joe's outburst.

"Oh, he's just chompin' at the bit to go and fight with no thought about me," Helga exclaimed. "What about our future? There won't be any if he gets killed in some stupid war."

"I know," Fiona answered. "They're all the same. My cousin Liam talks about it all the time. He's been doing very well working for Judge Flood. The Judge put him in charge of the horses and gave him a nice room over the stable. But all Liam talks about is joining up if there's a war. What is it in men's nature that finds war so exciting?"

"They're all just little boys at heart wanting to play soldiers," Helga sighed. "Let's pray that there won't be a war. Let the South go. Who cares."

Fiona had been lost in thought when she heard a voice from the yard next door. She looked over and saw Mrs. Birdwell hanging her laundry. Fiona stood up and waved. The Birdwells, a young family with three children, had moved into the Gross house. Several months ago Mr. Gross and his son Ralph had moved to Virginia. Fiona recalled her last meeting with Ralph. He told her that his father was offered a job in a slave catching business.

"He'll be traveling up and down the coast looking for runaways. He thinks he'll make a lot more money than working on his own." Ralph took Fiona's hand and said, "I'll never forget you and the mornin' we went to fetch the sheets from Ole Molly."

Fiona just shook his hand, smiled, and wished him luck. The Ritner household was glad to be rid of the slave catcher and his snarling dogs, but Fiona had felt a pang of pity for poor Ralph.

Fiona got up and went over to the fence to say hello to Mrs. Birdwell. She thought their new neighbor was well named. She reminded her of a tall bird. She was thin with a long nose and her actions were fluttery and bird like. The Birdwells were Mennonites and she always wore her prayer cap and dressed in plain fashion.

Fiona greeted her, "Good morning. Isn't it a lovely day?"

"Praise God, it is my dear. You looked like you were lost in thought. I hope I didn't disturb you."

"No not at all," Fiona replied. "You woke me up from my day dreaming, I have to get back to my duties."

When Fiona entered the kitchen, Mrs. Ritner was giving a list to Helga. "It's a long grocery list," she was saying. "I need you both to go. The order is too much to carry, so ask Mr. Hughes to deliver it. You're caught up on your chores, so take your time and visit if you like."

The girls thanked her and left immediately. They were happy to have an afternoon off. Fiona's melancholy mood lifted and they strolled through town with light hearts. After picking out the order at the grocery store, they looked in the shop windows and bought some penny candy at Granny Reisher's store. They crossed the King Street Bridge and climbed down the bank to the Falling Springs. The girls sat on the bank next to the water fall. Fiona loved watching that little water fall. The laughing waters always gave her a sense of peace.

Suddenly, the peace was shattered when they heard people shouting in the streets. The girls ran up to the bank to see what was happening. Crowds of excited people were headed for The Diamond. Fiona and Helga joined the crowd and asked what was happening.

"It's war. It's war," a man shouted. "The rebels have fired on Fort Sumter."

The crown headed for the telegraph office to wait for more news. Fiona and Helga sat down on a bench and held hands.

"Lord, Lord," Helga sighed, "What's going to happen? Oh Fiona, I'm mighty scared. What if the rebels come up here? Joe's gonna join up. I can't bear to loose him."

"Nothing is going to happen right away," Fiona said as she put her arm around Helga. "The fighting is down in South Carolina. I'm sure our army will stop them there."

There were more people in the streets now shouting "The Union forever down with the rebels."

Fiona noticed everyone joining in the chant even those who had sympathized with the South just a few days ago. Everyone was gleeful and excited. They formed a parade and surrounded the telegraph office shouting for news. Fiona took Helga by the hand and headed for Mrs. Gormley's house. Mrs. Gormley was happy to see them. She ushered them in, and closed the door.

"Dear God, everybody's going crazy," she said as she sat down and wiped her face with her handkerchief. "What a day! Sit down girls. What are they saying down town?"

"Only that the fort was fired on from Charleston this morning and a battle is going on," Fiona replied, then added, "Half of the town is waiting at the telegraph office for news."

"My, oh my," Mrs. Gormley sighed as she fanned herself. "What does it mean?"

Fiona stood up and walked over to the window. "They're saying it means war."

She gazed out the window and whispered, "God help us. "

Hattie came in with tea and they sat down and talked of other things, like how Judge Flood's wife was redecorating the townhouse. She had already redone the country manor house with elaborate French furniture. Agnes Flood was enjoying her new status as the wife of one of Chambersburg's most important citizens.

Mrs. Gormley lowered her voice and said, "I heard that she hired a new personal maid. She's a proper lady with an English accent."

Fiona remembered how Mrs. Flood had offered her the job and smiled. *I guess she didn't have to hire any Irish riffraff,* she thought. Mrs. Gormley then asked how Fiona's cousin Liam was doing.

"Very well," she answered. "He has charmed Mrs. Flood and is giving her riding lessons."

"That one could charm the birds out of the trees." Mrs. Gormley said with a fond smile.

When the girls returned to the Ritner house, the talk was of nothing but the war. Mr. Adamson came in with the latest news that the battle at Sumter was still going on. "They're posting bulletins on the board outside the telegraph office every hour. The commander of the fort, Major Anderson, can not hold out for long against the batteries of Charleston. The fort is not that well fortified. Mr. Lincoln is a wise man. He knew the North saw the fort as a symbol and that it should not be surrendered easily. The South will take it by force. The rebels fired the first shot and it will always be remembered that they started the war."

The next morning, Mr. Adamson went to the telegraph office and returned with the news that Major Anderson had surrendered the fort. He also carried the newspapers and the headlines screamed:

**Fort Sumter Makes a Vigorous Reply**
**The Fort in Flames**
**Fort Sumter Fallen**
**War Commences**

The next few days were ones that would always live in the memory of those who lived them. The people of Chambersburg were seized with a high fever of excitement. Flags, and red, white, and blue bunting were up on all public building and many people were wearing badges with the national colors. Lincoln issued a proclamation calling for 75,000 troops to serve for three months. In response to his call, many young men of the town volunteered their services.

On April 17, a meeting was held in the Court House to meet the emergency of the times. Many distinguished citizens gave long winded speeches. Judge Flood stood and declared his readiness to fight and said he would accept the rank of colonel. He pledged to support the Government by every means in his power and expressed his willingness to shoulder a musket if needed to save the flag of his country from dishonor. In the end, the Judge gave money to support the troops instead of going off to war. As always, it was the young men who were enlisted into the newly formed Chambersburg Artillery.

April 18 was a great day for Chambersburg. A pole, 120 feet high, was erected in the center of The Diamond. The whole town turned out for the grand occasion. With great ceremony the flag was run up the pole and it unfurled in the breeze. A group of ladies, with splendid red white and blue sashes across their breasts, stood on the balcony of the Franklin Hotel and sang "The Stars Spangled Banner." Many patriotic speeches followed.

Fiona, standing on the edge of the crowd with the other residents of the Ritner house, looked around at the people. Many were weeping. Some perhaps with patriotic fervor and some with sorrow. She noticed Mr. Hoke standing next to her. He was a prominent merchant and a friend of the Ritner family. Fiona always enjoyed talking to the older gentleman. She smiled at him.

He tipped his hat and said, "You know, Fiona, if Virginia adopts the order of secession, the seat of war will be right along our border. Here we are in the great Cumberland Valley that goes right into Virginia. Both of the contending armies could possibly pass through here. The rebel flag might one day fly from that pole." He looked at Fiona and shook his head as if to waken himself. "Oh, I'm sorry my dear. Pay no attention to an old man's ramblings. I'm sure we'll be safe here." He tipped his hat again and walked away.

Fiona was glad that Helga had not heard his remarks. She was a little further away holding on to Joe. That's all she had been doing since he enlisted. Fiona's cousin Liam Healy, Helga's brother Hans, and most of the young men of the town were joining the Chambersburg Artillery.

The next day, most of the town gathered again. This time at the train depot to see the cream of their youth off to war. The Chambersburg Artillery was leaving for Harrisburg where they would join their regiment. It was another brilliant day with more speeches and cheering. Father Mahoney and some of the Ministers stood in front of the troops and blessed them.

Fiona noticed Mr. Heneberger, one of Chambersburg's oldest citizens, standing on the train platform. Fiona remembered hearing about him when she first came to town. He had served in the Revolutionary War and she always wanted to talk to him, but was too shy back then. She was a different girl now and went up and greeted him. Mr. Heneberger looked at her and tipped his old battered hat giving her a toothless smile. His face was thin with a pointed chin. Fiona had never seen a face with so many wrinkles, but his pale blue eyes twinkled like a mischievous boy.

"Them boys is gonna be in for it," he spoke in a raspy voice. "They have no idea what they're a gettin' into. I went off to war like them with the bands playin' and the girls waving and throwin' kisses. I was thirteen years old. Thought it would be a grand adventure." He looked over at the volunteers. "Them boys is thinking the same, but they'll learn different. Them younguns will see some terrible things. Half a them won't come back." He shook his head. "Well I reckon there has to be a war every now and then. It gets folks's blood up and gives the survivors something to talk about when they're old men."

He walked away still shaking his head as the band began to play. The volunteers were ordered to form a line and prepare for departure. The boys were laughing and eager to go. Their parents, sisters, wives and sweethearts clung to them and cried.

Fiona found Liam with several girls hanging on him. She pulled him aside and hugged him. Her eyes filled with tears. She had become very fond of her rakish long lost cousin.

She held him close for a few minutes and whispered. "Come back to us."

"Never fear cousin dear. The North will win. We have more Irish on our side." He turned and saw Tom and his friend Barney who had just arrived. "Uncle Thomas, I'll be back and we'll work together and make a lot of money. I have big plans."

"Tom blessed him and said, "God go with you my son."

Barney shook his hand and said, "Fight like an Irishman me boy."

Fiona was about to ask her father about their big plans when she spotted Hans Myers and his parents. His mother was crying and his father looked stoic. She went up to them and wished them well. She hugged Hans and whispered. "Dear Hans, take care. I will write to you and pray for you and all our soldiers." He only smiled and nodded.

Joe had to push himself away from Helga's arms and promised "I'll be back by Christmas sweetheart. We'll whip them rebels in no time."

The troops boarded the train, the crowd waved as the train departed and the band played on through the fog like smoke and the screeching sounds. The crowd began to disperse each with his and hers own thoughts. Da had to get back to the farm. He wished Fiona goodbye and hurried off. Fiona walked with her arm around the still sobbing Helga and her thoughts were of another time. She remembered that first flurry of her love for John Kagi. She was almost jealous of her dear friend Helga because she had someone to love. Fiona sighed and wondered if she would ever have someone to love again. She wished that John were here once more walking with her by the creek. She would ask him about Mr. Hoke's dire warnings about the town's closeness to the southern border. He would assure her that she would be safe and she would feel protected by the warmth of his love.

As they walked home, there were shouts from the telegraph office about riots in Baltimore, Maryland, just a few miles down the road, Maryland did not secede from the Union, but it was filled with southern sympathizers. Soldiers of the Sixth Massachusetts Militia were attacked by a mob of those sympathizers as they marched through Baltimore to board a train. A riot ensued and four soldiers and twelve civilians were killed. It was the first bloodshed of the Civil War.

For the next few days, Chambersburg was filled with soldiers. Wagon loads of Union troops from Harpers Ferry arrived. Rebel troops had been advancing on the arsenal and the small contingent of Union troops quartered there had to evacuate. Before they left the troops under Lieutenant Jones, blew up the arsenal destroying, 15,000 armaments before the rebels could get them.

Next came news of the destruction of the bridges along the Northern Central and Philadelphia, Wilmington and Baltimore railroads. All travel stopped on these routes. Northerners were trapped in the South and Southerners in the North. Many availed themselves of the Franklin and Cumberland Valley Railroad. People of all sorts passed through Chambersburg. Senator Caleb Cushing of Massachusetts, returning home from Washington, was seen in town. One observer noted that many people with "southern looking features" were seen in town.

In the next few weeks more companies of soldiers arrived in town and were encamped on the Fair Grounds along the Pittsburg Pike west of town. This became known as Camp Irvin and units from Fannettsburg, St. Thomas, and Captain Eyster's Company from Chambersburg were camped there. Their own Chambersburg Artillery arrived in Harrisburg and was divided into two companies and attached to the 43rd Regiment Pennsylvania Volunteers.

Several more camps were set up and in May, Governor Curtin arrived in town. He reviewed the troops with much pomp and circumstance. As one newspaper observer noted:

> with his penetrating eyes firmly fixed upon them, and his countenance unmoved and firm like the condition of the country and the object for victory, the Governor of the Commonwealth moved steadily and silently along the line to which so many sons of labor had been called.

It was a very different scene a few weeks later when the defeated troops from Fort Sumter passed through. Fiona was crossing The Diamond on an errand for Mrs. Ritner when she watched them go by. The sight of them shocked her. They were covered in dust and their uniforms were ragged. These troops were tired and bedraggled from their long march. The expressions on their exhausted faces showed the reality of war.

Constant rumors circulated through town. Visitors from Williamsport, Maryland brought news that two regiments of Rebels had come through there and that the troops planned to march to Philadelphia in order to get provisions. Many more rumors went around at that time, but no Rebel troops appeared. At lease not yet.

# Chapter Twelve

For the people of Chambersburg, life went on as usual. The sun rose and set. People did their work and tended their homes. Babies were born and folks died. But soon many newcomers would come to town and their quiet little place would never be the same. At the Ritner house, the only permanent border in residence was Mr. Adamson. The young men were off to war. However, the rooms were soon full and Fiona and Helga were constantly busy with renters coming and going. Families visiting their sons at the camps, merchants selling supplies, farmers selling provisions, and businessmen of all kinds passed through. Even Mr. Monteith returned with his medicine show.

The town was busy and thriving and as Leopold Monteith explained "War is good for business." He also explained why he no longer had the Indians with him. "They were drinking too much of my medications."

In July, excitement ran high when the news came that Federal troops, under Irvin McDowell, were advancing south toward Manassas, Virginia. First came news that the Federals had attacked the rebels at Bull Run Creek and were victorious. Later news told of the arrival of Confederate reinforcements and a Southern victory. The Federal troops retreated and ran. Some ran all the way to back to Washington entangled with the carriages of sight-seers. One result of the rout was that General McDowell was replaced by the young George B. McClellan.

At home that weekend, Fiona and her father read about the battle and their spirits were low. They were revived by a letter from Liam. His unit was camped at Tennallytown, Maryland, where the young recruits' spirits were high. Liam could not wait to get into action and get the war over with.

Liam's letter reminded Fiona of something, "Da, what was Liam talking about that day at the train. He said something about the two of you making a lot of money."

Tom just laughed. "That boy has all kinds of schemes. Saving up a little money and investing it is one of them. He wants to make enough to buy a horse farm. That's one of his schemes. I let him have his dreams. Who knows what will come of them."

Helga also had a letter from Joe. "He's just itchin' to get into action," she told Fiona. The pivotal year of 1861 was coming to an end. Christmas came and went and the war was not over. It had hardly begun.

People realized that the war would not be over soon and the country prepared for a long war. In Chambersburg, the Ladies Aid Society was formed. They had fundraisers and collected money for the troops. They also prepared lint and bandages for dressing wounds. Mrs. Ritner was very active in the society and she recruited her daughters and Helga and Fiona to help.

One of the first fundraisers was a bazaar and ball to be held at the Franklin Hall that spring. Tired of making bandages, the girls were eager to help with the bazaar. They made cakes and jellies and crocheted doilies to be sold. The day of the event, they helped to decorate the hall. Then they rushed home for the most important project of dressing for the ball.

Laura Ritner, Helga and Fiona would attend the ball. The younger Ritners, Emma Jane, and Ella, were only permitted to stay for the bazaar. They were most unhappy about this, but were swept up in the excitement of helping the older girls to dress.

First they had to do their hair. The curling iron was heated in the fire place and Mrs. Ritner helped each of the girls to curl her hair. Fiona swept her dark hair to one side with long cascading curls. She secured her locks with the silver combs Da had given her. Laura and Helga had their hair curled and they were ready to dress.

Laura had a new dress of pink silk with a very wide skirt and tight fitting bodice. She donned her petticoats and hoops. Her mother and

Fiona had to stand on chairs to put her dress on and get it over the hoops. Her mother added her best lace cuffs and diamond broach. They all stood back in admiration. Fiona donned her best blue dress and added some lace borrowed from Mrs. Ritner. They all laughed when they helped Helga into her pale green gown. They had never seen her so dressed up before and told her how beautiful she looked.

"I only wish that Joe was here to see me," she sighed wistfully.

Mr. Adamson had hired a carriage and escorted them to the ball in style. It was a memorable night for all. The old hall had become a fairy-land. Two large gas chandeliers hung from the ceiling and hundreds of candles in sconces were placed around the walls. Beautiful flowers and red, white, and blue buntings were strung around the hall. Soldiers from the camp in their dress uniforms stood around admiring all the pretty girls and asked them to dance when the band struck up. Laura, Fiona and Helga danced every dance and Mr. Adamson watched from the sidelines as a chaperone. He even asked each of the girls in turn for a waltz.

A sweet young soldier walked across the floor and asked Fiona to dance. He introduced himself as Jim Thompson and said. "You're the prettiest girl here."

Fiona just laughed. After several dances, Jim asked Fiona to sit down for a while. He told her he was from New Jersey and lived in a small fishing village on the sea. Fiona was entranced and told him she always wanted to see the ocean.

"Perhaps I'll take you there someday," he teased. He said he would be leaving for Virginia soon and asked if she would write to him. Fiona agreed and he gave her his regimental address.

Helga came over to get Fiona at intermission and asked "Was he bothering you?"

"No, he's very nice. I'm going to write to him. He lives near the sea. Did you notice his sandy hair and beard? He lives by a sandy beach." After that, Fiona would always think of him as Sandy.

They joined the other girls for refreshments. As they sipped their punch, they giggled at all their admirers.

"This is fun. We're helping the war effort," Helga whispered. "I don't think Joe would mind me dancing with those boys." She suddenly stopped and exclaimed, "Do you think Joe is dancing with a girl somewhere?"

"If he is, I'm sure it's harmless. He's probably thinking of you," Fiona explained.

Jim asked Fiona to dance again and she enjoyed his company, but to her he was just a nice boy nothing else.

The evening was a great success and they headed home with beautiful memories of their first dance. Fiona and Helga lay in bed talking about the young men they had danced with.

"None of them could hold a candle to Joe," Helga whispered before she fell asleep.

*Nor to John*, Fiona thought before she drifted off. The boys had seemed so immature to her. She felt no spark of interest in any of them, even Jim. None of them were like John. He was so wise and kind. He had spoiled her for others.

The next morning they awoke to the news that McClellan was at last moving down the Virginia peninsula. "On to Richmond" was the cry heard in the streets. Excitement mounted with the news that the 43rd Regiment Pennsylvania Volunteers had been ordered to join the Peninsula Campaign. Some wondered why McClellan was taking such a round about way to get to Richmond, but hopes were high. Hopes were soon dashed when no word of victory came. Instead McClelland settled down outside of Richmond for a siege and demanded reinforcement before he would attack. Richmond was not captured.

Liam Healy put it best in a letter to Tom and Fiona. "Old Mac is a great leader. He likes to dress up and make a great show of reviewing his troops and showin' them off.

He likes 'em spick and span. Trouble is he won't use them; afraid of gettin' them dirty. There's no disgrace in getting beaten, but there is in not fighting."

The only good news that spring was the victories of Grant in the West. After his capture of Fort Donaldson, he was known as Unconditional Surrender Grant.

During the summer, many sick and wounded soldiers began passing through town and a temporary hospital was set up in the lower floor of the Masonic Hall and in Franklin Hall. The School House Hospital was later opened on King Street. Mrs. Ritner was on the committee there and recruited Fiona and Helga to help. They were only permitted to distribute food and write letters for the soldiers in the recovery ward. Women were not permitted in the receiving and operating wards. They were not considered proper places for women. That would soon change as the war went on.

In September of 1862, General Lee invaded Maryland and the war came close to Chambersburg's border. The horrific slaughter at near by South Mountain and Antietam resulted in a Union victory at last. The little hospitals in Chambersburg received many of the wounded. Fiona took care of a Union soldier in the ward. He was a very young freckled face boy with a bad chest wound. Fiona was drawn to him and spent many hours reading to him. He was so innocent and alone.

Slowly, he started to recover and began to talk. He told her his name was David Walters and he was from Philadelphia. He talked a lot about his older brother William who was studying to be a doctor. "His name is William the third and my Dad has always called him Trip. We can't call him that in front of my mother. She doesn't like it."

As he improved, plans were made to move David out of the ward as the beds were needed. He was still too weak to travel and some of the convalescents were being housed in private homes. There were only a few boarders at the Ritner house at the time so Fiona asked Mrs. Ritner if David could stay there until he could travel home.

Mary Ritner was a compassionate woman and quickly gave her permission. Before they could put their plan into effect, David's parents arrived from Philadelphia to take him home. Fiona and Mary Ritner were at the hospital when they arrived.

The Walters were well dressed and spoke in refined accents. They were both quite tall. Mr. Walters was a pleasant looking gentleman and spoke kindly. They had just come from the train. He looked a bit rumpled and dusty, but Mrs. Walters looked absolutely perfect. She was dressed in a spotless dark blue traveling suit that looked as if it had been freshly brushed. The lace at her cuffs was spotless and not a wisp of her up-swept auburn hair escaped under her large flowered hat. Her complexion was flawless and her eyes were ice blue.

David was overjoyed to see them and introduced Fiona. "Mother and Father this is Miss McKenna my nurse. She has been so kind to me. I would not have made it without her." He smiled up at Fiona. "And this is Mrs. Ritner. She is going to let me stay in her home until I can travel."

"What?" exclaimed Mrs. Walters as she removed her spotless white gloves.

The doctors did say that David wasn't able to travel yet, dear," Mr. Walters answered. He turned and said, "Mrs. Ritner, might you be related to our former Governor Ritner?"

"Yes, he is my father-in-law," she replied

At that reply, Mrs. Walters looked at Mary differently and consented to the arrangement. *I guess she sees Mrs. Ritner as more of her class now*, thought Fiona.

The next day, the hospital transported David to the house in the back of a wagon.

They settled him in the bedroom off the kitchen so he could be near-by. The doctor told them that all he needed was rest and some good food. Fiona liked having him in John's old room. She was sure they would help him get well.

Mr. and Mrs. Walters arrived soon after they had David settled. Mrs. Walters looked around with her perfect nose in the air. "I didn't know you ran a boarding house," she said with an edge in her voice.

"Yes," Mrs. Ritner replied. "It's lucky we have few boarders here right now so we can give your son our full attention."

"Indeed," she replied. She started to say something else when Mr. Walters interrupted.

"I'm sure he will be well cared for here. Thank you so much for your kindness. We have to catch the train soon." He turned to his wife. "Remember, dear, we have the party at the Ingersoll's tomorrow night. You don't want to miss that. All of Philadelphia society will be there."

"Please have some tea before you go," Mrs. Ritner invited.

They sat in the parlor and Fiona and Helga served them. Helga observed, "That Mrs. Walters is the most perfect looking woman I've ever seen, but I don't like her. Laura told me that so called lady was appalled when she heard you and I were servants. She couldn't believe we were treated like family."

After tea, Mrs. Walters kissed her son and reluctantly took her leave with a last disdainful look around the house. Mr. Walters hugged his son and shook everyone's hand thanking them profusely, as if to say pardon my wife.

David stayed with them for two weeks improving each day. Mrs. Ritner nourished him with chicken broth and beef tea. Fiona, Helga, and Laura read to him. Rufus, the eldest Birdwell son from next store, spent a lot of time with David. They were about the same age and he wanted to hear all about the war. When he was stronger they took turns taking him for walks. Fiona's father stopped in one day and took him for a ride in the country. When David was well enough to travel, Mr. Walters came back to take him home. He was a more relaxed man without his wife around. They all sat around the kitchen table eating the peach pie that Mrs. Ritner had made.

"David, I made an extra pie for you to take home."

He smiled and said, "Thank you, Mrs. Ritner, I'll enjoy that."

Before they left, Mr. Walters explained that David was only sixteen and had enlisted without their consent. "But I'm very proud of him and thankful to all of you for helping him to get well."

Mr. Adamson arrived with a carriage to take them to the depot. They said their goodbyes and hugged David and wished him well. His youthful spirit had filled the old house and they would miss him.

Later Helga told Fiona that she had overheard Mr. Walters whispering to David.

"Make sure you bring that pie in the back door and give it to the cook. You know how your mother is. Accepting home made pies is something common people do."

"Oh poor David with such a mother," Fiona shook her head.

Soon the rooms were again full with boarders. Between the housework and their work at the hospital the women were very busy. Life went on as usual until September when there was a threat of invasion. Pennsylvania Militia units took over Chambersburg and martial law was declared. Many citizens hid their valuable possessions or sent them away for safe keeping. However, no invasion happened. The military units pulled out and martial law was suspended. Chambersburg relaxed with the knowledge that the Army of the Potomac stood between them and Lee's Army. Little did they know that Jeb Stuart's army was heading their way.

On October tenth the war did come to Chambersburg. The farmers had been facing a drought and it looked like rain that day. For many years, the story was told of the first incident. A soldier rode up to Mr. Denig's Dry Goods Store. He hitched his horse and came in. He was wearing a blue overcoat, but the rest of his clothing was butternut. He walked up to the counter and asked for a pair of socks. He seemed in no hurry and looked all around the store.

Mr. Denig asked, "Are you from the Army of the Potomac?"

"No sir, "said he, "I'm from Virginia."

He paid for the socks in silver and left. The men in the store stared in amazement. Mr. Denig frowned, "I think he was an advance scout. The rebels must be nearby and none of our troops are anywhere close. We're in for it."

Later word came that the rebels were in Mercersburg and on the way to Chambersburg from St. Thomas.

Fiona was home with her Father that day. Mr. O'Brien came to the door and told them that thousands of rebel Cavalry were in St. Thomas and headed their way. "They're taking horses, Tom. You better hide your horse. I already warned them at the Judge's farm."

Fiona said, "I'll take her, Da." She took Rosin to the woods far behind the house and tied her to a tree. She fed her and put a pan of water near by. As she patted the dear old horse's nose, she whispered, "Stay here and be quiet. We're not gonna let any rebels get you. I'll be back for you soon."

By the time Fiona returned to the house, the neighbors were all lined up along the road. They could see a cloud of dust in the distance. Soldiers on horseback with flags flying soon came into view. They were led by a young man with a full black beard. He wore a grey cape with red lining flapping in the breeze. A yellow sash adorned his waist and an ostrich plume was stuck in his hat. He stared straight ahead and paid no attention to the taunts from the crowd. "Dirty rebels go home."

Tom looked at Fiona and said, "I think that's Jeb Stuart."

"He is magnificent isn't he?" she replied.

Other officers rode by and arrogantly tipped their hats to the ladies. Annie Kelly shook her fist and called after them, "I take no tip from you rebels!"

Fiona laughed. Annie had hard feelings for rebels since her husband Mike had enlisted.

"I'm enlisting before the draft gets me," he had explained to Tom. "I can get a three hundred dollar bonus."

It took a long time for the cavalry to pass. Tom estimated it to be 1,500 or more. Next came the artillery, followed by troops leading hundreds of captured horses.

"Some of those horses belong to the Judge," Tom observed. "He has so many they could never hide them all."

One soldier stopped and looked in their barn. He walked over and asked, "Where's your horse?"

Fiona looked up at him pleadingly, "Oh kind sir, we are so poor. We had only one horse. She was very old and she died yesterday. We buried her at the farm down the road. You can dig her up if you don't believe me. Now we have none. Could you give us one of yours?"

The soldier just looked at her, shook his head and walked on. Annie walked over and slapped her on the back. "Good one, Fiona."

As they watched the last of the horsemen disappear down the road, the country people feared for Chambersburg. They wondered what would happen when that great cavalry arrived in the defenseless town.

The next day Fiona was due back in Chambersburg. She desperately wanted to go and make sure her friends were all right, but her father hesitated. "Perhaps you should wait a few days darlin'. Wait and see what happens."

Fiona stationed herself out on the road to wait for any travelers with news. Soon a farmer came along and she hailed him. "Have you been in Chambersburg? How goes it there."

He stopped and got down from the wagon. "The town was warned they were coming. Just in time, George Snyder lowered the flag in The Diamond and cut the ropes so the rebels couldn't raise their flag. Soon after, a rebel cavalry came into town with cavalry with hundreds of stolen horses. They took over the bank and telegraph office. They commenced to strip the stores of clothes and shoes. I saw several rebels riding around wearing two hats and one had a ladies hat tied to his saddle."

Tom came out of the house and asked what happened. "Did the town surrender?"

The farmer went on, "They rode into The Diamond sounding their bugles and stopped in front of Judge Kimmell's office and went in. I was told that they informed the judge that General Wade Hampton with a force of 2,800 men and four pieces of artillery were on the hill west of town. They demanded the town's surrender."

Other neighbors were gathered around now and shouted, "Did they surrender?"

"Well, they did eventually," the farmer answered. "Not right away. Judge Kimmell and Col. McClure demanded to be shown this force. The officer in command complied and they all rode out West Market Street to the brow of the hill. Here they were introduced to General Wade Hampton and J.E.B. Stuart."

"I thought that was Stuart," Tom exclaimed. "Then what happened."

The farmer went on, "Well, the judge, being the only town official present, knew that none of our forces were near by and we didn't have a chance. He said he would agree to surrender if the rebels would assure him that unarmed citizens, women and children would not be harmed and that private property would be respected. "

They thanked the farmer and he went on. Folks stood around and wondered what would happen next.

Fiona didn't wonder. She turned to her father, "It sounds like it wound be safe to return. Please, Da, I want to make sure they're all right."

Tom understood that there was no stopping his daughter. Her sense of adventure compelled her to see what was happening in Chambersburg.

# Chapter Thirteen

Tom hitched up Rosin saying, "I hope they have enough horses by now and don't want an old one like her."

They started out and stopped each person they passed on the road for news. They first saw Jack Perkins from St. Thomas. He stopped and told them his tale.

He had been in town on business and was in the bank when some rebel soldiers entered and demanded all the money. "The cashier just walked over and opened the vault," Jack said, "It was empty except for a few coins. That bank president, Mr. Messersmith, had sent most of the money to Philadelphia when he was warned of the September raid. Them rebels sure were mad at not getting any money." Jack said. He started to drive away and called back, "Oh, and they also cut the telegraph wires."

Later down the road they heard tales that the rebels had cleaned out the bakeries of bread and the warehouses of supplies

"So much for respecting private property," Tom remarked as they entered town.

The Diamond was crowded with Confederate soldiers milling around. Fiona noticed that they looked rather content. Some even tipped their hats to her as she and Tom drove through town. They left the horse and wagon at the stable and Mr. Reisher assured them that the horse would be safe.

"I think them rebs have more horses then they need. I seen a whole bunch that I recognized as belong to Judge Flood," he remarked with a smile.

They started to walk to Kate Gormley's house across the square when they saw Judge Flood standing in front of the Franklin Hotel.

Seeing Tom and Fiona he called them over. "Generals Stuart and Hampton stayed here last night. I'm waiting to see them," he said with a growl. "I'm going to ask them to return one of my horses. You know, Tom, that valuable stallion I just purchased."

Just then, the two generals emerged from the hotel. They both looked well rested and were dressed in splendid uniforms. Fiona recognized General Stuart. He even looked more magnificent close up. General Hampton was older with a full beard and prominent nose. They both gave Fiona an eerie feeling. These men are our enemy yet they do not look threatening. They look like normal reasonable people.

The Judge went up to them and made his request in his demanding way.

They stopped and General Hampton said, "We're not horse thieves, nevertheless we do need horses and will retain yours."

They bowed and walked away. The judge muttered, "They are damnable thieves!"

Tom wanted to stop by the church and check on Father Mahoney. They found him standing in front of his house looking somewhat bewildered.

He looked up and said, "Oh Tom, the most extraordinary thing just happened. I was sitting on the porch watching the troops go by when a rebel soldier stopped and came up to me. 'Let's have it padre,' he demanded. "Have what?" I answered. 'Your watch,' he replied.' " I looked down and I saw that it was hanging out of my pocket. I hesitated, you see it was my father's gold watch, but he had a gun and I gave it to him."

"Thank God you weren't hurt," they both replied in unison.

"Well, I'm kinda sorry I didn't put up a fight," he said and laughed. "I guess I can count that as my sacrifice for the union."

After Tom and Fiona assured themselves that the priest was all right, they headed for Mrs. Gormley's. They found her in hysterics. "Oh Tom, I'm so frightened. What's going to happen?"

He put his arms around her and reassured her, "They won't be here long. I'm sure our troops are on the way. They just want supplies. They won't harm civilians." He turned to Fiona, "You go and check on the Ritners, I'll stay with Kate awhile."

All was calm when Fiona entered the house. Helga was washing dishes and Mr. Adamson sat at the table drinking coffee. They both greeted Fiona and assured her that all was well with them.

Helga sat down and said, "We did have a scare with the little girls. My sister Gertie was staying with me for the day. You know what a scamp she is. She was playing with Ella."

Mr. Adamson interrupted. "I came home with the news that the rebels were headed for town and advised everyone to stay inside."

"We thought the girls were upstairs," Helga went on. "We all sat here and waited for news. Later, Mrs. Ritner went up to check on the girls and found them gone." She stood up and began pacing. "You can imagine how scared we were. Mr. Adamson was ready to go and look for them when they came in the back door giggling."

Mr. Adamson laughed and said, "What a tale they told. "They heard us talking about the rebels coming and snuck out the front door to go and see them."

Fiona listened intently to the rest of the tale of how Gertie and Emma walked into town and sat on a bench in The Diamond to watch the rebels. No one was around. Soon one lone soldier rode into the square and stopped in front of them.

According to Gertie he said, "Where's the mayau of this town?"

"The what?" she replied.

He repeated, "The mayau, the mayau," he repeated.

They just shook their heads and the exasperated rebel rode on.

Fiona collapsed in laughter. "Well we don't have a mayor. We have a town council. I wonder how he would have pronounced that."

By nightfall all was quiet. Pa had calmed Kate Gormley and returned home. The Ritner household had gathered in for the night. Gertie and Ella were sent to bed and soon the rest of the household joined them.

The next morning, they woke to great noise and shouting in the streets. They all rushed to the front door in their nightclothes. People in the street told them that the rebels were pulling out. They were heading east across South Mountain. As a parting shot they had set fire to the depot house, the machine shops, and Wunderlich and Nead's warehouse. They first cleared the warehouse of all they could carry of government clothing, hats, boots and pistols. Mrs. Ritner was concerned about the wounded in the hospitals. Some were near the fires and there was fear the remaining ammunition would explode. They all quickly dressed and headed to the fire.

Fiona saw the last of the rebels riding out of town. Some were a comical sight; wearing three hats and carrying everything from live chickens to ladies dresses. People were trying to put out the fires, but were driven back by exploding shells. Mr. Adamson helped to move some of the wounded from the hospital near the fire. They were brought to the King Street hospital. Fiona, Mrs. Ritner, and Laura stayed and tended to them. Helga was dispatched to keep an eye on the little girls.

They heard that a cavalry force from the Army of the Potomac near Sharpsburg was sent to capture Stuart's army at Williamsport. However, when they learned that Stuart had not gone that way, another force was sent east, but too late. Stuart's army had already crossed the Potomac below Frederick, Maryland. Again McClellan's army did not pursue them. This brought no contentment to the people of Chambersburg.

Life returned to normal. They were thankful that Stuart's men had not been able to blow up the Cumberland Valley Railroad Bridge. It was constructed of iron and they did not have the explosives to destroy it. All the stores were empty and many people had lost horses, but no one was hurt. They were grateful for that.

Mail delivery resumed and Fiona received a letter from her friend Jim Thompson. They had been corresponding since they met at the ball. Fiona had started writing to him as Sandy because he had sandy colored hair and lived at the seashore. He liked the idea and signed his letters that way. They became pen pals. He knew that was all they were and he was all right with that. He enjoyed corresponding with his friend Fiona. He didn't write much about the war. He wrote about his family and life in the little fishing village where he grew up. She told him about the happenings in Chambersburg and the books she was reading.

Troops were constantly moving through town and singing their marching songs. One day Fiona was trying to cross the Diamond on her way to the grocery store. She was stopped by a battalion of troops carrying a flag of a Massachusetts unit. She began to cry when she heard what they were singing.

> *John Brown's body lies a moldering in the grave*
> *John Brown's body lies a moldering in the grave*
> *His soul is marching on.*
> *Glory, glory hallelujah*
> *Glory glory hallelujah*
> *His soul is marching on.*

Fiona didn't hear the rest of the song. She had to sit down on a bench. Her heart was full of sorrow at this reminder that her John was also in his grave and she didn't know where it was. She also felt a sense of pride that something that he had participated in was recognized as worth fighting for. She finished her purchases and went home with those stirring words ringing in her ears. "His soul is marching on."

Several days later, Fiona was reading in the kitchen when she heard someone sobbing and knocking at the door. She opened the door to their neighbor Mrs. Birdwell. She had tears running down her face and looked in great distress. Fiona pulled her inside and asked her what was wrong.

She tried to control her sobs and whispered, "It's my son Rufus, he's gone."

"Where, what happened?" Fiona said as she guided her to a seat.

Mrs. Ritner entered the kitchen looking concerned and put her arm on the other woman's shoulder. "What happened?'

"Rufus has gone to join the army. He must have left late last night. We found a note from him this morning saying he was going to Harrisburg to join up. His father has gone looking for him." She gulped and wiped her eyes. "He knows we don't believe in fighting. It is against our religion. How could he do this to us?"

Mrs. Ritner sat her down at the table and gave her a drink of water. Fiona remembered Rufus coming over a great deal when David Waters was staying with them.

He was very interested in David's experiences in the war and seemed excited about the army. He would soon be eighteen and ready for the draft. She heard him complaining to David about not being able to participate in the fighting. She remembered him saying he was afraid people would think he was a coward.

Mrs. Birdwell was speaking calmly now. She turned to Mrs. Ritner, "You know we Mennonites oppose slavery, but we are against war. Some of the men of our congregation have entered the war believing that the Union must be preserved, but most have resisted."

"I know," Mrs. Ritner replied. "Governor Curtin granted them exemptions. Many have chosen to work in hospitals or pay a fine. Did Rufus ever think about that?"

"We talked about it, but he refused. Said that was for cowards. But I never thought he would defy us and all that we believe in," she started weeping again.

"He is a young man," Fiona said. "They all think they need to prove themselves. Perhaps he'll change his mind. The governor has issued exemptions for those who don't believe in fighting. He could find something else to do."

Mrs. Birdwell just smiled and shook her head. "I must go home and wait for word from my husband. Thank you for your kindness."

The next day Mr. Birdwell stopped over and told them that he had arrived in Harrisburg too late. Rufus had already enlisted. He looked as devastated as his wife.

"We will keep him in our prayers," Mrs. Ritner assured him as the poor man left looking defeated,

Next came news that President Lincoln had replace McClellan with General Ambrose Burnside. He had grown inpatient with McClellan's slowness in following Lee's army after Antietam. The papers quoted Lincoln's order to McClellan, "If you don't want to use the army, I would like to borrow it for a while."

The people of Chambersburg agreed with Lincoln. McClellan's army had been no help to them. Fiona saw a sketch of Burnside in the Philadelphia newspaper, she had to laugh. He had a large bald head, a drooping mustache and great side whiskers that ran all the way down the side his face. He did not look like a hero to her.

December came and cold winds blew down the mountain passes. The cold winds of war continued. On December 13, the telegraph clicked out the news of a great battle at Fredericksburg, Virginia. Chambersburg waited for news. Their own 43rd Regiment was there. When the news came it was devastating. It was a defeat and again the losses were horrific. The 43rd had been the only division to penetrate the Confederate line. Chambersburg waited with dread for the list of casualties. When it came many local boys were on it as killed or wounded. Mr. Adamson brought a copy of the list home and they scanned it anxiously. There was great relief when the names of Liam Healy, Joe Leiss and Hans Myers did not appear, but many other friends and neighbors did.

John Oaks, the son of David Oaks who ran the warehouse, where John Brown had stored his weapons, was one of them. He was wounded and taken to a hospital in Washington where he died on Christmas day. His parents had rushed to his bedside when they received the news, but arrived too late. They escorted his body back to Chambersburg. The town gathered at Cedar Grove Cemetery for his burial. There would be many more.

Tom McKenna paid his respects at the funeral and, back at the Ritner house, he handed Fiona the latest letter from Liam.

He described the Union attempt to take Mayre's Heights at Fredericksburg." We might as well have tried to take Hell."

January of 1863 brought the good news of the Emancipation Proclamation. The document freed all slaves in the territories held by the Confederates and called for the enlistment of black soldiers in the Union Army. The war to protect the Union now became a war for the abolition of slavery.

Her Da was in town that night and he took Fiona to Wolftown where most of the colored people lived. They wanted to witness the celebration. They met Hattie, Enoch and Molly and shared in their joy. They stayed only a short time. These people were their friends, but Tom and Fiona realized that they could never fully understand their feelings at this time. They didn't want to intrude.

After the debacle at Fredericksburg, General Burnside was replaced by Joseph Hooker. He was known as Fighting Joe and everyone hoped that he would live up to his name. General Grant was placed in command of the Army of the West. He had proven himself to be a fighter.

The Chambersburg Regiment went into winter quarters and their loved ones breathed a little easier. However there was an unseen enemy killing solders on both sides that winter.

One snowy morning Fiona answered the back door and found Helga's father standing there. She gasped at the sight of him and knew something was terribly wrong.

She has always thought of him as a giant of a man who could weather any crisis, but today his strong face was grey and haggard. He tried to speak, but no words came out. Fiona took his hand and pulled him in to the kitchen while she shouted for Helga.

Helga came into the room and asked anxiously. "Papa, Papa what is wrong?"

He pulled a letter from his pocket and handed it to her. She read the letter and burst into tears.

"My brother Hans is dead," she screamed.

Mrs. Ritner came in just then and folded the girl in her arms. She asked them all to sit down and told Fiona to bring coffee.

"What happened, Mr. Myers?" she asked.

"He died from Camp Fever," he replied. "We haven't heard from him for several weeks and were starting to worry. I knew something was wrong. Helga, will you read the letter to us?"

Helga sat up straight, took a few gulps of air and started to read.

> *January 30, 1863*
> *Falmount, Virginia*
>
> *Dear Sir and Madam,*
>
> *It is my painful duty to inform you of the death of your son, Pvt. Hans Myers. He became ill a few weeks ago. He developed Camp Fever and was placed in the hospital tent. Please know that he was well cared for and every-thing was done to save him. Unfortunately, he could not be saved and he died yesterday January 29.*
>
> *Hans was one of the company's most faithful mem-bers and a young man of pure and innocent character. We buried him here in good rough board coffin in his uni-form. The headboard clearly states his name, company and regiment.*
>
> *My deepest sympathy to you and your family,*
>
> *Captain Hezekial Easton*

They sat around the table and spoke of Hans and his gentle ways. Mr. Myers said, "His mother regrets that he is buried in such a far off place. We cannot visit his grave."

Helga wiped her eyes and spoke, "We will go after the war Papa. We'll find his grave. We will always remember him. He will always be with us."

Mrs. Ritner put her arm around Helga, "Get your things together dear. You go home and stay as long as you want."

They saw the Meyers off with many tears and promises of prayers. Fiona went up to her room and had her own good cry. She remembered Hans as a sweet boy. She knew how much he had admired her. She had written to him often and would treasure the letters she received from him.

The next day Fiona received a letter from Liam. He said that he and Joe had been with Hans when he died and that they were at his burial. He stated that he also wrote to the Myers family and hoped that it would give them some comfort knowing that someone from home was with him.

A few days later, Mrs. Ritner, Mr. Adamson, Fiona, Tom, and Mrs. Gormley went out to the Meyers farm for a prayer service for Hans. The table was pushed back and chairs were placed around the large kitchen where many friends and neighbors were gathered. The Meyers family sat together their faces edged in grief. Fiona remembered the many happy times that she had spent with them and knew it would never be the same without dear Hans.

Their Lutheran minister the Reverend Klegg led the brief service in German. As the strange words washed over her, Fiona looked at Mrs. Meyers and saw that those words brought her some comfort. After the service, Mrs. Meyers got up and moved around in her brisk way serving streusel and coffee. They said their goodbyes and Mrs. Ritner told Helga to stay at home as long as she was needed.

Fiona kissed her dear friend good-by and said, "I will always be here for you."

Helga nodded and said, "I will need you."

Helga came back a week later, bur she was a different girl. The rosy cheeks and smile were still there, but there was a new maturity in her eyes. She went about her work with the same energy, but in her leisure time she was quiet. Fiona sat with her in those times and just held her hand. Helga drew comfort from her friend.

The war went on and had an affect on everyone. Mary Ritner called Fiona and Helga into the parlor one day to tell them of a decision she had made.

She asked them to sit down and began. "My two step-sons John and James are in the army and that is a constant worry. I also worry about my girls here. Ever since the raid and that terrible time little Ella was missing, I've been anxious about them. We are so close to the fighting here. I'm afraid of what might happen." She stood up and walked to the window. "My step-daughter Mary up in Connecticut has been urging me to send them to her. I have decided that this would be a good time before the school term starts." She turned and said with a catch in her voice. "They will be leaving next week."

Both girls went over and put their arms around her. Fiona sighed, "Oh I'm so sorry. I know you will miss them terribly and so will we, but it's for the best"

Helga in her practical way said, "Well, I guess we better start getting them packed. Don't you worry, Mrs. Ritner, we'll take care of everything."

Mr. Adamson came in and saw that she had told them. He went over and put his arm around Mary as the girls left the room.

In the kitchen Helga said, "Oh why doesn't he tell her how she feels and ask her to marry him."

Fiona smiled sadly and said, "Because he knows she wont. She's the kind of woman who marries only once." As she spoke those words, Fiona thought of her father, *I used to think that way about him, but lately I'm not so sure. She remembered the day of the raid and his tenderness toward Kate Gormley.* She smiled to her self, *If they would get together. It would make me happy.*

The house was bustling with activity for the next few days. Trunks were packed and tears were shed and the girls were put on the train to Connecticut. All three were sad at leaving their mother, but also filled with youthful excitement.

As Ella put it, "Oh Mamma, I'll miss you so much, but I'm happy to go on a train ride and see sister Mary.

Mary Ritner looked very downcast for the next few days, but one day she seemed to brighten when she came into the kitchen with a letter in her hand. "Fiona, you remember Mrs. Walters, the mother of the young soldier who stayed with us?"

Fiona smiled and said, "Oh yes, I've gotten a few letters from David."

"Well, she has written to me and invited us to come and stay with them in Philadelphia for two weeks. It seems David has been insisting. He wants to thank us for the care we gave him"

"I'm sure *she* didn't insist," Helga said with a laugh. "She didn't think much of us."

Fiona was happy that Helga was almost back to her old self. She knew that the sorrow of Hans's loss would always be there, but she and her family were dealing with it. They were strong people.

Mrs. Ritner looked down at the letter, "Well, it seems they are having a large party as a fund raiser for the troops and they want us to come for that. What do you think, Fiona?"

"Well, I would love to see David again, but how can we leave the house for two weeks?"

Helga chimed in. "Things are slow in February. I'll be glad to keep busy. I can take care of things here. We don't have too many guests right now. If I need help, I'll have my sister Maria come in. It will be a good change for her and Mr. Adamson will be here. You should go."

The decision was made and a letter of acceptance went off. Fiona conferred with her father and he gave his blessing.

"It will be a wonderful opportunity for you to see the city where you were born. You know it's funny, Judge Flood said something about his wife going to stay with a family in Philadelphia to attend a fund raiser. Could it be the same family?"

It turned out it was the same. Mr. Walters had business dealings with the Judge and Mrs. Flood was invited to the party.

A few days later, Mrs. Ritner called Fiona into the parlor to show her another letter from Mrs. Walters. "Fiona dear," she said, "the house in Philadelphia is quite a large one and the Walters are very high in society there. They live by certain standards." She looked at Fiona closely, "Mrs. Walters writes that you would have to stay in the servant's quarters."

Fiona just looked at her, "Well, I am a servant. I wouldn't expect to stay in the best bedroom. It should be interesting staying in a big house like that."

Mrs. Ritner smiled, "I do hope you will enjoy your stay dear. Mrs. Flood and her personal maid Barbara will be traveling with us. I will tell them you are also a lady's maid. You will get much better treatment that way. I hope Barbara will be company for you. Have you met her?"

"No, I heard she was English and that Mrs. Flood is very pleased with her."

Fiona was filled with excited anticipation for the next few days. She remembered little Ella's excitement about her trip and felt the same. She was going to have a long train ride and see Philadelphia. She had a feeling that something wonderful would happen there.

# Chapter Fourteen

On the train, Fiona found herself sitting at the back of the car next to Miss Barbara Clark, personal maid to Mrs. Agnes Flood. Mrs. Ritner and Mrs. Flood sat at the front. Mrs. Flood had insisted on this arrangement. Barbara Clark was young and attractive. Her bright red hair was swept up under a fashionable hat. He green eyes were large and bright and she had an eager look about her. She leaned back in her seat and put up her feet on the rail of the seat in front. She spoke very carefully in a chipped English accent that did not quite go with her demeanor.

"Well, Fiona, have you ever been to Philadelphia?" Fiona answered that she hadn't and Barbara went on. "I arrived here from England and stayed there until I was hired by Mrs. Flood." She smiled wistfully. "I enjoyed it then and look forward to seeing some old friends."

"That would be nice," Fiona replied, as she stared out the window taking in the passing scenery. "Actually, I was born in Philadelphia, but my Da took me to Chambersburg when I was just a baby. I'm looking forward to seeing the city of my birth."

"I hear your father is from Ireland and Judge also hired his nephew to tend the horses. I didn't get to meet him. He was off to the war soon after I started. What part of Ireland are they from?

"They're from a small place in County Kilkenny."

Barbara just nodded and looked down at her fine boots resting on the rail. The two girls chatted amicably and several hours later they heard the conductor announcing their arrival at Broad Street Station. When they stepped down from the train, they saw Mr. Walters and David waiting for them.

David ran up to Fiona and threw his arms around her. She held him out and looked at him closely. His face was beaming with joy, but he was pale and thin. Fiona looked over at Mr. Walters and he lowered his eyes.

They walked through the station and out the great doors to the noise and confusion of Broad Street. Fiona looked around in amazement. She had never seen so much traffic in her life. The street was full of elegant carriages, wagons, omnibuses, and men on horses, all traveling at great speeds. She covered her ears at the din of noise and laughed with delight at it all. Mr. Walters was leading the ladies to his carriage parked near by and David took Fiona's hand and escorted her and Barbara.

The carriage was plush with red leather seats and big enough for six. The driver sat high up in the front and they were pulled by two magnificent white horses. Fiona found the carriage ride invigorating. She looked about eagerly at the passing scenes as they trotted along the busy streets.

Mr. Walters told the driver to take them past Independence Hall and Fiona saw the Liberty Bell high up in the tower. They traveled up Market Street and she looked in wonder at all the many shops and tall buildings. The streets were filled with people walking in every direction and Fiona wondered where they could all be going. All too soon they arrived at Spruce Street and stopped in front of the Walters's home. Fiona looked up in awe. It was four stories tall and the facade was of fine brownstone. The many windows had lace curtains and broad marble steps led up to the front door.

A servant ran out and helped the ladies down from the carriage. Mr. Walters led them up the front steps and Fiona and Barbara were directed to the side steps leading down to the servant's quarters.

David called to them, "I'll see you later Fiona. My brother Trip will be home soon and you must meet him."

Fiona waved good-by and they went down and knocked at the door. It was opened by a little maid. Fiona had never seen such a wan little thing in her life. Her big eyes stared at them from a thin little face. She was dressed in a mop cap and apron and spoke in a thick Irish brogue.

"Hallo, I'm Lizzie the kitchen maid. Ye must be the ladees maids. Please come in. I'll call the housekeeper Mrs. Travers and tell her." She curtsied and walked away.

"What a creature," Barbara said with a laugh.

Lizzie soon returned with Mrs. Travers. She was a dignified looking woman with beautiful grey hair pulled back in a net. She wore a black gown with a starched white collar.

"Welcome girls. I'll show you to your sleeping quarters. You'll be sharing a room back here," she explained as she led them down a long hall way. She opened a door to a small room with two beds and a small chest. "This is the room we keep for our visitors' maids. Make yourselves comfortable. Charlie the footman will bring your bags in soon. When you're ready come back to the kitchen and I'll show you around."

Barbara replied that the first thing they needed was the privy and Mrs. Travers pointed them to the back door. The girls returned and washed at the wash bowl on the chest and saw that their bags had arrived.

"Great service," Barbara noted.

They returned to the kitchen where some of the other servants were seated at a large table. Mrs. Travers introduced them to Charlie, the footman, Livey, an upstairs maid, and seated at the head of the table, like a queen surveying her court the cook, Mrs. Brighton.

Mrs. Travers pointed out the bells on the wall. Each one had the name of a room printed under it. "Barbara, your lady, Mrs. Flood is in the Red Room. She will ring this bell if she needs you. Fiona, your lady, Mrs. Ritner is in the Yellow Room and there is her bell. You will go up the back stairs when they call and then up another flight to the bedrooms. The rooms have signs as to their names on the doors. Your only duties will be taking care of your ladies. Do you have any questions?"

"No questions," Barbara replied, "I'm sure my bell will be ringing soon." With that the bell did ring and Barbara was off with a sneer on her face.

"Doesn't she like her lady?" Livey asked.

"I guess not," Fiona replied with a smile.

They asked Fiona to sit down and Mrs. Brighton poured her a cup of tea. They all asked her questions about her lady and where they were from. Fiona found them a convivial group, but was careful in her answers. She was ever mindful that she was supposed to be a ladies maid not a boarding house servant. They told her about the household and the other servants. Billings was the butler and he was in charge.

They all looked up when Billings himself entered followed by David and a tall young man. "Mr. David and Mr. William would like to see Miss Fiona McKenna," Billings said with a look of disapproval.

Fiona stood up and Billings said, "You may use the servant's parlor" and led them to a room off the kitchen. He left with great dignity and closed the door.

David grabbed Fiona's hand and beamed, "This is my brother Trip"

Trip took her hand and looked into her eyes, "Davey has been talking about you for some time. He said that when he first woke up after he was wounded and saw you sitting next to him, he thought you were an angel. I can see why"

Fiona looked up at him and laughed. He was tall with dark hair and a neatly trimmed beard. He had a nice face, but it was his eyes that caught her. All she could think was that they were kind eyes. They were hazel and when he smiled they lit up and crinkled at the corners.

"I also heard a lot about you, Mr. Walters. David always spoke of you with such pride. Are you still in medical school?"

"First of all, please call me Trip, Fiona. I received my degree from Penn in January and now I'm a real doctor. I enlisted and will be called up soon."

"Oh, your Mother must be upset about that," Fiona replied.

"I can deal with Mother. She'll come around. I'm her favorite," he winked at David.

They sat down and talked for a while. Trip was very interested in the hospital work that Fiona was doing in Chambersburg. She found him very comfortable to talk to. She was disappointed when Mrs. Travers opened the door and announced that Mrs. Ritner was ringing for her. She got up to leave.

David called after her, "Fiona, we'll see you tomorrow. Trip asked Mrs. Ritner if you could have a day off. We're going to take you out."

Fiona hurried up the back stairs stopping on the first floor landing for a look. She looked down the long entrance hall to the large dark wood door. It was lined on either side with stained glass windows. Fiona had never seen stained glass out side of a church before. A red carpet ran down the hallway and she could see the carved curve of the banister of the staircase. She quickly ran up the stairs to the second floor. She was looking at the names on the doors, when she saw Mrs. Flood walking toward her. Fiona recalled the first time she had seen her in the hallway at the Ritner house. This time she acknowledged her with a nod.

"Well, Fiona, you certainly have come up in the world. Ladies maid indeed," she said with as she swept past her.

*Not very long ago you asked me to be your maid*, thought Fiona as she found Mrs. Ritner's room and knocked.

"Come in, Fiona I thought I should call you to unpack for me. That's what ladies maids do," she said and motioned her to sit down. "Are they treating you well downstairs?"

"Oh, yes, very well. This is quite a house. I've never seen anything so big. David and his brother came down to welcome me."

"Yes, William spoke to me about giving you the day off tomorrow. Of course I said yes. I want you to see as much of the city as you can"

Mrs. Ritner had already completed most of her unpacking. She was used to doing things for herself. Fiona helped her hang her gowns in the large chifforobe and looked around at the room. The walls were covered with flowered yellow wallpaper. The carpet was a pale green and the large four poster bed was covered with a yellow satin spread.

"I can see why they call it the yellow room," Fiona said and laughed.

They sat down on a yellow settee by a large window and talked of the trip to the city and the sites they had seen. Fiona mentioned her encounter with Mrs. Flood in the hall and how it reminded her of their first meeting.

"Pay no attention to her. She won't give you any trouble," Mrs. Ritner said. "She is so thrilled to be here and mingle in high society, she thinks of nothing else." She pulled back the lace curtain and looked down at the street below. "On the train here, she wanted to know all about the Walters family and where they fit in society."

"They seem to be very wealthy and quite high up in society," Fiona replied.

"Oh, yes, Mr. Walters's family is very old Philadelphia. Augusta Lawrence is from a newly wealthy family with not such a high position."

As she left the room, Fiona thought of Mrs. Walters and began to understand her. *She must feel very unsure of herself and always trying to live up to upper class standards. She may be afraid that people will think she's not good enough. In that way she is very like Mrs. Flood.*

William and David came down to the kitchen to call for Fiona the next morning. Downstairs they were all abuzz with the Master's sons calling for a maid. As soon as Fiona saw Trip, she immediately felt warm and comfortable. When he took her hand, she smiled and greeted him warmly.

"Is there anything in particular in the city that you would like to see?" he asked.

"I really don't know much about the city," she answered, "I'll leave it up to you"

Just as they were leaving, Barbara came running down the back stairs. "Well what do you know?" she grinned and said, "Mrs. Flood gave me the day off too. I guess she was afraid Mrs. Ritner would show her up." She headed for their room. "I'm going to get dressed up and meet some of my old mates."

Fiona waved as they headed out the door. Trip had a small carriage waiting and he took her hand and helped her in.

David climbed in and motioned toward the driver, "Fiona, this is Tim," Tim tipped his hat and smiled. David continued, "I've been trying to figure what you would like to see, Miss Fiona. There's a lot about the war. I thought you might like to see the Union Volunteer Refreshment Saloon down on Washington Avenue."

"Oh, yes, I read about that. They take care of the soldiers that are passing through the city." The horse took off quickly and Fiona was thrown against Trip. "Oh, sorry," she said.

"Not at all," he replied with a grin.

He took her hand and held it. Fiona didn't mind. She felt very comfortable with him. It was a warm day for February and she enjoyed the ride down Broad Street. Fiona marveled at the sights along the way. Trip pointed out the Academy of Music at Locus Street. Fiona gazed in awe at the magnificent building and imagined what it would be like to see an opera. David mentioned that the family had a box there. They turned on to Market Street and Fiona could soon see the Delaware River ahead. A ferry was crossing from the Jersey side.

"Here we are," David cried with excitement. "All of these buildings are part of the Refreshment Saloon. Over there is the dining hall where they are fed and behind that is the hospital for those who need treatment. The recruits come by train to Camden and cross the river by the ferry."

Fiona gazed about her. There were many building surrounding the pier. The one in front of them was a two story house with a porch on the second floor. The word UNION was painted on the roof beam above it. The house was connected to a larger building with a sign in front that read Volunteer Refreshment Saloon. High up on the peak of the roof stood a large wooden eagle. Fiona found all of the activity exciting. . Ferries were dislodging passengers. Wagons came and went and people were hurrying everywhere.

The carriage stopped and Trip helped her down. "We'll go into the dining hall and you can see where the men come when they first arrive. Some of them have traveled great distances from their homes and need food and rest."

They entered the hall that was filled with long tables and chairs. Garlands and flags hung from the ceiling and women with long white aprons and caps hurried about serving the young recruits.

An elegant older women in a starched apron stopped and greeted David and Trip, "Well, if it isn't the Messrs Walters" she explained. "What brings you here?"

"Hello Mrs. Morris," David replied. "This is our friend Miss McKenna. We're showing her around."

Mrs. Morris took Fiona's hand. "Welcome, Miss McKenna. I'm Mary Morris. Are you interested in volunteering here?"

"No, I'm sorry, Ma'am, I would love to, but I don't live here."

Mrs. Morris smiled and said, "Too bad we could always use a pretty girl like you to cheer up the troops. I keep trying to get Mrs. Walters to volunteer, but that's not her thing. She would rather hostess fund raising parties, but that's important too. Will you be at the party on Saturday?"

Fiona blushed. "Oh no, I don't think so." She started to say something more when Trip interrupted.

"Well, let's get started with our tour. We want Fiona to see everything. Thank you, Mrs. Morris."

They walked around the hall and Fiona saw a group that had just gotten off the ferry. They entered the hall and hesitantly looked around. *Oh how young they are*, she thought. The young men were all invited to sit down and were served sandwiches and coffee. They relaxed and began to chatter.

Trip explained that after the meal, bathing facilities would be available and writing material would be handed out. They boys would have an opportunity to rest before the next leg of their journey. There was also a hospital for those who needed any medical treatment.

Fiona was impressed with the cleanliness of the buildings and the kindness with which the troops were treated. "They are so young and most are away from home for the first time. It is good of the people here to give them such tender care before they face the horrors of the battlefield."

"Yes," Trip agreed. "As they go off to fight, it is our responsibility to provide them some comfort. However, Fiona, this is your day. Let's go and find some pleasant things for you to see."

The remainder of the day was spent riding around the city. They rode up to the Fairmount and saw the many old mansions. Trip pointed out Lemon Hill, the home of Robert Morris, a signer of the Declaration of Independence and a financier of the revolution.

Fiona asked, "The Mrs. Morris that we just met, is she a descendant of his?"

"Why, I believe she is," Trip replied. "Many of the old families are still around." He turned to David, "Well Davey, I can see you're getting tired. Let's head home and you can have a nap."

Fiona could see the fatigue in dear David's face and worried for him. He had not gotten his strength back.

When they arrived back at the house, David hugged Fiona, "I hope you enjoyed our day?"

"Oh, I did indeed, Davey, very much."

She watched him go inside and turned to go down to her quarters when Trip stopped her.

"Fiona, the day is still young. There is a tea shop around the corner. Will you join me in a little refreshment?"

She agreed and he took her arm as they strolled to the shop. As they walked, Fiona thought of David.

"Trip, is your brother going to be all right? He seems to tire easily."

"I don't know. We're very worried about him. That chest wound damaged his lungs. All we can do is to see that he gets plenty of rest. I don't think he would have survived the wound were it not for the good care he received at your hospital. They used the new method of closing the wound with metal sutures."

Fiona stopped and her eyes filled with tears. "Oh, Trip I'm so sorry. I care for him so much. He is such a loving boy. He will be in my prayers."

"Thank you, Fiona, Davey is so happy having you here. It means a lot to him. Here we are. Let's go in and talk of more pleasant things."

They sat in the tea room for hours. Fiona found it easy to talk to Trip. He wanted to know all about her and she talked freely. She even told him about John Brown's men and her feeling for John Kagi and the books he had given her.

Trip said that he also loved Emerson, Whitman and Thoreau. "You know what? When I first saw you yesterday, I was reminded of lines from a poem by Whitman.

*I draw you close to me, you woman,*
*I cannot let you go, I would do you good,*
*I am for you, and you are for me, not only for our own sake, but for*
*others' sakes.*

Fiona blushed at his words and he apologized, "I'm sorry, I just knew right away that we were meant to be.""

He told her about his family and the love that he had for them. "I know that my mother has not been all that kind to you and I'm sorry. You have to understand she is very unsure of her position in society. Unlike someone like Mrs. Morris whose family goes way back, her family are newcomers and she is always afraid she will make a misstep and not be accepted. Mrs. Morris can put on an apron and wait on the lowly, but mother could never."

"Yes, I understand, Trip. I will keep that in mind and not judge her. Your father has been very kind."

"Oh, yes, Father does not worry about his place because his family has always been accepted. He understands and that's why I asked him to get us tickets to the Academy of Music next week.

"To see an opera!" Fiona almost shouted.

"Yes, an opera, but we'll have to sit in the auditorium. I could not be seen sitting in our box with you. People would ask, 'who is that beautiful girl with William?' And when they found out that you were a servant girl, Mother would be mortified. I'm sorry, Fiona."

"Oh, don't be sorry, I don't care where we sit. I'll be thrilled to be there."

They walked back to the house hand and hand and Fiona felt like she was floating on air.

When she entered the kitchen, Fiona ran straight into Tim the coachman.

He whispered, "Bridie needs to see you in your room."

She looked at him and frowned, "Who?"

"I mean Barbara," he replied and led her to their room.

Barbara was lying on her bed and looked up with a silly grin on her face. "Hallo there, Fiona, I seem to be a little drunk."

Fiona was astonished. Her very proper British accent was gone and she was giggling like a school girl. She turned over and soon began to snore. Fiona turned to Tim for an explanation.

"She went to meet some of her old friends and they had a party. She liked to party in the old days when I first met her here."

Fiona sat down on the other bed. "Why did you call her Bridie?"

"That's her name, Bridget Clark. I recognized her the first day you arrived, but didn't say a word. The name Barbara and the British accent were put on to get a job as a ladies maid. She was born in County Cork."

He looked at Fiona. "We Irish have to stick together. We have ta help the poor lass."

Fiona just rolled her eyes and fell back on the bed.

# Chapter Fifteen

Fiona and Tim concocted a scheme. They would tell the housekeeper that Barbara was unwell. On her outing, she had eaten something that didn't agree with her. She just needed rest and Fiona would take care of her. Fiona would also help Mrs. Flood dress for dinner.

Fiona laughed when she told Tim about Mrs. Flood. "She thinks the Irish are riff-raff. I wonder what she would think if she ever found out that the very proper Barbara was Bridie Clark from Cork."

"Aye, that would be an event," he laughed.

Fiona brought a cup of tea and a piece of bread in to Bridie (as she though of her now.) "Come on, sit up and eat a little something. You'll feel better."

Bridie complied and took a sip of the tea and a bite of the bread. "Oh, Fiona, you are a darlin' for taken' care of me." She laid back down and said. "Oh, me head."

Fiona soaked a cloth in water from the basin and put it on Bridie's forehead. "I have to go and tend to Mrs. Flood now. Shall I give her your regards?"

"Tell the ole biddy I'm so sorry I can't be there to tend her every need, ha ha."

Fiona found Mrs. Flood waiting impatiently in her wrapper and under-garments. They went through the old routine of lacing her corsets. Fiona found it was harder than ever. She helped her on with the hoop skirt and black silk gown.

"It's a lovely gown, Mrs. Flood. Is it new?"

"Of course, I sent my measurement to a dress maker here in Philadelphia and had several gowns made. The Walters dress for dinner every night. I had a special one made for the ball tomorrow night. I didn't want to wear anything that came from Chambersburg. Barbara advised me on that. She is so sophisticated."

"Indeed she is." Fiona replied surprising a smile. "Shall we do your hair?"

"Yes, but I'm sure you don't know the latest styles like Barbara. Do the best you can."

When her hair was piled on her head to her satisfaction, Mrs. Flood, looking resplendent in her jewels, got up to leave. As she headed for the door, she turned to Fiona.

"You know, chasing after that Walters boy is not going to do you any good. You are not his sort. They marry their own kind."

Fiona said nothing as Mrs. Flood swept out the door. She stuck her tongue out as the door slammed, thinking, *I have no intention of marrying him. I just like him very much and enjoy his company.*

Fiona was relieved the next morning when Bridie announced she was ready to resume her duties with Mrs. Flood. She still could not believe how Irish Bridie had managed to fool everyone as the proper British Barbara.

In answer to her question, Bridie laughed, "Aye it was easy. Spent some time in England before coming over and picked up their talkin.' I saw an advert in the Philadelphia Inquirer for a personal maid with the ole No Irish Need Apply line."

She started out the door and turned, "I made up me mind to put one over on the ole girl and I did."

"How long do you think you can keep it up," Fiona asked,

"Oh, not too much longer. She pays pretty good and I'm saving me money. As soon as I get enough I'll come back here to Philadelphia. Chambersburg is boring."

"And what will you do."

"Don't know. Somethin' will come up."

Fiona laughed to her self as she got ready to go up to see to Mrs. Ritner. The lady was already dressed and sitting at the vanity fixing her hair.

She turned and smiled. "Oh, Fiona, I'm fully capable of dressing my-self, but I wanted to ask you something. You know the ball is tomorrow tonight."

"Oh yes, that's all their talking about downstairs. It's going to be a grand affair."

Mrs. Ritner got up and gestured to the bed. "Sit down, Fiona." She sat down beside her and began. "Mrs. Walters came to see me earlier. She is upset because some of the extra maids they hired for this eve-ning won't be here. She asked if Mrs. Flood and I could lend her our maids."

"Lend?' Fiona

"That's exactly what I said," Mrs. Ritter answered. "I told her I would have to ask if you would want to do it. That surprised her."

"I'm sure," Fiona responded."

"She said there would be a cloak room near the front door for the ladies. You would have to take their wraps and help them with any toiletries they may need." She took Fiona's hand and said. "I know she has not treated you kindly. You don't have to do it if you don't want to."

"Well, she hasn't acknowledged my presence since I've been here," Fiona replied. Frowning a bit, she thought for a while, and then quickly raised her head. "I don't think I will mind. It will be very interesting. I've never seen a ball in a grand house before. I heard that the most important people of Philadelphia will be there. It will be exciting."

"Oh, Fiona, you are a dear. The butler will give you instructions. I do hope it will be exciting for you."

Fiona ran into Bridie on her way downstairs. She informed her that she would also be working the cloak room. "Av course the ol biddy didn't ask if I wanted to do it. Just ordered me. And I have to go up earlier to get er ready. That's quite an endeavor in itself. But I'm thinkin' it will be a lark seein' how the quality parties tonight."

Fiona was the first to arrive in the cloak room. She was dressed in a black dress and white apron that Billings the butler had given her. That morning, she and Bridie had been instructed to take the ladies wraps and ask their names. Slips of paper would be on a table. They were to write the name, pin it to the wrap and hang it on the coat rack.

Billings had looked at them sharply, "You do know how to write don't you?"

Bridie started to say something and Fiona interrupted, "Yes, we do, sir."

Billings went on, "You are to curtsy to the ladies and refer to them as ma'am or miss. There will be no chatting. Only to answer questions as they are asked. Is that clear?"

"Very clear sir," Bridie answered in her stiff British accent.

Still alone in the room, Fiona looked around. The coat racks and table were there. Across the room were several vanity tables with chairs. Fiona walked over and saw each had a mirror and on the tables were toiletries, combs and brushes for the ladies. Through the open door to another room she could see several screens set up. She knew that behind them were commodes.

"The kitchen maids will take care of emptying them." Billings had stiffly informed them.

Suddenly Fiona felt a hand on her shoulder. She turned to see Trip's smiling face. She stepped back to admire him. He looked so handsome in his white tie and tails. It took her breath away.

He took her hand, "Oh, Fiona, you are the prettiest maid I've ever seen."

"Trip, you should not be in here," she exclaimed with horror. "Someone will see you.

He kissed her on the cheek and promised to steal a dance later. Just as he was leaving, the housekeeper Mrs. Travers entered. He bowed to her and smiled back at Fiona.

Mrs. Travers said nothing, but the sour look on her face told it all. The two maids that had been deemed presentable enough for cloak room duty came in after her. Mrs. Travers was lining them up for inspection when Bridie flew in and joined the line.

"It's like we're in the military," she whispered to Fiona.

Fiona started to laugh and stopped abruptly when she saw Mrs. Walters enter the room. At the sight of the lady of the house, Fiona felt her face grow hot. She was not sure why she felt so uncomfortable in her presence. Mrs. Walters inspected the line up of servants. Her eyes passed over Fiona without acknowledgement. She nodded to Mrs. Travers and swept from the room.

The guests soon began to arrive and the ladies entered the cloak room. To Fiona they looked like bright hothouse flowers fleeing the cold night air. Mrs. Travers knew most of them by name and announced them. Fiona recognized some of the names like Ingersoll, Biddle, and Cadwalader and knew they were from the most important families. The maids carefully took their fur stoles and matching muffs. Most of the ladies thanked them and smiled kindly. But, others looked right through them as if they didn't exist.

Fiona heard Mrs. Travers announce, "Mrs. Morris,"

She looked up to see the lady she had met at the Refreshment Salon. She curtsied and said, "Good Evening, Mrs. Morris."

Mrs. Morris took Fiona's hand and smiled, "Good evening, Fiona. It's so nice to see you again."

Fiona could feel Mrs. Travers's disapproving eyes on her, but she didn't care. She peeked out the door and watched the ladies ascend the stairs to the ballroom on their escorts' arms. The rich colors of their dresses gleamed in the gaslight. Soon the music began to play and Fiona felt herself swaying to the music picturing the dancers in the ballroom.

Fiona jumped when she heard, "Remember your place, girl, and get back to work," Mrs. Travers had come up behind her.

"Yes, Mrs. Travers, sorry." Fiona replied, and returned to the cloak room.

All evening the music and laughter from above filtered down. The ladies came and went to use the facilities. Some asked the maids for help with their hair. Falling tresses were fixed and noses were powdered.

Late in the evening, Mrs. Morris came in and asked for Fiona. She sat down at one of the dressing tables and Fiona stood behind her and asked what she needed.

She looked at Fiona in the mirror, "I have a message for you my dear. Trip is waiting for you in the hall. He says the next dance is his."

Fiona felt a thrill at the very thought of a dance with Trip, but knew she couldn't. "Mrs. Travers will never let me leave. "

Mrs. Morris stood up and said, "Don't worry dear, I'll take care of it."

She went up to Mrs. Travers and explained that she needed a maid to assist her with something. She did not explain. Such was her position in society that she never had to explain. Fiona followed her out and there stood Trip.

He bowed and said, "I believe this is our dance Miss McKenna."

Mrs. Morris waved to them as she went up the stairs the orchestra began to play a waltz. Trip grabbed Fiona in his arms and they twirled down the hallway and into the next room. Round and round they went and Fiona was deliriously dizzy. The music stopped and a slower waltz began. Trip held her very close and Fiona felt that she was melting into him. He sang softly in her ear:

*Beautiful dreamer, wake unto me,*
*Starlight and dewdrops are waiting for thee;*
*Sounds of the rude world, heard in the day,*
*Lull'd by the moonlight have all passed away.*
*Beautiful dreamer awake unto me.*

When the music stopped, he pulled her down on a sofa.

"Oh, Fiona, my dear dear girl, I have to tell you that I love you. I have loved you since the first moment I saw you. No, it was before that. It was from the first time Davey described you. I loved you already and wanted to marry you."

He wrapped her in a warm embrace and Fiona had the strange feeling that she was at home in his arms. He kissed her slowly and she felt a fire rage through her entire body. She pulled away and tried to catch her breath.

Fiona could not speak. She could barely breathe. Finally, she looked into his eyes and said, "Oh, Trip, I think I love you too, but it can't be."

Trip stood up and laughed. "Of course it can be. That is if you will have me."

"Of course I will have you, but your family…"

Trip got down on one knee and took her hand, "Fiona Mc Kenna, will you marry me?"

Fiona squeezed his hand, "Oh, yes, yes, I want to marry you, but I don't know how we can."

Trip stood and lifted her up, "We can, we can. I will marry you no matter what. I did not plan on asking you so soon. I should have spoken to your father first."

"My father? What about your father and mother?"

Just then Mrs. Morris appeared in the doorway and said, "I'd better be getting Fiona back, Mrs. Travers will be wondering. "

Trip hugged Fiona and said, "We'll talk tomorrow. Thank you Mrs. Morris, you have no idea what you have done for me."

She rolled her eyes and replied, "I can only imagine."

Fiona slept very little that night. All she could think of was Trip and she knew she loved him and wanted him. This was very different than her feelings for John. That had been like a fairy tale. This was real.

She turned things over and over in her mind. His family would object for sure. The formidable Mrs. Walters would object most strongly. She had not even acknowledged Fiona's presence in the house. It was as if she didn't exist. Her thoughts were also of her Da. She knew he would warn her of the difficulties they would face, but would want her to do whatever made her happy. She arose the next morning and knew what she had to do.

Bridie looked at her sheepishly and said, "What's goin' on with you? I heard you tossin' and turnin' and mutterin' to yourself all night."

"I was just overtired and had a restless night. Let's go to breakfast."

They were just finishing breakfast when Trip appeared and asked "to speak with Miss McKenna." In the servants parlor they sat side by side. Trip took her hand and said. "Good morning, Miss McKenna, I love you."

"I love you too, but please listen. I have made a decision. I want to marry you, but I don't think we should tell anyone yet."

"But I want everyone to know that I love you."

"Trip, please listen. You will be getting your orders soon. You don't know where you'll be going. I'm sure your parents are worried about David and will be upset about you leaving. Don't add to it. Just let it be our secret for now. We'll write while you're away and make plans."

Trip encircled Fiona in his arms, "I will do whatever makes you happy my darling, but we will be married."

She again felt that lovely feeling of being at home in his arms and kissed him with a surprising passion. "Oh what you do to me, Mr. Walters."

He jumped up and danced her around. "Tonight will be our night. We're going to the opera."

The next few days passed in a whirl of excitement for Fiona. That night at the opera, when she entered the Academy of Music on Trip's arm, she felt she was in a palace. An attendant in splendid livery led them to their seats. Fiona sat on the red velvet chair and gazed about her. The ceiling was painted with figures from allegories. A magnificent crystal chandelier hung above her ablaze with hundreds of gas lights. There was a gilded bust of Mozart over the stage and other gilded figures over the balconies. She felt she was in a golden haze. But when the music began, she was transported to another world, the world of Faust in 16th century Germany. She sat entranced by the story, the singing and the costumes. She had to hold on to Trip to believe it was all real. On the carriage ride home, she leaned against him and felt engulfed in love and happiness.

Fiona's last day in Philadelphia was a day for Davey. He wanted to see Dan Rice's Circus. Dan was one of the most famous men in America before the war; his circus had traveled all over the country and Europe. Dan Rice's Great Show was at the Walnut Street theatre. Trip got tickets for the three of them and they all felt Davey's excitement. When they entered the theatre, they saw that there was a great ring filled with dirt on the stage. It was a very different crowd than the formally dressed patrons of the opera. They were a rowdy bunch and stamped their feet waiting for Dan to appear.

He came out dressed in his usual costume of red and white stripped trousers, a star spangled coat, top hat and a white beard.

He called out in a booming voice his familiar phrase "Hey Rube" and the audience roared with laughter.

He went on to introduce acrobats, clowns, and the famous equestrian Ella Zoyara who performed acrobatic acts on a horse as it paraded around the ring. There were animal acts and they were amazed to see an African rhinoceros led out on stage. Davey stood on his seat and clapped with excitement. The finale was the appearance of the wonder horse Excelsior. At Dan's command, the beautiful white horse performed wondrous deeds. He answered questions yes or no by shaking his head. His great final trick was shooting a gun by pulling on ropes to pull the trigger. Fiona's greatest enjoyment was seeing the look of wonder and joy on Davey's face.

Fiona and Mrs. Ritner were to leave on the afternoon train the next day. Mrs. Flood wanted to stay a few more days to do more shopping. Fiona spent the morning helping Mrs. Ritner to pack. When she went down stairs to do her own packing, Bridie was waiting.

"So, you'll be off soon. I hope we'll be getting' together in Chambersburg when I get back."

Fiona took her hand, "Sure we will. We ladies maids must stick together."

"Hey, Fiona, I hope you play you're cards right with the young master of the house. I can see he's smitten with you. You can get some money out of him."

Fiona turned on her with anger, "I'm not interested in getting anything out of him."

"Have it your way, dearie. I meant no harm. Let's part friends."

"Of course, Bridie. We are friends. We just have different view points."

Bridie hugged her and wished her a safe trip home. Trip and Davey saw them off at the station.

Davey held on to Fiona and said, "I enjoyed your visit so much, maybe we can come to see you in Chambersburg soon."

"I would like that very much Davey.

Trip kissed Fiona good bye and whispered in her ear that he would see her soon.

Without the presence of Mrs. Flood, Fiona was glad that she and Mrs. Ritner could sit together on the trip home. But soon she was hearing the same warnings about Trip that she had heard from others, but in a much kinder way.

"I can see that he cares for you, dear, and I'm sure you are aware of the obstacles. Please don't do anything foolish."

"I do know the obstacles, Mrs. Ritner, and I promise not to do anything foolish."

Mrs. Ritner patted her hand and they sat back and relaxed for the rest of the trip.

Fiona closed her eyes and thought of Trip and the wonderful time in Philadelphia. She was filled with happiness. Soon the click clack of the train wheels lulled her to sleep.

Later, she awoke with a start with an overwhelming sense of foreboding. It seemed that the time in the city had been a dream and she was going back to the real world and all its sorrows.

# Chapter Sixteen

Fiona's father and Mr. Adamson were waiting at the station. Fiona's mood brightens as soon as she saw her father. She had not realized how much she missed him and she could not wait to tell him everything that had happened in Philadelphia. *Well not everything*, she thought, *I can't tell him about Trip,* as Da embraced her in a bear hug. Fiona had never kept anything from her father and she wasn't sure how she would handle this secret.

Mr. Adamson took Mrs. Ritner's hand and held it tightly. He smiled at her and said, "We all missed you very much, Mary."

She smiled at him and said, "It's good to be home. How are things at the house?"

"Getting busy. We have several new boarders checking in at the end of the week."

"Oh, there will be so much to do."

He patted her hand and said, "Don't worry. Helga and her sister have started getting the rooms ready."

Mrs. Ritner turned to Fiona and said anxiously, "I was going to let you go home with your father, but I'm going to need you sooner. I'm sorry. Mr. McKenna, you may have her for the rest of the day, but please have her back this evening. "

"That will be fine, Mrs. Ritner," Fiona replied.

She was relieved. She wanted to spend a few days at home with her father, but she worried how she would keep her plans about Trip from him. Da knew her so well. He could almost tell what she was thinking.

"Da, why don't we visit Mrs. Gormley. We can spend the afternoon there."

He agreed, but looked at her anxiously. Fiona knew that Kate Gormley would keep the conversation going, telling her about the happenings in town and asking Fiona all about her visit to Philadelphia. Da would not have much chance to question Fiona.

Kate did not disappoint. "Agnes Flood must have been in her element in that society. I hear they had a grand ball."

"Oh, yes," Fiona replied and went on to tell her in great detail all about the music, the people who attended, the gowns the women wore, and the grandeur of it all.

"And what did you enjoy the most Dear?" Da asked

Fiona told them all about the wonders she had seen and the magnificent home of the Walters. She went into great detail about what she saw in the city. She described the trip to the Refreshment Salon and the circus. She did not mention the opera. She would have to mention Trip and she wanted to avoid that.

Fiona paused for breath, then asked, "Well, what has been happening in Chambersburg, Mrs. Gormley?"

Kate went on about all of the latest gossip and the war rumors. Fiona noticed that her father sat very close to Kate. Soon it was time to leave. Fiona kissed her father good-bye and promised to be home the next week-end. Tom hugged her and said he would look forward to spending time with her then.

His parting words were, "Then we'll have a grand talk me darlin'."

Fiona was anxious to see Helga. They had exchanged letters while she was away, but she wanted to see her in person. Fiona was relieved when she saw Helga. She almost looked like her old self. She told her all about what had happened at the house while they were away.

"It was good having my sister Maria here. We could talk about Hans and laugh about the good old times. Mama doesn't talk much about him. That's how she keeps going."

Fiona was glad to talk about Hans, it kept the subject away from the events in Philadelphia.

And they all kept going.  Spring was coming, the armies were moving and more boarders were arriving. In March, Congress passed the Military Draft Act. It required all male citizens age twenty to forty-five and those immigrants who had applied for citizenship to register for the draft. Men who could pay three hundred dollars or provide a substitute were exempt.

On Fiona's next week-end home she discussed the draft with her father. He worried about the draft act.

"So many volunteered at the beginning of the war, but as it goes on people are discouraged. They see this conscription for poor men only. They are saying the blood of a poor man is as precious as that of the wealthy. But enough of this talk, tell me more about your time in Philadelphia. "

Fiona knew this was coming and she dreaded it. She tried telling him more of the splendors she had seen, but he kept asking about the Walters family and what they were like. She knew he meant no harm, but she also knew he suspected she was keeping something from him and she burst into tears.  The next thing she knew she was telling him all about Trip and the plans they had made.

He took her in his arms and asked, "Do you love him?"

"Oh Da, with all my heart!"

"You thought you loved John."

"I did, but this is different. It just feels so right and comfortable with Trip."

She went on to tell him how handsome, how manly, how kind, how sweet he was. She neglected to mention how he stirred a new passion within her. She told him about his family and how his mother would object and how he asked her to marry him and their pact to keep it secret.  He held her hand and listened intently.

"Thank you for telling me darlin'. I think it is wise to wait and keep it secret. It won't be easy, but if you both love each other you will find a way. I would like to meet this paragon."

Fiona knew she would have to tell Trip that she betrayed their secret and hoped he would forgive her. She would write and tell him that her

Father wanted to meet him. Perhaps he could come to Chambersburg before he left for his assignment.

The armies were moving and there were no letters from their troops. Since Hans' death, Helga worried about Joe constantly. Fiona tried to lift her spirits by talking of other things, but she knew Helga suspected she was keeping something from her. Fiona was relieved when she received a letter from Trip forgiving her for telling her father about their engagement. "It was your idea to keep it secret darling and any thing you want to do is fine with me." He went on to say that he would tell his brother Davey. "He is not well and the news would make him very happy." Trip ended with the news that he would be traveling south to join his unit in a few weeks and would try to stop in Chambersburg.

Fiona felt a surge of joy at she thought of seeing him again. She could wait no longer to tell her dear friend Helga of her happiness. They walked down to their favorite spot on the bank near the spring and she told Helga of her love for Trip. Helga's reaction was to jump up and down and hug her with all her might. "I am so happy for the first time since Hans died. Maybe we can have a double wedding after the war."

The girls returned to the Ritner house arm in arm and found Mrs. Ritner waiting for them. "We're having guests for dinner tomorrow night. My father-in- law Joseph Ritner and his friend Thaddeus Stephens will be here. I would like to have a very special dinner for them." She was sitting at the table making a list. "I saw a haunch of mutton hanging in the butchers yesterday. Ask them to deliver it. We still have some of the red currant jelly we made last summer. We can serve that with it. Oh, and we can have ox tail soup to begin. Get three tails from the butcher and tell him to cut them at the joint.

We will need potatoes. We still have some of the spring peas that we put up last summer. They will be good and we still have apples in the barrel. We can make apple compote for desert. Here's the list. Hurry back. We have a lot to do."

The girls set off, happy to see their mistress so excited. Fiona had never met Governor Ritner and asked Helga about him.

"I don't think he's been here since the war started. He's a very important man and a real gentleman. He was always involved in anti-slavery. Mr. Stevens was also, but I wouldn't call him a gentleman. He's kind of rough lookin' and wears this awful red wig on top of his head. Oh, and they say that the colored housekeeper that lives with him is his mistress."

"But he is an important man," Fiona chimed in. "He is a congressman and Da says he is pushing Lincoln to make an amendment to the constitution to end slavery. He still owns the Caledonia Iron Works in Green Township. The Judge has done business with him, even though he never agreed with his politics. Da says Stevens is a Radical Republican and an Anti-Mason. "

"Well, whatever that is," Helga replied. "I just know that he and the Governor are old friends and they were both in the Underground Railroad."

The ladies worked hard at getting the house ready and preparing for the dinner They were to dine early because Mr. Ritner had to get back to Cumberland County. When the guests arrived Fiona had the honor of answering the door. She showed them into the parlor where Mrs. Ritner and Mr. Adamson were waiting. Mr. Ritner was elderly, but still a fine looking man. He wore spectacles and was tall and stately looking. He shook Fiona's hand with a warm smile. Mr. Stevens was everything that Helga had described.

He walked with a limp from a clubfoot. She tried not to look at that thing on his head and fled to the kitchen to suppress a giggle.

The guests seemed to enjoy the dinner and complimented Mrs. Ritner and Fiona and Helga as they served. The girls smiled and thanked them with a curtsey. The party adjourned to the parlor and the girls were invited to join them after they finished the dishes.

They sat and listened to the conversations. Mr. Ritner sat next to his daughter in law. They talked of her daughters in Connecticut and her step-sons in the army. Thaddeus Stevens and Mr. Adams were discussing the war and Lincoln's plans. Mr. Stevens became very agitated and his voice rose as he discussed Lincoln.

"He should be waging a war of extermination. After the war there should be a re-colonization of the South and the old state lines should be abolished."

Mr. Ritner looked up and smiled. "My friend Thad does not agree with Mr. Lincoln on some issues." He rose from his chair, "Thad, it's time we should think about departing. I would like to get home before dark. My coachman should be here soon."

The coach soon arrived and they all said their goodbyes. Mr. Stevens went out first and waited. As Mr. Ritner descended the front steps, he stumbled and fell. Stevens and Mr. Adamson rushed to pick him up and he complained that his ankle hurt. They laid him on the settee in the parlor and Mr. Adamson ran for the doctor. By the time the doctor arrived the ankle was badly swollen. The doctor said it was sprained and he would have to stay off it far a few days.

Mrs. Ritner asked the girls to make the bedroom off the kitchen ready for him. "He should not climb the stairs." She wrung her hands and cried. "Oh, we should have been more careful with him. He's eighty four and blind in one eye, you know. He is such a dear man."

"We'll take good care of him," Helga assured her. "Thank goodness it wasn't broken."

Mr. Ritner was a good patient and didn't complain. Once again Fiona had someone in that room that she enjoyed talking to. He told her something about his life. He grew up on a farm in Berks County. His father was an immigrant from the German Palatine. Early on he saw the evil of slavery and fought against it. He felt his greatest achievement as governor was his expansion of the public school system in the state.

"Fiona, I believe everyone should have the right to an education. I support County School Superintendent Andrew McElwain and his Negro school. After the war, we must educate the slaves and the Indians. "

"Do you think we will win the war, Sir?" Fiona asked.

"Of course we will, my dear."

Fiona felt reassured by his words. In a few days his ankle was better and Joseph Ritner was ready to leave. He shook hands with Fiona and Helga and thanked them for their care.

He kissed Mrs. Ritner and said, "After the war, Mary, our family will have a grand get together."

She watched him drive away and said, "God willing he will still be around by then."

The April rains came and the troops were moving. Chambersburg's own troops were in Sufffolk, Virginia and news came of a battle there. The Federals had driven the Confederates out of their position on the river at Northfleet House. The good news of that victory was lost in the events at Chancellorsville in May. Joe Hooker had lost a horrific battle there with huge losses of life. The residents of Chambersburg rejoice that their troops had not been involved.

A few weeks later, Tom McKenna received a letter from his nephew Liam. He was coming home. He had been wounded at Suffolk. He gave no details on his wound and was not sure when he would arrive. It depended on when he could get on a train.

Tom rushed into Chambersburg to give the news to Fiona. A few days later they received a telegram stating that he would arrive on the tenth of May.

Fiona and Tom waited anxiously at the station, not sure what to expect. When the train pulled in, Liam was standing in the door balanced on crunches. He was not the same Liam that had left triumphantly so long ago. His face was thin and haggard. They rushed to help him down and he smiled his old cocky grin.

"It's so good to be home, my dears."

All they could do was cry and hug him. They took him home and put him to bed. Fiona stayed for a week to take care of him. He had a bad wound on his calf but it looked clean with no infection.

"You had some very good nursing, Liam," Fiona noted, "the wound looks good. Are you in pain? "

"Yep, a lot. But it's worth it. They didn't cut me leg off. I guess I'll have ta limp for life, but I'll manage."

In a few days, Liam insisted on getting up and moving around in spite of the pain. The weather was warm and he liked sitting outside on a bench by the door. One day, as Fiona was sitting with him, a carriage stopped and a woman got out. She recognized Barbara Clark, now known to her as Bridie. Fiona had not seen her since their return from Philadelphia.

Bridie sprang from the carriage. "Well, Fiona, how ya been. The old witch actually let me take the carriage into town to get her some supplies."

She stopped short and looked at Liam. He painfully pulled himself up and smiled at her.

"This is my cousin Liam, just home from the war. Liam, this is Bridie Clark who works for Mrs. Flood."

They shook hands and stared at each other. Fiona could almost see the sparks flying between them. *Oh my God,* she thought. *What have I done putting these two together?*

Bridie sat next to Liam and said she was sorry she didn't get a chance to meet him when he was working for the Floors. She told him all about her employment with Mrs. Flood and had him laughing at her posing as an English woman. Liam told her that he hoped to get his job back when he was well.

"It would be grand working with you me boyo," she said as she got up to leave. Fiona walked her to the carriage. "Fiona, why didn't you tell me your cousin was so handsome?"

Fiona laughed and said, "Go easy girl, he's hasn't gotten his strength back yet."

"I'll give him some strength," she called as she drove away.

When Fiona got back to Chambersburg, all thoughts of Liam and Bridie went out of her head. There was a letter from Trip. He would be in Chambersburg for a few hours between trains on Tuesday. Could Fiona and her father meet him at the station.? She was out of her mind with joy. She remembered that Da said he would be coming into town for supplies that day. It was meant to be. She asked Mrs. Ritner for a few hours off on Tuesday and the lady kindly asked her no questions.

Fiona and Tom were waiting at the station when the train pulled in. Luckily Tom had gotten into town early and Fiona had time to tell him of Trip's arrival. They made plans to take him to the hotel for lunch where they could talk in private. When Fiona saw Trip get off the train in his First Lieutenant's uniform her heart skipped a beat. He looked so handsome.

He came right up to Tom, took his hand and bowed. "Hello, Mr. McKenna. I am William Walters."

Fiona looked at her father and he was smiling. "It is a pleasure to meet you Lieutenant Walters."

They walked to the hotel speaking of his trip from Philadelphia and his new assignment. He explained that doctors were not permanently attached to any regiment, but sent wherever needed. He had been assigned to the 45th Pennsylvania under Colonel John Curtin. They were with Grant's Army of Tennessee. When they were seated in the hotel dining room, Trip began.

"Sir, may I have your daughter's hand in marriage? I love her very much and I want to cherish and care for her the rest of my life."

Tom answered, his voice trembling a bit. "All I want is Fiona's happiness. I understand that your family may not approve. That worries me."

"Not to worry, Sir. I know that they will come around when they get to know her."

"When do you plan to tell them?"

He turned to Fiona and smiled. "That's up to Fiona. I'm ready to tell them now."

She answered, "I still think we should wait. This is a bad time for them with you going away and Davey not doing well. You said you may be able to get leave in a few months. Perhaps we could go together and see them and ask their permission then."

"I don't need their permission, Dear. I will marry you no matter what."

The waiter came and they ordered lunch. Trip ordered some wine.

When the wine came, he raised his glass and said, "To Fiona. Mr. McKenna, I pledge to you to do everything in my power to make her happy."

Tom offered another toast, "May you have the hindsight to know where you've been, the foresight to know where you're goin' and the insight to know when you're goin' too far."

"Oh Da, you and your Irish quotes," Fiona said.

Tom smiled at them and said, "May the good Lord keep you, my children." He turned to Trip and said, "You have my permission, Sir, not that it would matter. I have a headstrong daughter who would do what she wants anyway."

"Oh, Da, I would always want your approval."

They ate their lunch and spoke of Trip's assignment. He was to join Grant's army in Vicksburg, Mississippi.

"As there is a siege going on there, I don't expect to be treating any wounded, but I understand there is a great deal of sickness in camp. The poor hygiene of the camps worries me. That is something I would like to improve."

All too soon it was time for Trip's train and they headed for the station. Fiona clung to him and hated to let him go. Tom hugged him and wished him well. As the train pulled out, Fiona was surprised that she felt engulfed by a since of calmness. Somehow she knew in her heart that they would be together again.

Her calmness was soon replaced by a sense of urgency. The house was busy with boarders coming and going. She felt swept up in a vortex of rumors: Lincoln would not be re-elected he was losing the war he would get us into a war with England, and the latest the rebels had crossed into Pennsylvania again.

# Chapter Seventeen

On June 15<sup>th</sup> there was a report of an engagement near Winchester. Fiona had been shopping in town when she saw Judge Flood coming out of the bank.

She stopped him and asked, "Mr. Flood, please tell me what is happening?"

"General Jenkins and his cavalry are on their way, Fiona. The bank is sending all of its valuable papers and cash to Philadelphia. The army stores are also on their way there. Our state is doing nothing to defend itself against invasion. Governor Curtin seems paralyzed and unable to act. And we can expect no help from Washington." He looked at her stricken face and said kindly, "You'll be all right Fiona, go back to the house and tell everyone to stay inside."

At the Ritner house all was quiet. They sat in the front parlor and Mr. Adamson read from the bible. Suddenly they heard a great clash of wagons and horses passing by. They heard shouts that the rebels were coming. Mr. Adamson ran out and saw a sight of mass confusion and terror. He returned to tell the frightened people in the parlor that they were General Milroy's troops retreating from Winchester.

"One man told me that an entire Confederate corps under General Jenkins had born down on them."

After that all was quiet again. They waited a long time and nothing happened.

Mrs. Ritner suggested that they go to bed. "There is nothing we can do now. We will need our rest."

They awoke early to the clash of many horses and wagons going by. They ran out in their night clothes to see greybacks marching toward the

Diamond. Behind one unit was a group of colored people being driven like cattle.

Mr. Adamson shouted out "Who are these people?"

"There're contraband, Yankee," a soldier answered, "we're takin' them home."

Fiona gasped when she saw a familiar face, "Enoch," she shouted, "where are they taking you?" He was shoved along before he could answer.

Fiona ran after them calling, "You can't take him. He's a free man."

Mr. Adamson grabbed and held her. "We'll go to the authorities. They can't hold him. He was born here. He's not a fugitive slave."

Fiona collapsed in tears and he helped her into the house. He told her to get dressed and that they would first go to Hattie's and see if she was all right. They found her in hysterics surrounded by neighbors.

Ol'Molly, the laundress, came up to Fiona and said, "He was just a standin' in front of his house and they came along and grabbed'em."

Suddenly, Fiona remembered one of Molly's predictions that "there would be big trouble comin' to this town."

Fiona tried to comfort Hattie, Molly and the others. She told her they would go to General Jenkins's headquarters and try to get Enoch released. She and Mr. Adamson ran to the Diamond and found the square swarming with greybacks. The soldiers stood on the courthouse steps issuing orders for all citizens to turn over their firearms. Fiona and Mr. Adamson were wondering what to do next, when Fiona spotted Barney Carney.

She had not seen her father's old friend for a while. Da had told her that Barney was doing well and had not been drinking too much. Barney was always around town and knew everything that was going on. He saw Fiona and came over.

"What are you doin' out here in this mess, Miss Fiona?"

She explained to him what happened to Enoch and asked if he knew where General Jenkins's headquarters was located.

"He's holdin' court in the Montgomery Hotel right now, my dear. The owner Dan Trostle told me they just walked in and took it over. To get Enoch released, you'll need a man of the cloth to testify that Enoch was born here. His colored pastor won't do. They won't listen to him and I'm not sure Father Mahoney will do. They don't like Papes." He turned to Mr. Adamson and asked, "You know anybody, sir?"

"I'll ask the Reverend Doctor Schneck. He is very well respected and he has known Enoch for years. I'm sure he will help."

Charles Adamson set off for Schneck's church and Fiona turned to Barney. "This isn't the first time you helped me when I was in trouble. You're a good man Barney Carney."

He just smiled and tipped his hat, "Anything for you mi lady. I gotta get goin,' the Reverend won't want ta converse with the likes of me. Good luck."

Mr. Adamson was back soon with the Reverent Schneck in tow and they headed for the hotel. The Reverend was an imposing looking man. He was tall with a stock of white hair and looked impressive in his long clerical robe and collar. They were immediately escorted into the hotel. They asked to see the general and were told to wait. An aide came out and said the general would see the gentlemen. The lady was to remain. *I guess females are not permitted to bother the general*, Fiona thought. She didn't have long to wait. The men came out smiling and announced that Enoch would be released immediately.

Reverend Schneck spoke first. "I assured the general that Enoch Williams was long a resident of this place and that he was not a fugitive slave."

Charles patted Schneck on the back and added. "They were holding two more of our citizens and he had them released also."

All Fiona could do was to shake the hand of the Reverend and say, "Thank you, thank you," again and again.

Jenkins and his army stayed in Chambersburg for three days. They stripped the countryside of horses and cattle. He ordered that all of the stores should remain open so that his men could buy what they needed. They would pay with worthless confederate script. On hearing word of an advancing Union force, Jenkins's troops made a sudden departure. On the way out of town, they set fire to the Oaks and Linn warehouse and destroyed the Scotland Bridge. The residents quickly put out the fire at the warehouse, but the bridge was gone.

Fiona was relieved to see her father at the door the next day. He told her that Judge Flood had lost many horses and cattle to the rebels. They went to see Hattie and Enoch and were greeted with joy. They hugged them and thanked Fiona for Enoch's return.

"It's the Reverend Schneck you should be thanking, and Barney Carney. He told us what to do."

They assured Fiona and Tom that they had already gone to see the Reverend and would also thank Barney.

On the way back, Fiona spoke of Barney. "I always thought of him as an annoying old drunk, but after the time he helped us when Mrs. Ritner was hiding the fugitive slave, I saw him in a new light."

"Aye, he's an old Irish rebel and a good man to have around in time of need. Fiona darlin', I fear there will be more times of need coming. There are rumors that Lee's army is comin' our way."

Fiona assured her father that she would take care and keep in touch with him. She went back to the house with a heavy heart. For the next few weeks they lived on news and rumors. Confederate General Jubal Early entered York. On the way, he destroyed the Caledonia Iron Works in Green Township owned by Thaddeus Stevens.

Liam stopped to see Fiona when he was in town for supplies. He confirmed the story of the destruction of the iron works.

"Early did it for revenge," he informed Fiona. "Stevens was always goin' on against slavery."

Fiona remembered his fiery rant against the South when he was a guest in the Ritner house. *He though Lincoln should be waging a wart of extermination and that should be a re-colonization of the South.*

Fiona was glad to see that Liam was looking better. His limp was not as bad and he seemed to be in less pain. Da had told her that he was seeing a lot of Bridie and Fiona was sure that had something to do with it.

Before he left, Liam reflected, "Ole Abe finally got rid of Hooker. Mead's the man now. The troops call him Old Snappin' Turtle. God help us."

Chambersburg was not without an invading army for long. On Wednesday, June 24th, long columns of rebel infantry and artillery, wagons and cattle streamed through the streets and headed down the Harrisburg Pike. Later that morning, a Confederate Lieutenant General accompanied by several aides was seen entering the Montgomery Hotel.

Mr. Bird from next-door came over to tell the Ritners what he had seen: "I was passin' by and saw him close up. They say his name is R.S. Ewell. He is a cripple with an artificial leg, but has the look of a gentleman. I waited around to see what would happen. He got down to business right away issuing orders. They raised a rebel flag on top of the courthouse."

They all gasped at that news. Mrs. Ritner said, "I fear we are under rebel rule now."

Mr. Bird reflected, "I was saddened when my boy went against our wishes and joined the army, but I feel proud of him now." He left with the news that the general had seized the school building on King Street for a rebel hospital.

The next day the town's business leaders were called to Ewell's head-quarters and many requisitions were issued to them. They demanded clothing, boots, saddles, horseshoes, lead, powder, ropes, pistols, salt, molasses, flour, and all kinds of foodstuffs to be delivered to the court house by 3:00 p.m.

The Ritner's friend Mr. Hoke later stopped by the house with an interesting story. One of the requests on the list of food was sauerkraut. "Our Southern visitors seemed to think that as they were among the Pennsylvania Dutch, that sauerkraut could be had year round. They didn't know that it was out of season and that sauerkraut was a home dish and never served to strangers."

Day after day, rebel cannons, wagons, and men passed through town. People were shocked at their appearance. There were ragged and dirty. Many were barefooted. There were rumors of an engagement near Carlisle and that the Rebs were driven back. However, rumors were all they had. The town was cut off from any information.

Fiona had no way of getting in touch with her father. Things were quiet at the Ritner house. They had no boarders. The few whom remained had fled as soon as Jenkins's troops left. Food was getting scarce with all the stores cleaned out. The Ritners still had the vegetables in the garden and a barrel of flour on hand. Fiona called on Kate Gormley to check on her. She said that Hattie and Enoch were staying with her and they had enough food for now.

"Oh Fiona, Fiona, they say a big battle is coming. Some are saying it will be the best thing to get the war over with. It seems the whole South is marchin' through our town. It's fearful seein' them march by and knowin' their going' to kill our men."

Fiona stayed with Kate for awhile trying to assure her that the town would be spared. On the way home she crossed the square to see what was going on. She heard people murmuring.

"That's him. That's Lee."

She saw him sitting on his white steed. He was a fine looking man with grey hair and piercing dark eyes. He wore a Confederate officer's uniform with many insignias on his collar. His hat was a soft black with a cord around the crown. It seemed like half the town was out crowded along the sidewalks and standing in doorways.

Fiona wondered, *would he be our conqueror?* Lee and his staff passed through town and set up headquarters in a grove that stood along the pike leading to Gettysburg. It was a place called Messersmith's Woods. Later Fiona returned to the house to report that General Longstreet was seen conferring with Lee at the grove.

On hearing this, Mr. Adamson reflected, "This could be perhaps the most important council of the war and the fate of the government may depend upon it. If Lee goes on down the valley, Harrisburg and Philadelphia are threatened; if he turns east, Baltimore and Washington are in danger. I think he must be stopped here."

Longstreet's corps were encamped south and north of town. Their plundering parties visited the town and cleaned out what was left of the stores. The troops kept busy destroying the Franklin Railroad. They tore down fences and made great fires to heat and twist the rails.

July 2nd dawned cloudy and very hot. Early that morning, the Ritner household was awakened by the rumbling of heavy wagons and marching troops. The rebels were leaving town and heading for Gettysburg. It took four hours for the line to pass through. The day before cannon fire was heard, and the townspeople knew there was a heavy engagement going on nearby, but they were cut off from any news of what was happening. Evening came and all was quiet and the people heaved a sigh of relief. Mr. Adamson ventured out to try and find out what was happening.

He returned with a copy of the Philadelphia Inquirer. He had received it from a friend who had just arrived from Harrisburg. He read from a brief article:

> There was a report of heavy fighting yesterday west of Gettysburg along the Chambersburg Pike. The blows were heavy but the Union army stood firm. Major General John Reynolds of Pennsylvania was killed. He was the Commander of the left wing of the Army of the Potomac. The fighting continued through the town of Gettysburg. The Union took up a good defensive position on the heights of Cemetery Hill.

The death of Reynolds was received with sorrow. He was from Lancaster and known by many in Chambersburg. He was considered to be one of the finest Generals in the Army.

Units of rebel Cavalry were still passing through town toward Gettysburg. They left their sick and wounded behind. The inhabitants of Chambersburg knew there was a fierce battle going on nearby. All they could do was watch and wait.

Refugees began pouring into town. Helga's family, the Meyers, appeared at the back door. Helga was happy to see that they were all right. They stumbled in the door looking exhausted and full of fear.

Mr. Meyers blurted out. "Them rebels took over our farm. They are camped all around the fields. They took all of our stock and crops. They fought all through town yesterday and the Union forces were driven back. They took a position on the other side of town up on Cemetery Hill. I think it is a good place to fight."

Mrs. Ritner bid them all to sit down and asked Fiona to make coffee. She asked, "Do you need a place to stay?"

Mrs. Meyers replied, "Could you please put the girls up here for a few days? They rest of us can stay with our friends the Schultz's."

Mrs. Ritner replied, "Of course I would love to have them here. I miss my girls so. Please let us know if you need anything else."

Mrs. Meyers, still grieving for her son, collapsed in tears. She recovered and blurted out, "We passed the Widow Thomas's house on the Chambersburg Pike. General Lee has taken it over for his headquarters. You know the Wades who live on Baltimore Street in town?" Not waiting for an answer, she went on. "Their young daughter Jenny was killed. She was kneading bread in the kitchen and a bullet went right through the door."

Helga put her arms around her mother. "We'll all be safe here, Mama."

Fiona and Helga got her sisters settled in the upstairs room and the rest of the family left for the Schultz house.

There were still a few squads of rebels passing though town. There was a tale going around that one squad asked the Mr. Reisher at the stable the way to Gettysburg. He sent them to Harrisburg. The sound of cannonading went on all day. The people of Chambersburg were engulfed in a fog of fear. Later that evening a rider rode into the square with some news. Battles had been raging around Gettysburg all day, but the Union still maintained their position on Cemetery Hill. The fight would go on tomorrow.

July 3rd dawned hot and dry. The streets were deserted except for a few rebel stragglers, thought to be deserters. The terrible sounds of canons went on and on. Fiona had not heard from her father. She knew that there was no fighting out his way, but she still worried about him. She heard a knock at the door and was relieved to see her father.

"Is everything all right here, dear? I've been worried about you. "

"Oh Da, me too, we're all right, but the Meyers farm was taken over by the rebels. Helga's sisters are staying here. They just went to see their parents at the Schultz's."

"I came into see you and Kate and report on the Judge's farm. The rebels were encamped there. I'm afraid there's a lot of damage. He'll want me to take him out there. I'll be back"

He kissed her and was off. Fiona felt the need to get out of the house. She walked to the Diamond and sat in the square. The distant roar of cannon fire went on and on. The heat was oppressive. She noticed that there were very few birds since the rebels had come. The flies and other insects had increased. She fanned them away with her hat. Women were emerging from their homes trying to find some food.

One lady passed by and said. "I got some milk at Mr. G's Grocer. His man went out to Stoltz's farm and got a few cans. Rebels hadn't been by there."

Another said, "I've been feeding the children bread and honey. I'm going to see if I can find something else."

Bridie came by next carrying a market basket. "Hey, Fiona, the ol' woman sent me out ta find some food. She's in a panic about their house at the farm."

"I know, my father took them out there."

"Liam was hopin' to get back with them tendin' the horses, but I don't tink there's any horses left."

Fiona just shook her head and Birdie went on.

Next Helga and the girls passed by and she told them that she was waiting there for her father.

Little Gertie looking dejected said to Fiona, "Helga was goina buy us some candy, but the rebels took it all."

"Just be glad we have something to eat." Helga scolded as she pulled her along.

Finally Fiona saw her Da driving the Judge's carriage. Mr. and Mrs. Flood sat in the back.

He stopped and Judge Flood jumped down from the carriage. Mrs. Flood began weeping loudly and crying, "We lost everything."

"Not everything, my dear, but we had a lot of damage," the Judge replied.

"They passed through my farm cutting holes in the fences and trampled down the grain. Some 40,000 men camped there over night. All of my fences are gone and about forty acres of oat. They broke into the house and stole food and clothing. A report was circulated that I was a colonel in the Union Army."

Fiona remembered that town meeting when war was declared and the Judge's boast that he would accept the rank of colonel.

"Those dirty soldiers took some of my most beautiful gowns," Mrs. Flood screamed.

Fiona suppressed a smile at the thought of rebel soldiers carrying off those gowns.

On July 4th rain broke the oppressive heat and all was quiet. Wild rumors circulated of a dreadful battle in Gettysburg. Later a lone soldier rode into the Diamond with news of a Union victory. It was the Sabbath and the churches were full. At about six in the evening, a part of General Milroy's Cavalry passed through town at full speed brandishing their swords. The townspeople stood and cheered, but still no official word from Gettysburg.

On July 5th the citizens of Chambersburg awoke to a great ringing of bells. It was official. The great contest had lasted for three days and was the most desperate of the war. The Union was victorious, Lee had withdrawn toward the Potomac leaving many dead and wounded along the way. There was news of skirmishes all along his route, but no news of his capture.

Most of the town gathered in the square where the Confederate flag was torn down and the American flag raised, a bit soggy in the rain, but still a beautiful sight. Most of the townspeople were happy, but some worried that Lee would escape.

Mr. Adamson expressed his fears, "If Lee is allowed to escape, this struggle will be prolonged. God only knows for how long."

Later that evening, a low rumbling sound was heard form the east. It was a wagon train of General Lee's wounded passing a few miles south of Chambersburg. The men lay in heaps on the rough wagon floors. The train wound through Franklin County to Williamsport. Some said it was seven miles long. The sight of the men in those wagons and their pitiful cries would live in the nightmares of the people who saw them for years to come. Several of the wagons were routed through Chambersburg and brought to the King Street Hospital that was already established. Later several others were opened.

Mrs. Ritner, Fiona, Helga and her sister Maria hurried to the hospital. They were greeted by gruesome sights. Dr. Senseny saw that vermin had already appeared in the wounds of some of the soldiers. They needed castle soap to wash the wounds. He sent word to Mr. Miller's Drug Store and they sent all the soap they had on hand. The women worked all day washing the wounds. At first Fiona found it sickening work, but gradually her compassion for the young boys took over. She smiled kindly at them and asked their names.

She was shocked when she asked the name of one soldier. He answered in a weak voice, "Don't you recognize me, Fiona? It's Ralph."

"Oh my God, Ralph Gross our old neighbor," she cried. She could see that his wounds were grievous, but she smiled and said, "Well, you're back home Ralph. We'll take good care of you."

"No, I know I'm gonna die, Fiona. I just want to tell you I'm so happy to see you again. I always thought about you and missed you. Please stay with me a while."

duties. When she returned his eyes were opened.

"Fiona, I never wanted to leave Chambersburg, but my father insisted and then the war came. He was proud when I joined the Confederate Army. All I ever wanted was for him to be proud of me. That's the only reason I helped him catch slaves. I know you didn't like it."

"Well, that's all over now," she replied. She took his hand and said, "We just need to get you better."

He looked at her and whispered, "No, I just want to say good-by. I love you Fiona." His hand slipped from hers and he was gone.

Her anguish knew no bounds and she cried with great hacking sound. "Poor, poor boy," she sobbed. She cried for all the poor boys this war had taken.

Mrs. Ritner and Helga reacted the same way when she told them about Ralph. They remembered him as that annoying boy always hanging over the fence: a boy who was only looking for acceptance.

Mrs. Ritner was asked if she could supply some bread and coffee. She was thankful that she had that barrel of flour in the larder and went home and began baking. She supplied the hospital with bread each day. Supplies began coming into town again and Mr. Adamson was able to acquire more flour.

The town bells rang once again with the news that Vicksburg had fallen. Fiona's thoughts were of Trip. She had a faint hope that he would be sent to Gettysburg where so many doctors were needed.

Fiona spent a great deal of time at the hospital. She gained experience and assisted Dr. Senseny in many ways. She sat with a young soldier with a severe wound just above the knee. The bone was fractured and he was in great pain. She cringed when the doctor said it would have to be amputated. The doctor asked her to stay with him and she said yes, but she wasn't sure if she would be able to handle it. She thanked God that they did have a little morphine on hand and the doctor administered it. The young man slept through most of the operation, but it was a horrific sight to behold. Fiona thought constantly of Trip and felt that the work she was doing somehow assisted him.

Reports came that Lee had crossed the Potomac at Williamsport. Mead had not pursued him. The war would go on.

The newspapers were full of retribution toward Mead for letting the rebels go. Several generals were quoted in their messages to Mead after Lee's retreat. Pleasonton minced no words.

"I will give you half an hour to show your self as a great general. Order the army to advance, while I take the cavalry and get in Lee's rear and we will finish the campaign in a week."

Mead's reply was "How do you know Lee will not attack again? We have done enough."

The same papers also had stories of the horrors of Gettysburg. They called it the greatest battle ever fought in the western hemisphere, with the greatest number of casualties. The people of Chambersburg knew full well of the horrors. The endless wagon loads of wounded passing through their town, the horrific reports from Gettysburg of bodies rotting in the sun, the wounded taken in and lying on the floors of every building and home in that town, were all too familiar.

One evening after reading all this, Mr. Adamson put down the paper and said, "Perhaps we have done enough."

# Chapter Eighteen

The hard work of the aftermath of war consumed the people of Chambersburg and Gettysburg. Care for the wounded and the burial of the dead were the chief priorities. The people of Gettysburg were left with an overwhelming task. Work crews were dispatched from Chambersburg to help with the burial of the rotting corpses. They were buried in shallow graves near where they lay. Horses were burned in great piles. Volunteers returned to Chambersburg with tales of a devastated land of horror where a terrible stench hung over that sad place.

Temporary hospitals were set up in churches, public buildings, and tents in Gettysburg. Houses were filled with wounded both Confederate and Union. They were laid out on the floors of homes side by side. Help from many places would come later, but for those first few days, the awful task was left in the hands of the people of Gettysburg.

Fiona had a letter from Trip. He wrote of the surrender of Vicksburg on the Fourth of July the day after the Union victory at Gettysburg. "We now have control of the Mississippi," he rejoiced. Her hopes of him coming to help at Gettysburg were dashed. He was now in Chattanooga with Grant's army.

Work at the King Street Hospital in Chambersburg went on. Fiona, Helga and her sisters were there everyday. Fiona had grown attached to one rebel officer who was gravely ill. His name was Colonel Richard Boyd and as he proudly boasted, his unit was the 10th Georgia Infantry. He was a philosophical man and he and Fiona had some interesting conversations.

"Oh, Fiona, some of our best and brightest southern men fought here and now most of them are gone," he sighed as a tear ran down his cheek. "You know, I was amazed when we first passed into Pennsylvania. It is such a green and beautiful land of plenty. I now realize that you in the North have unlimited recourses and man power. We can never win."

They never spoke of politics or slavery. Most of their conversations were about their families. When he spoke of his wife and children his eyes would mist up again. Sometimes he asked Fiona to pray with him. One day he asked her to sing a hymn for him. He loved the old protestant hymns of his childhood. Fiona smiled and remembered the hymn she used to sing in the Ritners parlor and began.

*Shall we gather by the river,*
*The beautiful, beautiful river;*
*Gather with the saints at the river*
*That flows by the throne of God.*

Colonel Boyd smiled and closed his eyes. Fiona kept singing quietly until he fell asleep. When she came back the next day, Doctor Senseny was walking away from his bed. He just shook his head. She sat down and took the Colonel's hand.

He looked at her and smiled faintly, "Thank you kindly for all you have done for me, sweet Fiona. I don't have much longer. I fear that they won't give me a Christian burial. I'm in enemy territory. What will they do with me?"

"Don't worry, Sir. We are good people here. We will take care of you."

After the Colonel's death, Fiona was shocked at the reaction of some of the so called good people of Chambersburg. The rebel dead were being buried in a mass grave outside of town. Several churches had turned down her request for the burial in their graveyards. Finally, the Reverend Burnett at the Methodist Church said the Colonel could have a place in the far corner of their graveyard. Fiona, her father, Helga and Mrs. Ritner were there. Father Mahoney came and gave a blessing. Fiona grieved for her friend buried so far from home. She thought of dear Hans also buried in a foreign place and cursed the cruelty of war.

There seemed to be no end to the cruelty of the war. Next came news of the horrific draft riots in New York. Tom McKenna was heartbroken by the actions of his fellow Irishmen.

"The Irish always resented the coloreds. They competed with them for jobs and housing. When the war came, the Irish were keen ta join up and prove themselves as Americans. But the war went on and on and so many killed and some lost heart. Then the Emancipation came and they didn't like the idea of fighting for the coloreds. The draft made it a poor man's war. The rich could pay but the poor had to go. But nothing excuses what they did. It was a horrible thing they did, burning a colored orphanage. For the first time in my life, I'm ashamed of being Irish."

Fiona sympathized, "I know Da, it gives me great pain too, but you can't blame an entire people for the crimes of a drunken mob."

A few days later, the mail brought more news of the war's cruelty. There was a letter from the mother of Fiona's friend Jim Thompson (her Sandy).

*Peck's Beach, New Jersey*
*July 15, 1863*

*Dear Fiona,*

*It is my sad duty to tell you of the death of my dear son James Thompson Jr. He was killed in Chancellorsville in May. I just received a box of his belongings with your treasured letters. He spoke of you often in his letters to me. Thank you for all of your kindnesses to Jim. I know he thought very highly of you.*

*Best regards,*
*Anna Thompson (Mrs. James Sr.)*

Fiona looked up with tears in her eyes to see Helga standing there looking distressed. She had just returned from getting her family settled back on the farm.

Fiona was very happy to see her friend. She pleaded, "Helga please come with me. I need to go for a walk."

They walked to their favorite spot next to the falls. Fiona told her about Sandy's death and her anguish over the war. Helga talked of her own anguish at seeing the destruction of her home.

"Our dear old farm is such a sad place. They took all the cows and horses and trampled the crops in the field. The house and barn are still standing, but with much damage."

"Oh, Helga, I'm so sorry for you and your family, first losing Hans, and now this. How will you survive?"

"Oh, we will survive. That's what Hans would have wanted. Papa had losses before, but he always comes back. We're not as bad off as some of our friends. The Trostle farm down the Emmitsburg Road was right in the line of battle. They had to flee for their lives. There was a battle right in their yard. They returned to find hundreds of dead horses everywhere and a great cannon hole in the stone barn and bullet holes all over the house."

Fiona took Helga's hand and sighed, "Yes, we'll all survive."

Helga pulled a letter from her pocket, "I had a letter from Joe. That's good news," she said. She went on to read:

> *When they got news that Lee was headed for the Shenandoah Valley, we were sent to join General John Dix's army headed for Richmond. When our home was being threatened we were sent to threaten Richmond. As usually we failed. We had the advantage of a large force at their doorstep. But it took ten days for Dix to get all the troops and supplies assembled and we lost the advantage.*

Helga stopped reading and said, "I'm afraid he uses some cuss words here describin' what happened." Then she blushed and said, "The rest is just for me."

Fiona laughed and said, "Thank God Joe is all right and let's be thankful our troops weren't at Gettysburg in that awful slaughter."

Helga jumped up and said, "Let's go wade in the creek."

They pulled off their shoes and stockings and waded in. They screamed and splashed and laughed. They were little girls again just having fun. They dried off and walked home arm in arm. Fiona decided to send her letters from Sandy to his mother and hoped they would bring her some comfort.

October brought news of General Grant's appointment as commander of all operations in the western theatre. Fiona remembered Trip's description of him in a letter:

> I saw General Grant passing by several times. There is no distinction about him. He sits on his horse a bit slumped over. His uniform is not neat and he wears an ordinary soft black hat. However, he has a look of great determination. I think he is a man of great will power and will lead us to victory.

In another letter, Trip wrote of his future plans:

> I think there will be a great western expansion after the war. What would you think of me staying in the army and going west? As an officer, I could take my wife with me. I think we could do some good out there. I know you have always been interested in the Indians. Perhaps we could set up a medical clinic to treat the Indians. It would be a great adventure to see the West.

Fiona wrote back immediately that she would love to. She always wanted to see the West and was excited at the prospect.

There was more great excitement with the announcement that President Lincoln was coming to Gettysburg to dedicate the new National Cemetery on November 19th. Fiona and her father were determined to see him. They hitched Roisin to the wagon early that morning and joined throngs of people on the road to Gettysburg. They passed the town square, where Lincoln was staying at the home of David Willis, and headed down the road to the cemetery. Tom then pulled over and waited along the road for Lincoln's party to pass by.

It was cold and damp, but everyone was in a festive mood, excited to see the president. They finally saw the beginning of the procession coming down the road and there was Lincoln seated on a horse. To Fiona he looked a comic figure on the small horse. In his stovetop hat, he towered over the horse and his long legs were close to the ground. Fiona thought, *Why didn't they get him a carriage or a bigger horse?* He bowed and tipped his hat to the cheers of the people. When he got close, Fiona felt that he looked right at her with a modest smile on his careworn face.

After the procession passed, they joined the crowd headed for the cemetery. All along there were traces of the great battle. They saw destroyed barns and houses, rifle pits and broken fences. And strewn over the ground were pieces of wagons, canteens, and scraps of clothing both grey and blue.

It took a long time for the great throng to reach the cemetery, but when they arrived Edward Everett, the principle orator, was still speaking. He went on for two hours. Finally, President Lincoln stood up to speak. Fiona and Tom were far back in the crowd and could barely see that tall figure on the stand. He did not have the ringing tones of Everett the great orator and they could not catch every word. When he stopped speaking there was a great silence. People didn't realize the speech was over, but when they did there was a thunderous applause. Fiona and Tom stood in awe. They knew that they had heard something magnificent.

All the way home, snatches of the speech drifted through Fiona's thoughts, *These dead shall not have died in vain...a new birth of freedom.* That evening in the parlor, Mr. Adamson read the entire speech from the newspaper and Fiona hoped she would be able to tell her grandchildren that she had been there to hear it.

Trip had been with Grant's army during the successful Chattanooga Champaign. The Union now had control of the Gateway to the lower South. He wrote:

> *Those battles were horrific and we treated thousands of wounded and buried many dead. When our Chaplin asked*

*General Thomas if the dead should be buried by state he replied, "Mix 'em up, I'm tired of states rights." We're all very tired my darling.,*

In Chambersburg, folks were trying to get back to normal after the momentous events of the past few months. The boarding house was busy again with families visiting the wounded and travelers from everywhere coming to the Gettysburg battlefield. Fiona found it hard to understand why anyone would want to see that place of death.

Mr. and Mrs. Flood were staying in town and Tom and Liam were very busy trying to scavenge what was left of the farm. They were back and forth to town a lot, and Tom always managed to call on Kate and Liam always found time to be with Bridie.

Fiona wondered to Helga, "You know something? I think they are both courting."

Her thoughts were confirmed one day when Da asked her to meet him at Kate Gormley's house. When she entered the house, Da and Kate were sitting side by side. He stood up and announced there was something he wanted to tell her.

"Fiona, my darlin' girl, I have asked Kate to be me wife. I hope it will make you happy. "

She screamed with joy and said, "Oh, it makes me very happy. It's about time." And she hugged and kissed them both. "It will make it a little easier to leave you now that you have each other."

Thomas McKenna beamed at his two girls and said, "I'm just a slow mover. This wonderful woman was here all along and I was too blind to see."

He then asked Fiona to sit down and went on to tell her of their plans. .He and Liam had been thinking of buying up some of Judge Flood's land and starting a horse farm. "I have some money saved and Liam will be getting his pension from the government. We can put some money down an' we're hopein' ta get a loan for the rest. Liam wants ta buy some horses for a start. He'll be here soon and can tell ya the rest."

Just then Liam and Bridie came in the door hand and hand. They had made no announcement, but they were obviously a couple now. Liam made an elaborate bow and announced to Fiona, "Yur Da and me are gonna make millions."

Hattie was standing in the kitchen doorway all this time and said, "Dis calls for a celebration."

She returned with a tray of wine and cookies and they all sat down. Fiona was full of questions. When were they getting married? Where was Liam going to buy horses? The answers came back: the weddings would be soon. Liam was going to scout the county looking for the best horses. Bridie would keep working for Mrs. Flood until the deal on the land went through. They couldn't aggravate Mrs. Flood.

Fiona's next question was, "Is this a good time to keep horses when the rebs could come through anytime and steal them?"

Tom chimed in, "We'll only be startin' wit a few. If the rebs come again, we hope ta get a warnin, an hide them in the woods like you did with our Roisin when Stuart's men came. And you can stand in the road an charm the troops again."

"Oh, grand plans indeed." Fiona said with a laugh.

Liam took the floor. "Fiona, I don't wanna breed just any horses. I want to raise thoroughbred racin' horses. They just opened a race course in Saratoga, New York. That's where the good horses will be. Some day I wanna go up there an talk ta people. I had some experience in Ireland wit racers. I know what ta look for."

Liam added, "It'll be a long time afor we can make any money on the horses. Meantime we'll plant crops and raise chickens on the land."

"Chickens!" Fiona exclaimed.

Later when Tom was walking Fiona home he put his arm around her and asked. "I hope you're all right with all this. I wanted to have somtin' of me own to offer Kate and Liam has his ambitions. We all have our dreams."

"Oh, Da, I love you and want only your happiness. I just worry that Liam knows what he's doing. I hope all your dreams come true."

December brought cold weather and fewer visitors. Things were quiet in the Ritner house again. One day the quiet was shattered by a banging on the front door. It was the boy from the telegraph office saying there was a telegraph message for Fiona McKenna at the office.

Fiona pulled on her coat with her mind racing. *Who would send a telegraph message to her? Had something happened to Trip?*

Almost out of breath, she arrived at the telegraph office not even realizing that Helga was right behind her. She ran up to the counter and gave her name. The clerk gave her a piece of paper with a message written on it.

*Miss Fiona McKenna, Son David critical. Wants to see you. Please come Philadelphia soon as possible. Have arranged money for fare from Chambersburg bank issued to you. William Walters Sr.*

She sunk down in the nearest chair and handed the paper to Helga. "I don't understand. Why do they want me? Should I go?"

"You have to go. It sounds like the boy is dying. He wants to see you. They want ya to come. There sendin' money. I'm not sure how."

In a trance, Fiona walked back to the house with Helga. She was glad to see Mr. Adamson and showed him the message. He read it and asked if she wanted to go. She suddenly remembered Davey's sweet face and replied that she did.

Mr. Adamson took her to the bank where they were told that Mr. William Walters of Philadelphia had arranged a payment of five dollars for Miss Fiona McKenna. She signed a paper and they gave her a five dollar US National Bank Note. It was a green back. She had never seen one before. They then went to the depot and bought a ticket for the next day.

Mr. Adams said, "It's lucky that the army has the tracks repaired. They are very much needed for the transfer of supplies. And for Miss

Fiona to get to Philadelphia," he said with a smile. On the way back he stopped, "We should send a telegram to Mr. Walters and tell him what time you will be arriving tomorrow."

With that accomplished, Fiona said, "Thank you for your help, Mr. Adamson; I had no idea what to do. I have to stop at Mrs. Gormley's and ask her to let my father know. I'll see you at the house"

As soon as Kate opened the door, Fiona fell into her arms. All of her anguish about David, seeing the Walters, not knowing what to expect and wondering if Trip knew, poured out of her.

Kate sat her down and put her arm around her. She knew all about Fiona and Trip's plan to marry and his family's objections and said, "You know my dear, the unfortunate illness of poor David may bring some good to you. He cares for you and wants to see you. They must realize that you're a good person and they'll want to make him happy."

"Oh, I just want to get there in time to see Davey. That's all I'm going to think about."

When Fiona arrived in Philadelphia, Mr. Walters was waiting at the station. He answered her questioning look with, "Our beloved boy is still with us and he is waiting anxiously for you. Thank you for coming. It means a great deal to Mrs. Walters and me."

Tim the coachman was waiting for them. He tipped his hat and said, "Hello Miss McKenna," with a smile and a slight wink.

Mr. Walters looked tired and worn and his hair was greyer, but he still had that same kindly look about him. He told her that they had sent a telegraph message to Trip's commanding officer, but had not received a reply. When they arrived at the house, Mr. Walters helped Fiona down from the carriage. She stood there and hesitated unsure of where to go. He took her arm and guided her to the front door.

# Chapter Nineteen

Fiona walked into the stately hall, and for a moment, felt Trip's presence there. He was dancing her round and round the hall and whispering in her ear. She was startled by a voice and turned to see Billings the butler saying, "May I take your coat, Miss?"

She murmured, "Thank you."

Mr. Walters said, "We'll go up to David's room now."

She followed slowly and unsurely, thinking, *This is a very different reception from last time.* When they reached David's room, and she saw him lying on the bed so still and white, all other thoughts went out of her head. She ran right up to him and took his hand.

"Davey, Davey, my dear boy, I'm here."

He looked up at her and smiled, "Oh, Fiona, I knew you would come. I so wanted to see you."

She was startled to hear a voice from the other side of the room. "That's the first time he smiled in days."

She turned to see Mrs. Walters sitting there and jumped up. "I'm sorry I didn't see you ma'am."

She got up and said, "That's all right, Fiona. He's been waiting for you. I'll leave you alone for a while." She went out and closed the door.

Fiona gasped in amazement, but soon turned to Davey. "Oh, Davey, how are you?"

"Better now that you're here. You want to know something funny? Now that I'm dying they want to grant my every wish."

"No, no." she replied

Eileen Dougherty Troxell

"It's all right Fiona; I just want to leave everyone happy. I told them that you and Trip want to get married and that's what I want too. I think they'll come around."

Darkness came and a maid came in to light the lamps. Fiona kept by his side and they talked of Trip and the wonderful times they had. He had to pause to catch his breath now and then and she waited. He asked her about Chambersburg and everyone there. Mr. and Mrs. Walters drifted in and out of the room like ghosts. He finally dropped off to sleep with a slight smile on his face.

Mrs. Walters came in with a nurse and said, "Fiona, this is Nurse Watson. She will stay with David for the night. You must be tired. I'll show you to your room." Fiona followed her down the hall to a lovely bed room. Mrs. Walters showed her in and said, "Mr. Walters and I have already eaten dinner. We didn't want to disturb your time with David. I'll have a maid bring you a supper tray." She smiled stiffly and left.

Fiona looked around and saw that her bags had been unpacked and her clothing hung in the wardrobe. The maid soon arrived with the tray. Fiona didn't recognize her from the last time. She must have been new. She set up a small table and chair and left.

Fiona had just finished eating when there was a knock at the door. She said, "come in" and Mr. Walters entered.

"Good evening, Fiona, I hope I'm not disturbing you?" he said as he stood in the doorway."

"Not at all, please come in and sit down. Thank you for your kind hospitality."

He took a chair next to her and began. "We thank you for coming. I can see how happy you have made David."

"I love him and would do anything for him. May I ask, sir, is there no hope?"

"No, my dear, I'm afraid not. We have had the finest doctors in Philadelphia on his case. His lungs were damaged from his wounds. My son William has told us that he would have not have lived as long as he did were it not for the excellent care the people gave him in Chambersburg."

She began to cry and he put his arm around her. "I can see that you are tired. We'll talk in the morning."

The next morning, Fiona awoke with a start, unsure of where she was. She looked around the strange room and remembered. Her first thought was of David. She got up and was glad to see there was a commode. She washed at the basin and dressed in a clean skirt and waist. She had started down the hall when she encountered Mr. Walters in front of David's room.

"Good morning, Fiona." he greeted her. "The nurse is bathing him right now. Please come down and have breakfast with us."

She followed him down to the breakfast room where Mrs. Walters was seated at the table. She looked up and said. "Good morning. Breakfast is laid out on the buffet. Please help yourself."

With trembling hands, Fiona poured a cup of coffee, put a biscuit on a plate and joined them at the table. After Mrs. Walters's polite enquiries of how she had slept, Mr. Walters began to speak.

"Fiona, David and William have both spoken very highly of you. I consider both of them very good judges of character. David has told us that William has asked you to marry him."

Fiona paused and said, "Yes, he did, and I love him very much, but I asked him to wait and keep it a secret. I am vey much aware of the difference in our stations in life and can see there will be problems. Before he went away we met in Chambersburg and he asked my father for my hand. My father consented, but he also is very aware of the problems we face."

Mrs. Walters turned and for the first time looked directly at Fiona, "David asked us to consider the possibility of the marriage and we could not refuse him. We will do that for his sake. Our only wish is the happiness of both of our sons."

The nurse then appeared in the doorway with the news that the patient was asking for all of them. The three sat with him all morning and into the afternoon. He was growing weaker and his speech did not come as easily. Later, they heard a disturbance downstairs and footsteps running up the stairs. The door burst open and Trip ran in. As soon as Fiona saw his dear face, she wanted to run to him, but she held back. He went to his mother first and kissed her. He shook hands with his father then gave him a great bear hug.

He then turned to Fiona and enfolded her in his arms and whispered, "Oh my darling, I'm so glad you're here." She felt his strength go through her body.

They surrounded David's bed and his pale tired face beamed at them. "I'm so happy. Everyone I love is here," he whispered.

In the evening, the doctor came and examined him. He asked to see William and his father in the hall. Fiona and Mrs. Walters looked at each other across the bed and knew what he was telling them. They stayed at David's bedside all night and just as the sun was rising, he opened his eyes.

He looked at each one of them individually and whispered, "I love you." Then he said in a strong voice, "Mother and father, don't forget your promise."

And he was gone.

The next few days passed in a blur for Fiona. The house was busy with preparations, for the funeral. She had nothing to wear and Mrs. Walters had the seamstress alter a black gown of hers. Trip sent a telegraph message to her father and Mrs. Ritner to tell them of David's death. The funeral was held at St. Marks's Episcopal Church on Locus Street near Rittenhouse Square. Fiona was impressed with the beautiful church and found the service very similar to a Catholic mass. Trip sat right next to her and held her hand.

He whispered that his father's family were originally Quakers, but found it more fashionable to be Episcopalians.

After the burial there was a luncheon at the house. Fiona was introduced as the nurse who took care of David after he was wounded.

Mrs. Morris took her hand and said, "I know you are much more than David's nurse, dear."

Trip introduced her as his fiancé to his best friend Sam Cadwalader. Sam was on leave from the Philadelphia Brigade. They had been at Gettysburg. "Sam and his boys were waiting on the top of the hill when Pickett's men came charging up," Trip later told her.

Trip had to leave in a few days to get back to his unit and Fiona was anxious to get home.

The next day her bags were packed and ready in the hall. Trip stood waiting to take her to the station. When she came down, he told her that his parents wanted to see her in the parlor.

Alone, she entered the parlor. Mr. Walter stood up. "We just wanted to say good bye and wish you a safe journey, Fiona. Please sit down."

Mrs. Walter began, "I feel I must apologize for my past behavior toward you. I know it must be hard for you to understand my feeling of the differences in our positions.

David was very fond of you and I can see that William loves you. I made a promise to David to consider the possibility of the marriage and I will do that."

Mr. Walters broke in. "I think we will do more than consider. Please come and visit us again soon so we can spend more time together."

Fiona got up to leave and Mrs. Walters took her hand, "Fiona, I must say you have conducted yourself like a lady these past few days."

"She is a lady," Mr. Walters interjected as he walked her to the door.

At the station Fiona and Trip clung to each other and hated to let go as the train pulled in. She promised to marry him as soon as the war was over. Trip put her on the train, waved good bye and shouted, "I love you" over and over as the train pulled out.

Her father and Mrs.Gormley were waiting for her at the station in Chambersburg and they wanted to know everything that happened. She told them of the Walters' consent to the marriage. "Well sort of a consent on Mrs. Walter's side, but she is coming around. We will get married after the war no matter what."

Those words kept repeating in her head all the way home. *No matter what anyone says, no matter what happens in the war, Trip will come home and we will be married, no matter what.*

Back at the Ritner house, Fiona repeated her story to Mrs. Ritner, Helga, and Mr. Adamson. They grieved for Davey and remembered that brave boy who stayed with them. They were filled with happiness for Fiona and Trip and wished them well.

As she left the room, Fiona turned to Mrs. Ritner and said, "Mrs. Walters' said that I had conducted myself as a lady. Do you know how I learned to be a lady? I learned by watching you."

Christmas Eve day they had their usual tree trimming party at the Ritner house with Mrs. Ritner, Mr. Adamson, Fiona, Helga and one lone boarder. The boarder, Catherine Henderson, was visiting her son in the hospital. Away from home, she was glad to have some companions for Christmas. They trimmed the tree and sang carols, but it wasn't the same without the girls there. They were greatly missed, but Mrs. Ritner still felt she did the right thing in sending them away.

Helga's father came to pick her up and reported that the farm house was somewhat restored after the damage from the rebel occupation. Fiona wished them all a Merry Christmas and headed for Mrs. Gormley's house. She and her father and Liam and Bridie were spending Christmas with her. They were all family now.

They had a wonderful Christmas Eve. Tom had invited his friend Barney and they all sat around the tree and sang the Irish carols. They sat down to the traditional Christmas Eve dinner of fish with white sauce and potatoes that Kate had prepared. Hattie was spending Christmas at home with Enoch. Bridie surprised everyone by serving a Christmas cake she had made.

"I had to sneak over here yesterday to make it," she explained. "It's me muther's recipe."

"It's delicious," Fiona exclaimed. "I didn't know you were so domesticated."

Later they had a long talk. Bridie was happy that Fiona and Trip were getting married, but she had some advice.

"Don't let them change ya. All this time I've been pretendin' for the ol bat Mrs. Flood. Pretendin' ta be sometin' I'm not has been hard. But it's much harder now that I have Liam and bein' wit all of you, me own kind. I don't know how much longer I can do it."

Mrs. Gormley overheard and chimed in, "I don't know how you do it, Birdie, putting on that British accent. You're like an actress on the stage. "

"Let's hear it," Barney said

Bridie went on for quite a while entertaining them with her proper British accent and decorum. Saying things like, "Ma deaar, I am so vary pleased to meet you" as she performed a perfect curtsy.

"That one should be on the stage," Barney commended.

"Don't worry. I won't change. I'll still be myself," Fiona said, when she stopped laughing.

Through the winter, work at the hospital went on. They still received some wounded, but most of the patients were suffering from diseases. Typhoid, pneumonia, measles, and tuberculosis were the most prevalent. Fiona divided her time between the boarding house and her work at the hospital. In her letters to Trip, she sometimes discussed her cases. He sent her reports that he had received from the Sanitary Commission. They recommended cleanliness, clean water, good food, and fresh air. Things that were hard to come by on the battlefield.

In Chambersburg, the doctors and nurses were trying to provide them. Mrs. Ritner, and many other ladies of the town, helped by providing the good food. Mrs. Henderson, who had stayed at the Ritners as a boarder over Christmas, sent a generous contribution of money to the hospital. "In thankfulness for the recovery of my son and for the wonderful care you gave him."

March brought the news that President Lincoln had appointed General Grant to command all of the armies of the Union. General William Sherman would become Commander in the West. Grant had losses but he was a different kind of general. He kept moving and waging a war of attrition.

Thomas McKenna and Katherine Gormley were married at Corpus Christi Church by Father Mahoney on a beautiful April morning. They walked down the aisle together both radiant in their happiness. Tom wore his best suit and Kate looked lovely in a mauve gown. Fiona was the Maid of Honor and Barney the Best Man. The wedding party and their guests: Liam and Bridie, Mrs. Ritner, Mr. Adamson, and Helga adjourned to the hotel for a wedding breakfast. After the breakfast, Mrs. Ritner invited them back to her house where many toasts were offered. They discussed their plans. Tom would move into Kate's house and travel back and forth to the farm. Liam would stay at the cottage. It was a happy day that they would look back on in the terrible days to come.

May and June brought horrific news of great casualties in the Wilderness, Spotsylvania, and Cold Harbor. But Grant didn't turn back. He kept going. The people of Chambersburg waited for infrequent letters from their loved ones.

After many weeks Helga finally had a letter from Joe informing her, "We are digging holes and livin' in them near Petersburg, Virginia."

Fiona's letters from Trip were even more infrequent. He had been moved from one battle field hospital to another treating the wounded. He tried to be upbeat in his letters, but sometimes he poured out his anguish to her. "I believe the most dreadful thing ever invented is the Minie ball. It causes gaping wounds that soon fill with dirt and pieces of clothing. It cuts a straight path through the body and when it strikes bone it causes it to shatter. Usually the only treatment is amputation. I don't know how many I have done. Please pray for me, my love."

In July there was news that Sherman was attacking Atlanta. That news was soon forgotten by the people of Chambersburg when the war once again came to their doorstep. Confederate General Jubal Early's forces had defeated Union General David Hunter at Lynchburg, Virginia and drove him into West Virginia. General Early sent troops under John McCausland north of the Potomac to capture Hagerstown, Maryland.

Early himself reached the outlying defenses of Washington on July 11th. Union troops were diverted from the Virginia front to save Washington and old Jube withdrew back into Virginia. He had come closer to Washington than any other previous rebel force.

McCausland occupied Hagerstown and demanded a ransom of 20,000 dollars in greenbacks. The ransom was paid and the town spared. McCausland later realized that he had misread Early's orders and missed a digit. Early had specified 200,000 dollars.

Rumors spread that the next target was Chambersburg. On the morning of July 30, 1864, the people of Chambersburg awoke to the sound of cannons. Fiona looked out the attic window and saw Confederate cavalry lined up on the hill west of town. The household gathered in the kitchen and waited, not sure of what was coming next.

Mr. Adamson observed, "They were shooting over the town. It was just a warning. Most of our forces under General Couch have been diverted to Washington. We have no defense. I think Couch did at least slow McCausland's advance. Most of the military supplies and money from the bank were sent out of town." Just then they heard the Court House bells ringing. Mr. Adamson said, "I'll go up and get dressed and go over to see what's going on. The rest of you stay here."

When he came down, they were all dressed and waiting. Fiona said, "We all want to see what's going on."

When they arrived at the Diamond it was filled with Confederate soldiers.

Townspeople stood around the perimeter. Someone told them that McCausland had the bells rung to call fifty of the towns leading men to the square. They saw several men begin to gather on the courthouse steps. Fiona noticed that Judge Flood and Mr. Hoke were among them. General McCausland began reading a statement to them. They could not hear what he was saying. The men disbursed and Mr. Hoke walked toward them.

He looked at Mr. Adamson and said, "They're demanding a ransom of $200,000 (McCausland got the decimal point correct that time) in gold or the equivalent in greenbacks or they will burn the town. You know there is not that amount of money in the bank. We have to see what we can raise."

The reaction of the people of Chambersburg was one of defiance. They had been visited by the rebels before. Jeb Stuart, Jubal Early, and Lee's army had come through. They had robbed and pillaged, but did not destroy the town. They did not take the threat seriously. There was no way they could raise that amount of money in so short a time. The ransom would not be paid. An enraged McCausland read General Early's ultimatum to pay the ransom or burn the town.

They could hear Judge Flood's plea, "The town has no money available to give."

"So be it," was McCausland's reply.

Most of the crowd started to disburse and head for their homes. They wanted to be there to defend them. The Ritner household did the same. Fiona saw her father and Kate across the square heading to their house. She called to them, but they didn't hear her. She could not get to them in the crowd. They all went home and waited.

It started slowly. They had all the windows opened in the heat of the July morning. The heat grew more intense. They then began to smell smoke. They ran out the front door and saw flames shooting up from the Diamond and drew back in horror. Great crashes and screams could be heard. Streams of people were running down the street away from the Diamond.

One man shouted, "They're burning all the buildings around the square. I saw them devils place barrels of kerosene under the stairways of the courthouse. The whole building is aflame. The soldiers are going into houses and looting them before setting the fires. The streets are filled with drunken soldiers."

The crowd surged down Second Street and crossed the creek into Cedar Grove Cemetery away from the falling debris of the buildings. The residents of the Ritner house followed them. Fiona looked back at the house and wondered if she would ever see it again. In the cemetery, they watched in horror as the burning masses converged around the Diamond and a great whirlwind of smoke swirled over Market Street. The children screamed in terror.

Fiona was not sure how long they stayed there sitting on the ground. She held the shaking Helga in her arms and Mr. Adamson sat with his arms around Mrs. Ritner. Fiona looked up to see Liam making his way through the crowd and called to him.

"Liam, Liam, have you seen my father?"

He came over, his face was flushed and sweaty and his clothing was covered in soot. "No, I haven't seen Tom or Bridie. I just come inta town when I heard it was afire.

Had to go this way around the Diamond. Good God, what a sight. Like Hell itself with fallin' walls and blindin' smoke. Never felt such a heat. Are you folks all right?"

They nodded and he fell to the ground beside them. They remained that way for a while. Later people came around with buckets of water from a nearby well. They passed the buckets around and drank greedily from the shared dipper. The next thing Fiona remembered was a man shouting.

"McCausland and his troops are moving out. Averill's troops are on their way from Greencastle."

People stood up and began cheering. The crowd slowly moved in the direction of town, fearful of what they would find. Fiona and the others headed for King Street and were relieved to find the house still standing.

"Thank God they didn't get this far. My home is still here," Mrs. Ritner said with tears in her eyes.

Fiona and Liam were anxious to find their family on the other side of the Diamond and soon headed that way. They were happy to see the King Street Hospital still there, but when they got to the Diamond all was devastation. They had to walk around it. Walls were still falling. The buildings were still smoldering. All they could see were ruins of all those magnificent buildings. The Court House, the bank, the Mansion House, the Franklin Hotel, the Town Hall, the stores; all were smoldering ruins. As they crossed Market Street they could see devastation all along there. Suddenly Barney Carney appeared like a cloud of smoke.

"I been lookin' for yer. The folks are all right," he greeted them. "They burned the Judge's house, but Kate's is saved. They're all there."

"Thank God, Thank God," was all Fiona could say as they saw Kate's house still standing.

Fiona and Liam walked into a scene of chaos. Mrs. Flood sat on the sofa weeping profusely. The Judge was walking up and down shouting profanities. Bridie and Kate stood in a corner laughing and Tom ran up and hugged them.

"Is everybody all right at the Ritners?" he asked. "Is the house still there?"

They reassured him that all was well and asked what was going on there.

"I'll tell you what's going on," the Judge shouted. "Those bastards set my house on fire. We barely escaped with our lives."

"Bridie brought them here," Tom explained. "And thanks to her Kate's house was saved."

"How did mi darling girl save it?" Liam asked.

Tom laughed and said. "When she saw tem coming up ta the house, she grabbed a broom, hit the first greyback over the head and knocked him off the porch. Then she shouted ta me inside to get the gun. Didn't have one, but they didna know that. She said 'If you come near this house you will regret it.' They backed off and moved on."

Liam picked her up and said, "That's me girl!"

Bridie had given up any pretence of her British accent, but Mrs. Flood didn't seem to notice. Tom and Liam went out to scout around and find out what was happening.

Fiona and Bridie got the Floods to calm down. They made coffee and sat around the table.

Mrs. Flood even said "Thank you."

The Judge's face was as ashen as the buildings across the square. His hands shook and he rambled on about his losses. "The house on

Market Street is gone. I already lost much of my stock and crops in the last raid. I find myself in very reduced circumstances. What am I to do?"

Fiona was shocked to see the always confident man in such a state. She tried to comfort him. She looked at him and said "Sir, do you have fire insurance on the house?" He nodded yes and she went on, "They moved the money out of the bank before the rebels came. So you still have your money. "

Bridie chimed in. "Liam and Tom are working very hard ta restore yer fields and they are gonna buy some of yer land. So yer not so bad off."

Both of the Floods looked at her in astonishment. Mr. Flood asked, "Why are you talking like an Irish woman?"

"Because I am an Irish wamen," she replied.

The Floods did not have time to speak as Tom and Liam returned with Barney in tow. They had a grim tale to tell.

All of the buildings around the Diamond as well as most of the properties on Market and Franklin Streets were destroyed. The number of building burned totaled in the hundreds. One exception was the Masonic Temple. The story going around was that McCausland was a Mason and ordered that it be saved. They would have fired the whole town were it not for the news that Averell's Cavalry was on its way. As McCausland moved out, he sent a column to burn the home of School Superintendent Andrew McElwain. McCausland had heard that he taught Negroes.

Tom added, "The church is still standing and Father Mahoney is all right. We checked on Enoch and Hattie. They weren't harmed. Thank God the rebels didn't get over there. I tink they've of burned the whole town were it not for Averell's Cavalry coming. "

Barney went on. "Mr. Miller's Drug Store is gone as well as Mr. Hoke's building and mi friend Daniel Trostle's Hotel. They even got down to the Paper Mill and the Edge Tool Factory." He looked at Mr. Flood and said, "They burned Mr. Trostle's brick building where I have me room. You and me is both homeless, Judge."

The Judge said with a humf, "Hardly, I have another home. Tom will you please take us to the country house?"

Tom replied, "There's still a lot of work to be done there since the raid."

"I don't care. Just get me out of this town."

"Oh yes, yes, let us go," a still shaken Agnes Flood replied and added, "Barbara, please come with me. I need you."

Bridie, shocked at Mrs. Flood needing her and saying please, hesitated. "You know my real name is Bridie and I'm not English."

"I don't care." She replied. "I need you to look after me"

A surprised Bridie (Barbara) accompanied her mistress to what was left of her country home.

# Chapter Twenty

The people of Chambersburg slowly recovered from the devastation of their town. The entire inner core of the proud Diamond had been leveled. They walked through the ruins in disbelief. The great pillars of the bank still stood like the ancient ruins of a Greek temple. All the rest was gone. A pall of smoke from the smoldering ruins hung over the town for days. They took comfort in the fact that there were no fatalities. The exception was an old man, named Daniel Parker, who refused to leave his house, and later died of smoke inhalation.

Some people moved on to other towns, but most stayed. They moved in with friends or relatives and tried to get their lives back together. Some enterprising shop keepers set up open air stalls to sell whatever goods they could get hold of. All too soon fall was upon them and they had to get ready for the approaching winter. Private homes that had survived around Market and North Second Street were turned into shops. Temporary sheds for places of business were set up along Second Street from Queen to King. The bank opened in the first floor of the Masonic Hall. Post Master J. W. Deal operated the Post Office out of his home. In a few years, most buildings would be rebuilt. Chambersburg would rise from the ashes.

And life went on. The Ritner household was busy once again with new boarders. Some were ghoulish sightseers coming to see the ruins. Others were men to work on the construction of new buildings. Fiona, Helga and Mrs. Ritner were busy running the household and nursing at the hospital. The fall of 1864 brought nothing but good news. In September, Sherman's Army captured Atlanta. "Atlanta is ours and fairly won." He telegraphed Lincoln and began his long march to the sea. One good thing came out of McClausland's raid on Chambersburg. Grant finally brought all the scattered Union forces in the Cumberland Valley under one commander, Philip Sheridan. The competent and aggressive Sheridan defeated Jubal Early at Fisher's Hill, Third Winchester and Cedar Creek. By March, all Confederate forces were driven from the Cumberland Valley. All of these victories helped Abraham Lincoln to be re-elected in November. As one pundit put it: "Long Abraham a little longer."

Helga heard from Joe Leiss. He and the Cumberland 43rd Regiment were camped outside Richmond. Fiona had an interesting letter from Trip:

> *I have been sent to Atlanta to check out Sherman's Troops. He is splitting his army for a long march. We must check each man for illness or injury. Those found unfit will be sent back to Nashville with General George Thomas.*

Bridie and Liam were quietly married by Father Mahoney. They didn't care for any fuss. The deal to purchase the land went through for Tom and Liam. Judge Flood was lenient with the terms. Tom and Liam agreed to continue working on his farm and Mrs. Flood wanted Bridie to continue working for her. The events of the past few months convinced the Floods that they needed these people. Bridie and Liam moved into the cottage and Kate and Tom gave Barney a room over the stable. He would be a working partner in their endeavors.

Sherman reached Savannah and offered it to Lincoln as a Christmas present. Everyone in the North felt it was a Christmas present for all of them. Their army was finally winning and the end of the long ordeal was in sight. January brought the good news of the passing of the Thirteenth Amendment to abolish slavery. The people of Lancaster and Franklin Counties took pride in the fact that their own radical Thaddeus Stevens had proposed the Amendment and fought to have it passed.

In February, Fiona received a letter from the Walters inviting her to come and stay with them for a few days. She was sure that Trip had asked them to extend the invitation. She felt very nervous about spending time with Trip's family by herself, but felt she had to go.

"Why don't I go with you as your lady's maid?" Helga volunteered. Fiona laughed and said, "I would love it," she replied. "But they know my circumstances and they certainly know I don't have a maid."

She accepted the invitation, but declined their offer to send her the money for the ticket. She assured them that her father would pay the fare. Mr. Walters met her at the station as usual and greeted her warmly. She looked at him closely and saw that those same kind eyes like Trip's were touched with sorrow. He looked older. The loss of his youngest son had taken a toll. It had been over a year since David's death. He no longer wore a black arm band, but he was still in morning.

When they arrived at the house, Mrs. Walters had tea ready. She looked elegant as she sat pouring the tea. She wore a blue gown that fell in soft folds over her slim form. However, she looked different somehow. The haughtiness was gone from her expression, replaced by a look of sadness. Fiona felt an urge to reach out and comfort her.

Instead they spoke of everyday things. They asked Fiona how things were in Chambersburg. They had been concerned about her and her family. They wanted to know when she had heard from William. Fiona had to remember not to speak of him as Trip. She told them she had brought his last few letters and would read from them later. *Not everything,* she thought, *some of the things he says in his letters are too personal and may shock them.*

A maid came in to clear the tea things and Fiona recognized her from the time she had stayed below stairs. "Hello, Livey," she said in a friendly way.

Livey just smiled and curtseyed. Fiona felt very unsure. She was relieved when Mrs. Walters suggested that she go up to her room and rest. Livey showed her to her room. It was the same one she had stayed in when Davey died. The memory brought tears to her eyes.

"You all right Miss?" Livey asked

"Yes, just a little sad, thinking of Mr. David," she answered.

"We all miss him." Livey answered. "He was a darlin', boy. "

Fiona asked Livey to sit down and asked, "How is everyone downstairs? I'm sure they're all abuzz about me staying upstairs."

"Indeed they are, Miss. They're sayin' you'r gonna marry Mr. William. Is that true?"

"Yes, he has asked me. It will probably be after the war."

"Good, this house needs sometin' happy. It's been a sad place. I must go now Miss."

Fiona had seen the sadness in both of David's parents and wished she could do something to comfort them. Fiona rested and read until another maid came in to light the lamp and announced.

"You're expected in the drawing room, Miss. There is company for dinner."

Fiona dressed for dinner in her best blue gown and went downstairs. She was surprised to find Mrs. Morris alone in the drawing room.

She got up and took her hand, "Fiona, I am so glad you are here. I'm very worried about both of my friends, Augusta and William. They've kept to themselves since David's death. This is the first time they invited me or anyone for dinner. I hope you can help them."

"Oh, Mrs. Morris, what can I do?"

"I'm not sure, but I think just your being here will help."

Just then, Mr. and Mrs. Walters entered the room and they talked of other things. The dinner was pleasant and they talked of the Great Sanitary Fair that had been held on Logan Square in June.

Mrs. Morris exclaimed, "The crowds were enormous and we raised a great deal of money to buy bandages and medicine for the troops."

"Oh yes, I read about the fair," Fiona replied. She turned to Mrs. Walters and said, "It must have been wonderful."

She just shook her head and said, "We sponsored one of the booths. I wasn't up to going."

After dinner, Fiona read to them from some of her letters from Trip. He talked about Davey a lot in his letters and she could see how it affected Mrs. Walters. She seemed eager to hear anything about her son. But Mr. Walters looked away and changed the subject.

At the end of the evening, they wished Mrs. Morris good night and Mr. Walters said, "We must have company more often. We've been to ourselves too long."

He excused himself and went up to bed. Mrs. Walters lingered and invited Fiona to join her in a night cap.

She poured them some wine from the tray and they sat in silence for a while.

Finally, Fiona turned to her and said. "How are you doing? I can see that you have been having a hard time since David's death?"

Fiona was startled when the always proper Mrs. Walters collapsed in uncontrollable sobs. She took her in her arms and tried to comfort her. It took a long while for the sobs to ease up.

Fiona kept saying over and over, "I'm so sorry, I didn't need t upset you."

"No no," she answered. "I needed that." She sat up and dried her eyes with a handkerchief. "It's been so long. My husband's way of getting over our son's death is by not talking about it. We've just been going through the motions of life since then. It's like he never existed. Hearing you read William's words about David made me feel like he was still here. I need to talk about him."

"Of course you do. He was a wonderful boy. He brought a great deal of joy to your life and you'll always have that. You can always remember the good times."

They had another glass of wine and spoke of David. Mrs. Walters even laughed when she told Fiona about some of his antics as a boy. Fiona was enjoying the conversation and for the first time felt at ease with Mrs. Walters. However, she was feeling the effect of the wine and had trouble keeping her eyes open.

Mrs. Walters noticed, "Oh, my dear, it's been a long day for you. I'm sorry for keeping you up." She stood up and said, "You must go to bed."

Fiona stood up and did not hesitate to embrace her, "You must talk to Mr. Walters and explain how you feel. He is a good man. I think he will understand."

"You are right, Fiona. I will do that. Good night."

As tired as she was Fiona could not sleep. Thoughts of death and its effect on people kept turning over in her mind. She thought of her father and how he mourned her mother. He had talked about her somewhat when Fiona was young, but not a lot. He found it too painful. Suddenly, she remembered the night Liam first came to them. He had brought letters that Tom had written to his sister in Ireland about his family in America. Tom read the letters to them and Fiona remembered: *He read the letters, telling of his marriage to Kathleen, their happy times together and the birth of their daughter. He read aloud, but it was almost like he was reading to himself. Sometimes he would stop and the tears would flow. He read of his pride in taking care of his little family and finally of his Kathleen's tragic death from Tuberculosis. Fiona realized that was a healing time for him that enabled him to get on with his life and marry Kate.*

Fiona also thought of Helga's mother and her inability to talk about her son. She hoped that Mrs. Meyers would some day get past that. Fiona thought *we need to cherish the memory of our loved ones. In that way they will always be with us.*

When Fiona came down the next morning, the breakfast room was empty. Charlie the footman came in and asked if she wanted coffee.

As he poured, he said, "It's good to see you again, Fiona. The Mr. and Mrs. are not down yet. Help yourself to the breakfast on the buffet. You must come and visit us downstairs. You're all the talk you know. "

"I will, Charlie," she answered.

She finished eating and wondered what to do next. She sat and read the newspaper for a while. She was just about to leave and go back to her room, when the two Walters walked in arm and arm.

"Good morning," Mrs. Walters said, "I'm sorry we were not here to join you for breakfast."

Fiona noticed a change in both of them. Mrs. Walters looked almost radiant and he looked at peace. They helped themselves to the food and joined her at the table.

Mr. Walters spoke first. "Fiona, we both want to thank you for doing us a great service. You got us to talk about our feelings and David's death. It made me realize I was wrong in suppressing his memory. Somehow, I thought it would be two painful for both of us."

226

"There is no need to thank me, Sir. I can see you both worked it out on your own. I hope you can find comfort in dear David's memory."

Mr. Walters took his wife's hand and said, "Gussie and I talked all night. Something we haven't done in a long time."

Fiona smiled. She had never heard him refer to her as Gussie before.

Mrs. Walters laughed. "They used to call me Gussie as a young girl. After we were married, I didn't think it was proper. I worried a lot about what was proper."

"You did my dear," he answered. "I failed you there too, by not reassuring that if you would just be yourself, people would accept you."

Augusta turned to Fiona and said, "I was so afraid of losing my place in society. That meant everything to me. I realized that it was nothing after David died. Fiona, I'm so sorry for the way I treated you. I saw you as a threat to my standing. Please forgive me."

Fiona got up and kissed her and said, "Of course I do. I never blamed you. I love Trip and I know I will love his parents." She hesitated and added, "Sorry for calling him Trip."

They both laughed and Mrs. Walter said, "It is much less regal than William the Third."

Fiona was surprised when they started talking about plans for their wedding. Mr. Walters started with, "Fiona, there is something you don't know. Trip has been writing to me about becoming Catholic. He wanted to surprise you. He has been taking lessons with the Catholic Chaplin he's been serving with."

"He didn't have to do that," she gasped.

"He wanted to do it for you," his mother replied. "William has always had a deep faith and I think the Catholic religion appeals to him. He always said we were just social Episcopalians," she said with a smile.

"So you and Trip can get married in your church either here or in Chambersburg. It's up to you." Mr. Walters added. "If you got married here, the Drexels would probably be the only ones to come. They're the only Catholics."

Augusta interrupted. "Stop teasing, Will, you know William would not want a big society wedding."

There was another subject that Fiona hesitated to bring up. That of Trip's plans to stay in the army and go out west. She didn't want to cause them anymore pain. They had lost one son and the other had been away for a very long time. The thought of Trip going out west and another separation would be too painful.

However they weren't surprised. Mr. Walters said that Trip had hinted at something like that.

And Mrs. Walters said, "I always knew that William would not stay here and be a society doctor." She turned to Fiona and asked, "How do you feel about it?"

"I can't wait. It will be a great adventure," she replied.

"Well, then that's it," Mr. Walters concluded.

Fiona was amazed at how easy it was to talk with her future in-laws now. They took her for a carriage ride in the afternoon and stopped for lunch at a fashionable restaurant. They were greeted by several friends and all expressed that they were happy to see them out again. Fiona was introduced as Young William's fiancée. If any of them were shocked, they didn't show it.

Fiona thought, *It's almost as if the Walters are saying this is our son's intended and you can like it or not.* She had to smile.

Before she went home, Fiona had to descend the stairs to greet the servants. In a way, that was harder than meeting the high society folks. These people were her kind, but she was afraid they would feel some resentment toward her. She knew that there was sometimes a reverse snobbery. However, as soon as she entered the servant's hall, she was received with excitement.

Lizzie the kitchen maid ran right up and gave her a great hug. "Yer gonna be a great lady, Miss, I'm proud ta know ya."

Tim the coachmen exclaimed, "It's a great day for the Irish. How's Bridie?"

"She married my cousin."

"Awe, it's a sad day for the lads round here."

The others gathered around and offered their congratulations. Mrs. Brighton the cook invited her to sit down and have tea with them. Even Billings the butler offered his stiff congratulations. Fiona was amazed at the knowledge of the below stairs staff. They knew that Fiona was not a lady's maid, but a boarding house maid, that the young master of the house was turning Catholic, that all of Philadelphia society knew of the coming wedding, and that the master and mistress of the house were doing much better since Fiona came. She pondered, *if you want to know what's going on in a household, just ask the servants.*

Mrs. Travers the housekeeper was the exception to the enthusiasm. She made her appearance just as Fiona was getting up to leave. She took Fiona aside and said, "I must warn you that a boarding house maid like you will never be able to perform the duties of mistress of this house or take your place in society."

Fiona pulled away and replied, "To tell you the truth, I haven't thought that far ahead, but I will be Mrs. William Walters the Third. Thank you and good day, Mrs. Travers."

# Chapter Twenty-One

When Fiona arrived back in Chambersburg, she felt a difference. She had only been gone for a week, but the town looked cleaner. Most of the rubble had been cleared away and the winds of March had blown away the acrid smell of smoke. Some of the new buildings were rising and the spirits of the people were rising with them.

In her own family, she also found spirits high. Tom and Liam were hard at work on their farm. They were getting the fields ready for planting the spring crops of cabbage, corn, onions and peas. Liam and Bridie were settled in their cottage and Bridie was thrilled to have a home of her own for the first time. After working out a deal with Mrs. Flood, she was able to go to her own home at night.

"It wasn't easy," she told Fiona. "The ol' biddie depends on me for everything. Ever since they burnt the house, she's been a little crazy. I'm the only one can calm her."

Tom and Kate were also settled in their house and it was truly theirs. Kate's house was transformed with Tom's presence. It was no longer the house of a lonely widow, but the home of a happy couple. And Barney was comfortably installed in rooms over the stable.

April brought the good news that Lee had evacuated Petersburg and Union troops had raised the stars and stripes in Richmond. Sunday April 9th had been a quiet day. That evening, the residents of the Ritner house had gone to bed with high hopes. Victory was in sight. They were aroused from their beds by shooting guns and ringing bells. They rushed into the street to hear shouts of "Lee has surrendered."

"Thank God, thank God," they all prayed. The ruined town erupted in joy. People stood on piles of bricks and gave speeches. Others danced and hugged. Many brought out bottles and offered toasts "The Union is saved and the war is over," was the resounding cry.

For women like Fiona and Helga, the cry was, "Our boys are coming home." They hoped it would be soon, but it would be a long process. It would be months before Joe was mustered out. Fiona only hoped that Trip would get leave when he re-enlisted. They needed time to get married and then they would begin their great adventure out west.

Helga and Joe had their plans. Joe had worked at the tool factory before the war. The factory was destroyed in the fire and had not yet re-opened. Helga's father offered them a small cottage on the farm. It was where he and his wife had lived when they were first married. Joe would help on the farm, but also use his mechanic skills to repair tools. He had dreams of starting his own repair business.

A week later, Fiona and Helga were sitting at the kitchen table still in a blissful mood and talking of there plans for their future. They looked up and Mr. Adamson was in the doorway. His face was white with a stricken look.

"What's wrong?" Fiona asked.

"They have killed the President," he pronounced.

They all reacted with horror. It was a death in the family. Father Abraham was dead. They later heard all the horrendous details. He was shot right in front of his wife while attending a play. The actor John Wilkes Booth was the assassin.

The Burgess of Chambersburg issued a proclamation that all businesses should be closed. Church bells tolled all day. That night Fiona cried herself to sleep, remembering the day of the dedication of the Gettysburg Cemetery. Lincoln had passed right by her and she remembered the sad smile on his careworn face. She spent the next day with her family and they attended a special mass for the president. Father Mahoney prayed that "Mr. Lincoln would at last find peace."

By the next day most buildings were draped in black and Chambersburg, with the rest of the nation, went into a period of deep mourning. They read of Lincoln's funeral and the capture and death of Booth. The long train ride that carried the body of the slain president stopped at major cities and then at last took him home to Springfield, Illinois.

The joy of Lee's surrender was replaced by the sorrow of the death of Abraham Lincoln. Fiona had a hard time dealing with it. A letter from Trip helped. He quoted a poem from Rumi, a 13th century Persian poet:

> *Sorrow prepares you for joy.*
> *It violently sweeps everything out of your house,*
> *So that new joy can find space to enter.*
> *We will find new joy soon my darling. Make plans for our*
> *wedding. I hope to be home soon.*
> *All my love, Trip*

As they waited for their loved ones to come home, life went on. Things were going well at the farm and Liam decided that it was his time to make his fortune. He had heard of a colt that had been sired by a champion horse in Saratoga. He wanted to travel up there and buy it from the owner, Mr. Van Steffen. He had it all worked out.

"We have our crops planted and they're coming along. I still have some of mi pension from the army. I can put that as down pay. I'll go up there and make a deal wit Van Steffen. My investment will be to raise the horse and train him and they will share in the profits of his wins."

All were skeptical of his plan, but Tom gave him the go ahead. As he had said long ago, "Let him have his dreams."

They all saw him off at the depot with high hopes. There were hugs all around and good luck wishes. Bridie said, "We'll all be standin' here waitin' when ye come back wit the little horse."

Weeks went by with no news from Liam. Tom was worried. He confided in Fiona, "I thought we would have heard from him by now. What coulda happened? I put me trust in him. It was your money too. You always gave me most of your pay and I tried ta save it. Kate even gave him some of her money. I know he's not a writer, but he did learn some since he came here. I expected a letter. I don't know what to do."

Finally, there was a letter. They were all gathered at Kate's and Tom tried to read from it. "Liam's writing is a bit hard to decipher, but here's the gist of it."

> Arrived safe and went straight to work. Met with the Van Steffens and gave him my pitch. Said he would think it over. Didn't want to spend any of the deposit money, so I took a job working in a stable. I wanted to show them that I was good with horses and that I could do any work, even though I'm a cripple. They gave me a bed in the loft. Last I heard the man is still unsure. I told a little lie about having some wealthy backer, but not sure he believed me. I'm going to stay here for a while and try to convince him.

Tom looked up and said, "I don't know what to tell him."

Bridie answered, "Tell him to stay where he is. Help is coming."

"What help?" They all asked.

"Me," she answered and went on to explain.

She would go to Saratoga and put on her act as the cultured British lady.

She would convince Mr. Van Steffens that she was the backer and would guarantee his investment.

Tom, Kate, and Barney just stared at her in silence. Finally, Barney spoke up.

"I tink it's worth a shot. I've always been a gambler. Tell ya what. I have a little bit put aside. Little lady, I'll pay your fare and expenses to Saratoga. That will be mi investment."

In spite of their unease in the whole situation, the rest of them agreed to the plan. Bridie "borrowed" an outfit and some accessories from Mrs. Flood. She told her she had to visit a sick relative and was off the next day. More days of unease followed.

A week passed with no news. Finally, when hopes were failing, they received a brief telegraph message.

*Returning home Tuesday with a friend.*
*Liam and Bridie*

On Tuesday they waited anxiously at the depot. The train pulled in and Liam and Bridie made their decent from the train steps. Tom, Fiona, Kate, and Barney just stared at them with questionable looks. Liam just pointed to the box car at the end and started walking toward it. A rail yard worker slid the car door open revealing a low stall containing a beautiful little colt. His coat was a shining red chestnut. He looked frightened after his long trip, but there was a look of pride in his eyes. Fiona thought he seemed to be saying, *I will be a fine horse. You're lucky to have me.*

Tom helped Liam to climb up on the car and he led the horse from the stall. Liam spoke soothingly to the animal and put a halter on him. The yard worker placed a wooden ramp against the box car and Liam led him down.

He stood holding the reins and said, "Hello to all. This is Dearg, that's Irish for Red. He is home. Let's get him to the farm and will tell you our tale of how we got 'em."

Tom pulled the wagon up. He had built up the sides with boards so that it would be easier to transport the horse. They led him up planks to the wagon and started home. The rest followed in Kate's carriage. They made a parade down Main Street and out to the farm.

They got the horse fed, watered and settled in the barn. Liam wiped him down and crooned to him in Irish. Once he was satisfied Dearg was settled, they went to the cottage to celebrate.

Tom brought out the whisky and poured everyone a glass. Barney stood up and said, "We must wet the babies head or make that the horse's head."

They all raised their glasses and Tom said, "God bless our Dearg. May he have a happy life here with us."

"And make us lots of money," Liam added.

Then they all sat down and waited for the tale.

Liam started, "Me darlin' girl out did herself. She charmed tem all with her looks and airs. She demanded respect wit her superior British distain. And they all believed her."

"But did she have to sign anything? Was it legal?" Tom interjected.

"Perfectly legal," Bridie replied. "Liam signed his name. I told tem I was a married woman, but had money of me own that me father left me. I told em I had to keep the investment secret from the husband. He didna approve if horses. They would have ta take me on me word."

"And they agreed to that without a signature?" Kate asked.

"They did indeed," Liam replied. "Oh, I wish all of ye couda been there. She was magnificent. They even agreed ta pay for the transport of the horse."

Bridie added, "I gave mi name as Barbara Clark and mi address as the Flood's manor house here. If they write me, I'll get the letter."

They rest just stared at her in disbelief and prayed it would all go well.

Fiona returned to the Ritner house and resumed her duties, but there were few boarders. One day Mrs. Ritner asked Fiona and Helga to come into the parlor. She looked very serious and they wondered what it could be. Maybe it was about hiring new girls to replace them Mr. Adamson was already there and they all sat down.

Mrs. Ritner began, "I just wanted to let you know that I have decided to sell the house and move to Connecticut. The girls are settled there. Laura is to be married and will be living in Bridgeport. They have asked me to come up there and live with them. Now that both of you girls will be leaving, I thought it would be a good time."

Helga was the first one to speak, "Laura getting married? How old is she?"

Mrs. Ritner smiled and said, "She's nineteen believe it or not. Her husband to be is Frank Ripley. Do you remember him? He was wounded at Gettysburg and we nursed him here. He was from Connecticut and I used to talk to him about my daughters living up there. When he got back home, he looked them up and now he will be my son-in-law. You never know how things will turn out."

Fiona could not help looking at Mr. Adamson and wondering how he was reacting to this announcement. She could see that he was not surprised. Of course Mrs. Ritner would have talked it over with him. *But how can he endure it,* was all she could think.

The girls got up and hugged Mrs. Ritner and wished her well. They were happy for her. She assured them that she would not be leaving until after their weddings. They went back to the kitchen and exchanged looks. Both were thinking, *What about Mr. Adamson?* The two talked about it for a while then Helga had to leave. She was meeting her father in town and going out to help at the farm for the day. Later, Mrs. Ritner came through the kitchen and said she was going out to do some shopping.

Soon after Mr. Adamson came in and sat down with her. Fiona looked at him and saw the pain in his eyes. He answered her puzzled look. "It was never to be, Fiona. I'm not sure if you know this, but I have a wife. She has been in an insane asylum in Baltimore for many years. I can't divorce her. I love Mary Ritner, but I cannot marry her."

Fiona gasped and her eyes filled with tears for this man and could only imagine the pain he was going through.

He patted her hand and said, "It's for the best, Fiona. Mary cares for me as a very dear friend, but I don't think she could ever love me. She loved only her husband. I think her going away is best for both of us."

"But what will you do, Mr. Adamson?" she asked.

"Oh, I'll be fine. My carpentry business is doing well with all this new building going on. I'm thinking of building a little house for myself on the outskirts of town. If you ever come back to Chambersburg, you can visit me there."

"Oh, I will come back and visit you," she assured him.

He hugged her and said, "You and I have always had a special relationship. I wish you all the best in your marriage and your great western adventure." He said he had to go out to attend to some business and Fiona was left alone.

She walked through the house as if in a trance. It had been her home for six years. She went from room to room remembering all that had happened there. She looked in the parlor and saw them all gathered there; Mr. Adamson reading and Laura playing the piano, while Mrs. Ritner sat sewing. She walked passed the front door and saw John Brown standing there asking for a room. Through the kitchen and there was the frightened slave girl sitting at the table. She looked into the yard and saw Helga and herself hanging clothes and laughing with poor Ralph looking over the fence. She entered the little room off the kitchen and John Kaigi was sitting at the desk working. Later, she was attending to Davey as he recuperated from his wounds. She went back to the parlor and sat for a while. *What a time it was,* she thought. *I grew up here and learned so much, but now we are all moving on. I hope there will be good times ahead for all of us.*

The weather was getting warmer and some of the early crops were being harvested. Young Dearg was happily romping in the meadow and sometimes danced around old Rosin who watched patiently. Tom, Liam, and Barney were working hard on both farms. Everyone was amazed at the change in Barney. He had gone from the town drunk to a sober hard working respectable citizen.

Tom wasn't surprised. "I always knew he was a good man. He just needed a chance, a purpose in life. Now he has it."

Fiona wished she had a purpose. She wanted to plan her wedding, but she did not know when it would be. In his last letter, Trip said he would get a long leave before his re-assignment to the West, but he was still needed in his last assignment at a hospital in Virginia. They would have to put the wedding on hold for a while. They had decided to have a small wedding in Chambersburg. The rebuilding was going well and there was a new hotel that would be open soon. Trip's parents would come for the wedding and stay there. But when would it be?

Luck intervened and gave Fiona a purpose. Joe Leiss was coming home and she and Helga had their wedding to plan. Helga wanted to get married at her family farm.

"I always wanted to have an outdoor wedding," she confided to Fiona. "I remember seeing one when I was a little girl. The couple got married under an arch of flowers. I would love that."

"If someone can make an arch, we can gather flowers and tie them on it," Fiona suggested."

"I'm sure Papa can build one," Helga answered. "Just pray that it doesn't rain."

"If it does, we'll just move it inside." Fiona assured her.

It turned out to be a beautiful June morning without a cloud in the sky. The arch, adorned with roses and white flowers called appropriately bridal veil, was ready in the yard next to the house. A small altar had also been set up with rows of chairs in front.

Fiona peeped out the upstairs window and saw the guests gathering.

Suddenly, Fiona had a fit of nervous giggling. She turned to Helga and said, "I was just thinking of the pretend wedding we had in Mrs. Ritner's parlor so long ago."

Helga laughed and said, "That was the first time that I knew I wanted to marry Joe. Now it's for real."

Helga's mother came to the door and said, "Its time Helga, dear."

The sisters Maria, Madeline, and Gertie came in and admired the bride. She looked lovely in the simple white gown her mother had made. But it was the radiance that beamed from her countenance that made her such a beautiful bride.

Fiona as maid of honor wore a lovely lilac gown made by Kate her step-mother, but she thought of her as her mother now. Fiona and Helga's sisters walked up the aisle and gathered around the altar. Everyone stood as Helga walked up the aisle on her father's arm. Joe and his attendants, Helga's brothers Peter and Johan, stood waiting. Joe looked nervous, but broke into a broad smile when he saw Helga.

The Lutheran ceremony was brief. Fiona could not remember what was said. All she could think of was her memories of Helga: *the first time she saw her in the Ritner's kitchen pounding the bread dough, the times they giggled together in that big old bed in the attic, the times they consoled each other in bad times, and laughed together in good times. Helga was the sister she never had and soon they would be parting and she wasn't sure she could bear it.*

The ceremony was over and everyone was smiling. Fiona wiped the tears from her eyes and followed the couple down the aisle. Tables were set up around the yard and soon Mrs. Myers and her friends started carrying out trays of food. Fiona thought Mrs. Myers looked happier than she had seen her in a long time. She followed her into the kitchen and she turned to Fiona and said. "Dis id a gud day. We have had many sad days. We mus be happy with the gud times to get us through the bad times. Hans would want us to be happy."

Fiona remembered the line from Trip's poem; *Sorrow prepares you for joy,* and hugged Mrs. Myers and said, "I think Hans is with us today."

Fiona went out and mingled with the other guests. She felt restored. She and Helga would be separated, but they would always keep in touch. They would have a wonderful correspondence telling each other about their lives and she would be with Trip. He would be her best friend then.

She sat with her Father, Kate, Liam and Bridie. She smiled at Mrs. Ritner and Mr. Adamson at another table. They spoke of the recent surrender of the Confederate General Smith who had been commander of the troops west of the Mississippi. The war was truly over. It was a time for their new lives to begin.

Helga and Joe were getting ready to leave. She and Joe were going to spend a few days in a hotel in Greencastle. As always, Helga's parting words made her smile. She whispered in her ear, "I'll tell you all about the wedding night so you'll know what's in store for you.

# Chapter Twenty-Two

At last the letter came. Trip would be home in two weeks. He had been assigned to Fort Kearney on the Platt River in Nebraska. He had a month before he had to report.  He was coming right to Chambersburg. He would write to his parents to ask them to come there and "Let's have the wedding as soon as possible. Make the plans."

Fiona already had the plans. Father Mahoney would marry them at Corpus Christi Church. She would make reservations for his parents, and their guest at the new Union Hotel on South Main Street. There would be a wedding breakfast at the hotel and a small reception afterward at Kate's house. Then Fiona and Trip would leave for their honeymoon. She didn't know where that would be. That was to be his surprise for her.

Fiona read the letter as she sat on the porch at Kate's house. She re-minded her self to call it Kate and Da's house now. She was staying with them until the wedding. She was still engrossed in the joyous message of Trip's letter when she looked up and saw Helga coming up the walkway.

Fiona ran down the steps and grabbed her. "You're back," she shout-ed. "I'm so happy you're here and Trip is coming home."  She spun Helga around with a dance of joy.

"Whoa," Helga squealed. "Remember, I'm a married woman now and must act proper."

"We'll never be proper," Fiona announced.  "Let's go for a walk."

They headed for their favorite spot by the falls. Helga said, "I stopped at Mrs. Ritner's first. It was kinda sad seein' the old place for the last time."

"I know.  I felt the same way just thinking of everything that happened there.  I will miss all of them.  Did Mrs. Ritner tell you Rufus Birdwell was home?"

"She did and said that the family welcomed the poor boy with open arms. They forgave him for joinin' up."

They arrived at the falls and sat on the grass as Helga started talking about their honeymoon. The hotel was very grand for Greencastle and they had a wonderful dinner in the dining room. Then she paused and looked at Fiona and began to giggle.

"Well, I kinda knew what to expect. I was raised on a farm and I'm not so ignorant. But it was nice. Joe was so dear and sweet. He got very excited and told me over and over how much he loved me. I know what love really is now. I'm so happy!"

Fiona hugged her and said, "Soon I'll be happy too."

The first week went by swiftly and everything for the wedding was in place. The Walters would be arriving from Philadelphia on Thursday evening and the wedding would be on Saturday. They would be bringing their friend Mary Morris and Trip's best friend Sam Cadwalader. Sam would be best man. Everything was in place except the groom. Fiona had not heard from him since the letter announcing his arrival and was getting anxious. She spoke of her worries to her father.

"What will we do if he's not here by Saturday?"

He just shrugged and said, "Then we'll just move it up."

"Oh, that's a typical male answer. Just move it up like it's nothing. What if something happened to him?"

"Fiona you know the trains are all overcrowded and running late with the returning troops. He's probably stuck somewhere."

"He could have sent a telegram. I'm going to check the telegraph office again."

Tom just shook his head as she walked away and said in a whisper, It's not like Fiona to get so wrought up. I hope he gets here soon or she'll have us all crazy.

"I heard that," Fiona called back.

A few more days went by with Fiona's anguish growing. She kept busy packing, going over her clothes, and wondering if she was taking the right things. Kate had bought her some beautiful outfits for her trousseau. She would bring them, but wasn't sure if she would need them out west. Plain lawn dresses and skirts and some sturdy boots were packed and some books. She couldn't bring all of them. Her other books and trinkets and mementoes would be left behind with Da. Fiona could not help but think she was leaving her old life behind with them.

They were to leave Chambersburg right after the wedding. They would stay at a hotel in Philadelphia the first night and then leave for the honeymoon. They would come back to Philadelphia and leave for the West from there. Her father and Kate would come to Philadelphia to see them off. All plans were in place except for the groom.

All anguish finally ended on Wednesday when Trip just appeared at the door. Hattie let him in and called to Fiona. When she saw him standing in the parlor, she didn't know whether to kiss him or hit him.

She decided on the former and threw her arms around him with cries of, "Where were you? I was so worried. Why didn't you let me know where you were?"

He just grinned and said, "I had to wait a long time between trains, but I'm here now."

"Why didn't you send a telegraph message to let me know?"

"I'm sorry, Darling, I just thought you knew I would be here. And here I am."

He pulled her down on the sofa and kissed her with passion as the rest of the household came in.

The next few days were busy with last minute preparations. The Walters, Mrs. Morris, and Sam arrived. They showed them around town and the Philadelphians were impressed with all of the new building going on.

Fiona was glad to have some time to get to know Sam. He and Trip had known each other all their lives. She could see why they were friends. He was like Trip, kind and easy going. Unlike Trip, he wasn't staying in the army. He was going to study law. They sat and talked in Kate's parlor one afternoon.

"Everyone in my family is a lawyer, so I might as well be one too," he told her. "After Gettysburg, I knew I didn't want to stay in the army. I was in the Philadelphia Brigade. We stood up on Cemetery Ridge that day and watched Pickett's men come marching up that hill in formation with battle flags flying. It was a beautiful sight. Then we mowed them down row after row. It is something that will forever haunt my dreams."

She patted his hand and asked, "Do you have a girl, Sam?"

He answered, "No, but I'm looking. Do you have a sister?"

The night before the wedding, Kate had a nice dinner for them all. Fiona felt that they were coming together as a real family. They were dissimilar people from different backgrounds, but they had Fiona and Trip in common. She hoped that would keep them together.

Fiona woke on the day of the wedding with a thrill of realization. *This is the day. After all the waiting through the war years, it is finally here.*

Da came in and kissed her good morning. He pulled a small package out of his pocket and handed it to her. "Before she died, your mother asked me to give this to you on the day of your wedding."

Fiona opened the package and saw a beautiful lace handkerchief. She held it to her face and it smelled of lavender.

Tom sat down next to her and said, "She carried it on our wedding day and wanted you to carry it on yours."

"Oh, Da, thank you so much. I'm so happy to have this special memory of my mother. I think she will be with us today." She got off the bed and put on her robe and turned to her father, "Da, I will miss you so much. When I think about it, I feel like my heart is breaking. But, when I think about going off with Trip, my heart seems to skip."

He just smiled and said, "That's just normal. I felt the same way when I left my family in Ireland to come to America."

She sat on the bed beside him, "Da, thank you for taking care of me and making a good life for me and thank you for letting me go."

At that thought, they both burst into tears. Their tears soon subsided and they talked happily until there was a knock at the door.

Kate entered with a breakfast tray and announced, "Breakfast in bed for the bride."

Fiona laughed and got back into bed, "Thank you, Kate. You have been so kind. I just got used to having a mother and now I'm leaving you."

"I'll always be here for you," Kate answered. "I'll write and give you motherly advice whether you ask for it or not," she said with a laugh.

The rest of the morning was left to the women. Helga and Bridie arrived and joined Kate in preparing the bride for her big day. When all the preparations were finished, the ladies stood and admired the bride. Kate had insisted Fiona's gown would be from a dressmaker and not homemade. She stood before them in a beautiful gown of white tulle trimmed in lace. Her hair was pilled up under a crown of orange blossoms that held a long lace veil.

"You look like a princess," Helga clapped her hands and exclaimed.

"Just for today," Fiona said and laughed. "Soon I'll be a frontier woman."

When Fiona went down the aisle of the church, holding on to her father's arm, she felt like she was floating. It was like a beautiful dream as she passed so many dear faces who smiled at her: Mrs. Ritner, Mr. Adamson, Barney, the Birdwell family, Mike Kelly, home from the war, and Annie, the Meyers family, Hattie and Enoch, Doctor Senseny from the hospital, Joe Leiss, Mr. and Mrs. Flood, Mrs. Morris, and Trip's parents. They had all been part of her life and she was so happy they were with her today.

And then there was Trip standing with his arm out to reach for her. Da kissed her and handed her to Trip. Fiona felt a sharp pain for an instant, but smiled tenderly when she looked at Trip. Helga and Bridie and Sam and Liam stood on either side as attendants. Father Mahoney put their hands together and the ceremony began. Fiona and Trip kept their eyes on each other all through the ceremony.

When Father Mahoney finally pronounced them man and wife, Fiona's eyes filled with tears of joy. He whispered a final blessing to them. "May God enfold you in the mantle of his love."

The breakfast at the hotel was formal, but the reception at Kate and Tom's house was not. There was a great buffet spread in the dining room with whisky and beer on the side table. The furniture in the parlor was pushed to the side to make room for dancing. Music was provided by Mike Kelly and his fiddle.

Trip waltzed Fiona around in their first dance. Then Mike broke into a jig and Trip bravely took her arm and tried to jig. The rest of the company joined in and the old house shook with joy. It was a great party and Fiona could see that Trip's parents were enjoying themselves. They had lost their inhibitions and even joined in some of the jigs.

Mrs. Morris took Fiona aside and said, "This wedding has been the best thing for William and Augusta. They have been sad for so long. I know it is going to be hard on them with you and William gone. I will do my best to get Augusta involved in some charity work. I think that will be the best thing for her."

"Thank you, Mrs. Morris, you are a good friend to them."

Tom stood up and offered a final toast.

*May joy and peace surround you both,*
*Contentment latch your door,*
*And happiness be with you now,*
*And love to cherish evermore.*

All too soon, it was time for Fiona and Trip to leave. Fiona started up stairs to get ready and Helga and Kate followed. Fiona turned to Kate and whispered, "I need to be alone with Helga for awhile."

Kate shook her head in understanding. This would be the last time they would be together.

Helga helped Fiona out of her gown in silence. She turned to get her traveling dress out of the wardrobe, but collapsed in tears.

Fiona went to her and put her arms around her and they both stood crying. Fiona led her to the bed and they sat until tears subsided.

Helga began, "I didn't think it would be this hard. I don't know what I'll do without you."

"I know. Me too, but we'll be all right. It will be different. Before we needed and depended on each other. Now we have husbands. We can depend on them.

"I love being with Joe, but I can't talk to him about everything like I can with you."

"We can write letters. We'll tell each other about everything. You can tell me all the gossip in Chambersburg and I can tell you about our adventures out west."

"I won't have any adventures to tell you about in Chambersburg."

"Hey, you never know, we've had plenty of adventures here the past few years. Even everyday things will be interesting to me. What new buildings are going up? How are Bridie and Mrs. Flood getting on? How is Mr. Adamson doing? Is Barney staying sober? What's Rufus Birdwell doing? Will the Mennonites take him back? That will all be exciting news to me."

Helga nodded, "Ya, I guess." Then she perked up. "Well, I hope we'll both be having children. That will be exciting."

"You bet. We'll both save our letters and hand them down to our grandchildren. Now you better help me put on my traveling clothes or I'll be catching that train in my shift."

They said their goodbyes on the platform at the depot. The group from Philadelphia were staying for a few more days. They wanted to tour the Gettysburg battle field and the rest of the countryside. They would be seeing both their parents in Philadelphia before they left for the West. But for everyone else it was really goodbye.

Liam and Bridie, Mrs. Ritner, Mr. Adamson and Barney were all there. Fiona and Helga had already said their goodbyes. They couldn't take another one. Fiona hugged each one and thanked them for all they had done for her. They got on the train and she sat by the window. As the train pulled out, she kept waving until they were no longer in sight. She wondered if she would ever see them again.

She turned to Trip and thought now it will just be the two of us. She settled into a mood of blissful joy. They arrived in Philadelphia and checked into the Continental Hotel at Ninth and Chestnut Streets. Fiona looked around the palatial lobby in amazement. A bellhop led them up the grand stair case to their room. They entered the room to find a beautiful bouquet of roses on the table. Trip took the card, read it and laughed.

"It's from Mrs. Morris, she says, Fiona and Trip, Do you remember the night of the ball at the Walters? I retrieved Fiona from the cloak room for you and the rest is history. I was proud to be a part of it. I wish joy to you both. Love, Mary Morris."

"She was the first one to believe in us," Fiona remembered.

They dressed and went down to dinner. Fiona wore one of her trousseau outfits and felt like a queen as they entered the elegant dinning room. They dined on lobster and roasted oysters and lots of champagne. Fiona had never eaten such food.

"Enjoy it now," Trip teased. "God knows what we'll get to eat at the fort."

She did enjoy it, and after much pleading, Trip finally told her where they were going on their honeymoon. "We're going to Cape May," he informed her.

"Cape what?"

"Cape May. It's in southern New Jersey on the ocean. I know you always wanted to see the ocean."

Fiona was thrilled and full of questions, "What is a cape? Is it far? How will we get there? Where will we stay?"

He answered patiently. "A cape is a strip land that sticks out in the ocean. We'll go by train from here. We leave here tomorrow morning and will be there by late afternoon. We are going to stay at the Congress Hall Hotel. It's a grand hotel that overlooks the ocean."

Back in their room, Fiona felt intensely happy filled with champagne and anticipation. Trip led her to the bed and said, Oh, my sweet, sweet girl."

They came together with love. They took pleasure in each other and were truly one. They fell asleep in a warm cocoon of love.

The next day on the train, Fiona still felt embraced by that love. She was also wild with anticipation to see the ocean. When they arrived at the Cape, they took a carriage that dropped them off at the back of the hotel. Trip walked her straight through the lobby and out the promenade where they could look at the sea. Fiona was filled with exhilaration looking at the waves crashing on to the sandy beach. Overhead seabirds flew in circles and their cries sounded like laughter. Her senses were filled with the tangy smell of the sea, the sights and sound of the beach.

She wanted to run right into the water. But she looked around at the elegantly dressed people and held back. The ladies with parasols and the gentlemen in top hats strolled along the promenade hardly glancing at the magnificent seascape before them. They politely nodded to others as they passed. Fiona thought *they are more interested in being seen than seeing the sea.*

Trip took her arm and they strolled down the promenade away from the crowd. They sat on a bench and took in deep breaths of the magnificent air. Fiona closed her eyes and just let her senses take it all in.

Trip squeezed her hand and said, "I have another surprise for you. Tomorrow I'm going to hire a carriage and we're going to another beach. It's a place call Peck's Beach.

"Peck's Beach!" Fiona exclaimed, "That's where Sandy lived."

"I know you always wanted to go there. I wrote to his mother and she is expecting us tomorrow. I think you will find it a very different beach from this one."

Peck's Beach was an island just off the coast. They had to leave the carriage at a stable and take a ferry across the bay. When they arrived in Peck's Beach, Fiona recognized it from Sandy's letters. It was a small fishing village with only one main street that led up from the bay. There were a few small shops along the way and several side streets with houses. They found Mrs. Thompson's house on one of the side streets.

The exterior was weathered grey clapboard, but it had a cheery look with starched white curtains in the windows and red begonias in the front yard.

The door was opened by a little grey haired lady who smiled warmly when she saw them. "Oh, Fiona, Fiona, it is such a joy to see you. I feel like I know you from your letters. And this handsome fellow must be Mr. Walters."

"Please call me Trip," he answered as she showed them in.

Mrs. Thompson had a beautiful tea laid out on a table by a window that looked out on the bay.

"Our family has lived here for generations," Mr. Thompson told them as they sipped their tea. "My late husband was a fisherman as was his father before him. Jim was our only child and we wanted more for him."

Fiona put a piece of cake on her plate and said, "Yes, he told me he wanted to go to school when he got out of the army. He was a very intelligent boy. I think he would have gone far."

"Yes, but it was not to be. God had other plans for him. Fiona, thank you kindly for sending his letters to me. They help to keep his memory alive."

"It was hard to give them up. I treasured them, but I thought it would be good for you to have them."

Trip cleared his throat and said, "It is important to keep the memory of our loved ones alive. I lost a brother and there isn't a day that goes by that I don't think of him," He paused for a minute and asked, "Is there any thing that we can do for you Mrs. Thompson? Do you have any other family?"

"Yes, I have kinfolk who live nearby. They come and see me often and I spend holidays with them. I have kind neighbors who look in on me. You know, I don't mind being here alone. I have happy memories. They are good company. People are always searching for happiness, but you can't be happy all the time. But you can be content. I'm content and I think that is more important."

They both smiled at this. They finished their tea and told Mrs. Thompson of their plans to go out west and she promised to remember them in her prayers. Fiona looked around the warm room and could feel the contentment of the place. When it was time to leave, Mrs. Thompson walked them to the door. They said their good-bys and started down the path. Trip stopped and went back and spoke to Mrs. Thompson for a moment. She nodded and pointed down the road.

"What was that" Fiona asked.

"I was asking her where the best beach was and I'm taking you there," was his reply.

They walked down the dirt road to the ocean side of the island. They then followed a path through a wooded area. They passed through the trees to a wide expanse of a sandy beach and there was the sea. It took Fiona's breath away. The white beach went on forever and there was no one in sight. She felt like they were the only people on earth standing there watching the crashing waves. The sun sparkled on the water like diamonds.

Trip took off his coat and laid it out on the sand. He sat down and started taking his shoes off and said, "Take your shoes and stockings off, dear, and hike up your skirts. We're going wading."

She soon complied and they ran hand in hand down the beach. When they reached the water, she tucked her skirts into her waist and Trip rolled up his pants. They joyfully waded in and it took her breath away. The water was cold and she screamed with delight at the movement of the water around her feet. At one point, she almost lost her balance and Trip caught her. Her feet sunk into the wet sand and she felt the swirl of the in-coming and outgoing waves. The sea gulls screamed overhead as if to say, you are invading our territory.

They came out of the water and lay on Trip's coat to let the sun dry their clothing. Fiona sighed with contentment.

"That was wonderful. Thank you for taking me to the ocean," she whispered. "I could stay here forever looking at this view. It is amazing looking out at the vast ocean. When I look at how it ends at the horizon, I can see why primitive people thought it was the end of the world."

"Maybe some day we'll get to see the Pacific," Trip mused. He turned to her and went on. "Fiona, I really don't know what lies ahead for us. You are such a brave girl for going with me. It won't be an easy life on the frontier. Sometime I wonder if I'm asking too much of you."

"You could never ask too much of me. I would go with you to the ends of the earth. I always wanted to see the West and I can't wait. It will be our big adventure."

They stayed there until the sun started sinking and they had to catch the last ferry.

# Sources

Alexander, Ted, Conrad, William, Neitzel, Jim & Stake, Virginia, *Southern Revenge,* White Mane Publishing, Shippensburg, Pa, 1989

Appletons' Cyclopedia of American Biography, *Massasoit,* 1900, *Joseph Ritner 1888*

*American Transcendental Web*, "Ralph W. Emerson Poems," vcu.edu/engweb/transcentalism/authors/emerson

Carlyon, David, "The Great Dan Rice," Wisconsin Magazine of History, Summer, 2005

Celtic-lyrics.com/lyrics/336/html

Classiclit.about.com/library/bi-etexts/wwhitman

Clark, Shanet, "John Brown 1859," *The Education Forum,* April 27, 2006

Connelly, William Elsey, *The Conspirators' Biography's,* Crane and Company Topeka, 1900

Cooper, John M., *Recollections of Chambersburg,* A. Nivin Pomeroy Publisher 1900

Cormany,Rachel,Diary1863,ValleyoftheShadowPrivatePapers, valley.lib. virginia.edu./papers/FD1006

Desmond, Frances, "American Indians and their Music," Minnesota Historic Society Publishers, 2009

1st Light Artillery Battery A, pa-roots.com/pacw/alrillery/1startillery/1star batta.html

Franklin Repository, Local Items, "A Word for Chambersburg," October 26, 1859

Frenchlearner.com/songs/fere-jaque

Heyser, William, *Diary 1862-1863,* Valley of the Shadow Personal Papers, valley.lib.virginia.edu/papers/FD1004

Hoke, J., *Historical Reminiscences of the War and Chambersburg,* M.A. Foltz, Chambersburg, 1884

Howe, Russell, *Letters 1862,* Valley of the Shadow Personal Papers, valley.lib.virginia.edu/papers/F6028

Keagy, Franklin, *Biographical Sketches of John Henry Keagy,* Boyd B. Stutler Collection, West Virginia Archives.

Kittochtenny Historic Society, Franklin County

Marotte, Maurice L. & Pollard, Kay, *Images of America, Chambersburg,* Arcadia, 2005

McPherson, James M., *Battle Cry of Freedom,* Oxford University press, NY, 1988

Niven, Alfred D.D., *Men of Mark of Chambersburg,* Fulton Publishing, Phila. 1876

Of-Ireland.info/holidays/carols.html

Rosenburg, Matt, *The Mason-Dixon Line Divided north and South,* about. com guide.

Ross, Anna Marie, *Volunteer Nurse, Brief History of the Refreshment Salon,* Temple.edu/awaskie/anna/maria/ross/ civil/war.

Stake, Virginia Ott, *John Brown in Chambersburg 1859,* Franklin County Heritage, Champersburg, 1977

*Tithe Wars 1831-1836,* Wikipedia.org/wiki/tithe_war.

United States Census 1850, Mary Ritner Family, ancestry.com

Wikipedia.org/wiki/Beautiful_Dreamer

Wray, Tina Brewster, "Patient Medicines," *Newsletter of White River valley Journal,* Auburn, WA, August 22, 2011.

Eileen Dougherty Troxell received her degree from Pennsylvania State University and lives with her husband, Gene, in Ardsley, Pennsylvania. She is the author of *The History of St. Malachy's*, the story of an old church in Philadelphia that welcomed Irish immigrants in the nineteenth century and African Americans in the twentieth.

Made in the USA
Middletown, DE
29 October 2016